Yahudit

A Novel

Yahudit

A Novel

Sammy Goldman

TOUCHFEATHER

Hillsborough ♦ Seoul ♦ Bangalore ♦ Cebu

Hardcover: ISBN 978-1-59689-082-4
Paperback: ISBN 978-1-59689-148-7

(USA) Library of Congress Control Number: 2009900306

Write-To Address:

TouchFeather
Suite 318
601 Route 206
Hillsborough, New Jersey 08844
The United States of America

For Ahava

Yahudit

1

She sat there and wondered what was to be. It wasn't like she just woke up, yesterday, and realized that something was wrong. She knew for a long time that something was not right. But she did not want to believe that there was anything wrong. She did not want to doubt. It cost too much to doubt. It cost her her peace of mind.

She thought back to that day. It was a day of jubilation. It was a day of elation. It was a day of enlightenment. But on the other hand, it was a day when she lost something. A day when she lost everything. It was a bittersweet day which she cherished.

She started to read her Psalms in Hebrew. She was the best student in her Hebrew school. She went faithfully every week and did the homework faithfully each time. She valued her acquired knowledge of Hebrew. She liked the fact that her parents complimented her on her Hebrew skills. It made her feel important. It made her want to learn more.

As she read her Hebrew text, she felt like she was hearing a voice. It was a familiar voice. It was a voice that had calmed her many times. It was the voice of Carlos. "You are wonderful!" She smiled as she imagined his voice.

Yahudit

Carlos was not Jewish. Carlos did not care about anything Jewish. In fact, Carlos hated Jews. But Carlos loved her, and she knew that this was a fact truer than the fact that there is gravity. It certainly was truer than the story of Moses and of Abraham. It was truer than what her rabbis taught her. It was the ultimate truth that she felt to be completely true.

Yahudit met Carlos incidentally. She could not even remember when she actually "met" him. Carlos was working in the kosher fast food place in West Los Angeles. It was the fast food place where all the Hebrew Sunday school students went for lunch. They had kosher pizzas, kosher falafel, kosher salads, kosher juices, kosher everything. It was glatt kosher with the visible certification of kashrut printed on the wall for all to see.

When Carlos serviced her, Yahudit thought that he was a Jew from Iran. There were many Jews from Iran in West Los Angeles, and they have dark skin like Iranian Muslims. Yahudit was an Iranian Jew. Her grandfather had come over to the United States at the time of the Revolution. He had been in the Iranian army as an officer. He used to brag that he was a general. Yahudit did not believe him, but humored him nonetheless.

Yahudit had always been ambivalent about her Iranian descent. She thought it odd that her grandparents had so many Iranian Muslim friends. Did they not know that they were Jewish and that Jews were in conflict with Muslims? For God's sake, Iran was conniving to nuke Israel, the Jewish state. Didn't her grandparents care?

They were not particularly religious. But her grandparents kept all the Jewish holidays. Especially during the Pesach season, they kept the house immaculate. They made sure that the house did not become defiled in any way. This puzzled Yahudit because her grandparents were not particularly religious. At least, it did not seem that way to Yahudit. And they had many Iranian Muslim friends. They seemed to get along better with Iranian Muslims than with Ashkenazi Jews down the street.

Yahudit

Yahudit thought her parents more consistent. They were strict about all Jewish observance, and not only about Jewish holidays. They made sure she went to Jewish Hebrew school and learned to read Hebrew. They made sure that they attended the synagogue on a weekly basis. And they seemed to have only Jewish friends who were observant of Jewish laws and religious traditions.

The weekly synagogue attendance was a hallowed event for the Kashiri family. But Yahudit dreaded going to the synagogue. Her synagogue had a clique of Ashkenazi princesses who made fun of the color of her skin. It was a local Conservative synagogue, and they lived in a predominantly non-Iranian area. So, when her parents wanted her to go to Hebrew school, Yahudit made one condition. They had to drive her 30 minutes to an Iranian Jewish Sunday School. Her parents did not like the idea of spending over 1 hour on Sundays driving. Actually, if they counted the two round trips for dropping her off at the Sunday school and picking her up from Sunday school, it was more like 2 hours of driving. But when the mom said they could make couples time out of the interval, her father relented.

Yahudit's father was the weaker link. He kept Jewish traditions because Yahudit's mother was religious and observant. In fact, if it were not for her mother, her father would have gone completely secular. Yahudit was convinced of it. Her father had too much of Gentile-love that her grandparents had. Yahudit took her mother's side. Jews should stick together. Gentiles are not to be trusted.

Yahudit's father worked as a movie executive at Sony Pictures. But he kept his word and shielded his family, especially Yahudit, from the movie industry. Thus, Yahudit only saw kosher Jewish friends of her parents visiting their home for meals. It was a Gentile-free environment at her home. It was so different from her grandparents' place, where Iranian Muslims seemed to be constantly around humoring her grandfather. Her mother did not like her visiting her father's parents.

Yahudit

When she saw Carlos at first, Yahudit imagined him to be the splitting image of her grandfather when he was young. He was smiling constantly. His hair flowed naturally and uncombed. And he looked so Iranian. Quintessentially Iranian just like her grandfather.

But he was not. Carlos was a Mexican who was working at the kosher hang-out. And the word on the street was that he was an illegal.

"He can't be illegal!" Yahudit said to her friend from Sunday school one time the topic was brought up.

"Of course, he is." Judith retorted. "Why do you think that he can hardly speak any English? He's like right out of the bus."

"Yeah," Janice agreed. "He probably rode a bus without air-conditioner from all the way south of the border. Do you see the way he walks? He walks like Igor."

"Igor! Igor!" Judith said, laughing. She got up to imitate his walk. Janice joined her.

"That's mean!" Yahudit said.

"Oh, you have a crush on the illegal, don't you?" Janice said sardonically.

"No," Yahudit said. "The Torah teaches us to be kind to the aliens in our gates, doesn't it?"

"Yada, Yada, Yada," Janice said, putting her hand up against Yahudit.

"Whatever!" Judith chimed in.

Yahudit did not understand why her best friends were so mean to Carlos. The day that she found out that he was not Iranian, the day that she found out that he was a Mexican, the day that she found out that he was an illegal scorned by her best friends, was the day that she fell in love with him.

She snapped back from her digression and thought about the day of bittersweet jubilation. She remembered the sound of his breathing. It was more beautiful than any song that she heard sung on the radio. It was a special song to her. It was a raw and honest testimony to his feelings for her. Song of

Yahudit

Carlos, as unintelligible as it was in human language, was the song of the Muses, Yahudit was convinced.

It seemed like, yesterday, when she first heard that song. That song has kept her spellbound for many weeks. It had kept her wanting more. She wanted to hear the song live, rather than in broadcasts by her memory. She was not yet sure if she regretted her private concert attendances or not. Even after what has transpired, she was not sure.

She remembered the first day that she said "hello" to Carlos. It was a weird day. In Hebrew class, they read a Hebrew passage about how Dana had fallen in love with Hamor and how she had planned to marry him. Her brothers promised her marriage to Hamor if he circumcised himself and his people. He kept his end of the bargain and circumcised the males. And Dana's brothers broke their end of the bargain and slaughtered Dana's lover and his people when they were in pain from adult circumcision. She thought it was cruel, unjust, and evil.

But her Hebrew teacher saw it in another way. It was righteous of Dana's brothers' to do to keep the Jewish race pure. Jews should not mix their blood with unholy races all around them. Jews are God's chosen people and they must keep their race pure. Even if it meant killing Gentile lovers under the guise of friendship, using the worse kind of deception possible, it was worth it to preserve the Jewish race.

Yahudit couldn't believe her ears. The Jewish race? Pure bloodline? Pure race? Was this teacher kidding? Yahudit searched each millimeter of the teacher's face to see if she were kidding, but it was obvious that she was dead serious. It seemed like cruel irony. Here she was, a teacher of Iranian descent with a dark skin, who was talking about the purity of the Jewish race. Did she presume that the Ashkenazi princesses in her synagogue were of the same race as she and her grandparents from Iran? She should know better because she is Iranian herself and has dark skin.

She found the whole Hebrew class infuriating. She was not so mad when she thought about the story of Esther because she knew that killing of Haman was justified. After all, he wanted to wipe out all the Jews of the Empire. But Hamor? All he wanted was love. He loved Dana truly, madly, and deeply. Hamor loved Dana enough that he was willing to convert for her. He went through the painful ritual of adult circumcision. Not only was he willing to convert for Dana and be circumcised, he was willing to force all of his people in his position as a ruler to convert to Judaism and be circumcised. What did Dana's brothers do? They blatantly tricked honest Hamor and his people and killed them in cold blood. Did they not care about love? Did they not appreciate the pain Hamor and his people were willing to endure to make Dana and Hamor's love possible? Was love not important? Were Jews to celebrate breaking up of pure love? It was not like the Capulets and Mantagues who hated each other. They started with altercation and they killed. With Dana's brothers, they accepted Hamor's hand of friendship. In fact, Dana's brothers did not have to do anything. It was Hamor who did everything. He converted. He was circumcised. He got all of his people to convert to Judaism. Even when Hamor kept his faith, Dana's brothers wanted to kill him and his people. Were they not technically Jews after the conversion? How could the Hebrew teacher stand there and praise such an act of cruelty, a crime against love and humanity, and deception. Is this what Judaism was all about?

Yahudit was mad. She was furious. In fact, she was angry beyond words. But she knew that her friends shared the views of the teacher. It would be pointless talking to them about her angry thoughts. So, she did the next best thing. She said "hello" to Carlos just to spite her friends and all the observant Jews in the small quicky-food place.

"Hello," Yahudit said. Her friends stopped what they were doing and just stared at her.

"Hi," Carlos said.

"What's your name?" Yahudit asked, trying to force a smile through all her angry thoughts. She felt the painful nudge of an elbow on her right side. She tried to ignore it. Then, she

Yahudit

felt a painful nudge from her left side. She tried to smile through the sharp pain.

"My name is Carlos," he said.

"My name is Yahudit," she said.

Carlos smiled.

"It's nice to meet you," Yahudit said.

Carlos smiled.

Yahudit smiled and went to their usual spot. Her friends seemed to be in a state of shock. They had been accustomed to ignoring him all the time. The very breaking of the pattern unsettled Judith and Janice. They hesitated for a moment, looked at each other, then sat down.

They were silent. For some reason, Yahudit felt a flood of contentment rushing into her heart and felt that a heavy burden was being lifted.

"What did you think about today's class?" Yahudit asked, wanting to confirm her thoughts.

"Torah is Torah," Judith said.

"I thought she was right on the ball," Janice said.

"I thought so," Yahudit said, and uttered no more.

That was the first day. There was evening and morning; the first day of creation. She saw that it was good.

All throughout that night, she thought of the first day. It was the first day that a contact was made. It was the first day of Carlos and Yahudit. It seemed like she created something beautiful. Anything was pure compared to the story of Dana and Hamor and her brothers. Carlos and Yahudit. It was pure compared to that Torah story. From the first day of creation, she began to believe. Yahudit believed in the purity of the greeting. She believed that it was far more pure than the tainted love and insincere promises that the Jewish world offered.

She snapped back from the digression and remembered the day. The day of bittersweet jubilation. But again, her thoughts were interrupted by a digression.

She wondered how her mother came to be modern orthodox. She was strict about observance. She wanted the household to be religious. What was the impetus behind her religiosity? The question seemed to open up a world of mystery especially because Yahudit knew for sure that her mother's parents were secular, rabidly secular. Her maternal grandparents seemed like they were still living in the 60s. Whenever Yahudit visited them, grandma Friedman tried to get her to join her in Tai Chi.

"You gotta fly, baby!" Grandma Friedman would always say.

"Fly, grandma?" Yahudit would always respond.

"Yeah, fly!" Grandma Friedman's answer was always the same. "Fly like a free bird. Don't let a birdcage hold you in; don't let a bird net capture you; and above all, don't let a bird hunter kill your spirit."

"Okay, grandma," Yahudit would always say.

Yahudit wasn't sure if Grandma Friedman knew she was repeating herself or if all those years of acid in her youth had fried her brain. Grandma Friedman never talked about having done drugs, but Yahudit was sure of it. In fact, she was sure that her maternal grandparents were still doing it. But of course, not when she was visiting. At least, not in plain sight. They were Jewish grandparents after all.

"Want some home baked cookies?" Grandma Friedman asked one day.

"Yes, grandma," Yahudit said. And thus began a conversation she would not forget until her dying day.

"How did you become such a free spirit, grandma?" Yahudit asked.

"Free spirit? Ha, ha," grandma Friedman seemed to like that.

"Yes, a free spirit, like a free bird," Yahudit pursued.

Smiling, giggling, grandma Friedman said, "It started in my college days."

"Yes?" Yahudit wanted to encourage her.

"When I went to Berkeley, I was a naïve little girl, a child of holocaust survivors from Poland," Grandma Friedman said as she seemed to fall into a reverie. "I grew up with my parents telling me never to trust the Goyim. The gentiles will betray you, every time, they always said. When I was young, I was sick of hearing it over and over again. I thought that they were mean and hateful. I loved them, but I could not understand where all the hatred came from. All the gentiles living around us were so nice that it was hard for me to imagine that they were evil. But my parents assured me that they hated Jews, too. Everyone did."

"Really?" Yahudit said.

"Yeah, that's what they said," Grandma Friedman continued. "When I asked them for proof, they said that they were the proof. They survived the holocaust. It was their next door neighbor who ratted them out to the Nazis. In fact, they were happy about them being arrested and being sent to be executed. And they had been friends all their life. They went to school together. In fact, dadda's first kiss was with the woman who ratted him out. When I heard the explanation, I saw their perspective. I understood."

"Oh, so did you hate the Goyim?" Yahudit asked.

"No, baby," Grandma Friedman answered, laughing. "I said that I understood them. But I did not agree with them. I knew what I knew. And that was that my gentile friends were really nice to me, and we were true friends."

"Oh, what did they feel about it?" Yahudit asked.

"Well, they didn't say anything, because I learned to keep my thoughts to myself," Grandma Friedman replied. "I figured that it did them no good for me to tell them my views which I knew would hurt them."

"I guess that's wise," Yahudit said hesitantly.

"It's the only way, baby," Grandma Friedman said. "Love and peace. It's the only way."

"So, what happened?" asked Yahudit.

"Oh, yeah, right. I will continue on with the story," Grandma Friedman said and took a sip of the lemonade in front of her. "When I was a Freshman at Berkeley, I started to question my Jewish identity and everything my mom and dad had taught me."

"What did they teach you?" Yahudit asked.

"Nothing really," Grandma Friedman said. "They had renounced God after the holocaust. Dadda kept saying, 'There is no God in Heaven. If there were, this would not have happened to the Jewish people!' Although mama would not say much during those rants by dadda, she would nod vigorously. They did not teach me anything Jewish because they renounced their Jewish beliefs."

"Oh, so did you become religious at Berkeley?" Yahudit was curious.

"No, baby. I went the other direction. Although dadda and mama renounced Jewish religion, they were moral people. Old Traditionalists. And they were strict. In fact, I was not allowed to go to any of the school dances. Their orthodox ways in Poland remained with them, I guess. But when I went to Berkeley, I thought about their hypocrisy. If there weren't God, then were there any moral regulations? In my logical mind, there wasn't. It was God that required morality. Humans are free apart from a supernatural being who imposed his laws on humans. So, I began to experiment."

"Experiment?" Yahudit asked.

Grandma Friedman paused for a second and looked at her young granddaughter. "I did a lot of tings I should not have done, I guess. But I went with the flow. And the flow at Berkeley was quite liberal and open at that time. And in the midst of all the experimentation, I met your grandpa."

"Really?" Yahudit said excitedly.

"Yeah, baby. We met and fell in love at first sight. Well, actually, at first … first personal encounter."

"Encounter?" Yahudit wanted clarification.

"Yeah, when, we, we got to know each other … personally," Grandma said with a sigh of relief. "And we decided to get married."

Yahudit

"Yes, grandma?" Yahudit had never heard this story before.

"Okay, baby, that's not the complete truth. I wanted to get married with him, but he was not so thrilled about it at first. He said, 'Why do you want to go tying a knot around the beautiful thing called love?' Such a poet, ain't he?"

"I guess so," Yahudit said hesitantly. It was obvious that she was still in love with him.

"Your grandpa was such a romantic. But I was a Jewish girl after all and wanted a marriage. It turned out he was Jewish as well. I guess I should have known with a name like Friedman, but in those days at Berkeley, everyone was just psychedelic, you know. And his parents were holocaust survivors as well, so both of our parents were thrilled when they found out we were married."

"You told them afterwards?" Yahudit said with eyes wide open.

"Yeah, baby. It was the 60s. No one cared about institutions, parents, society, and all that jazz. We loved each other, and we wanted to keep it simple and pure. Without all the hoopla. And so we got married in the city hall in Berkeley. It wasn't like we were not already a couple. It was a formality. And Danny did it just for me. We were in love. What can we say?"

"Wow, mom never told me about this," Yahudit said.

"No, baby. Your mom wouldn't tell you something like this. She's ashamed of us. She wants us to be more religious."

"Really?" Yahudit asked, curious.

"Yeah, baby. You see how she sends you to Hebrew school and keeps kosher and all that? Oh, I better not criticize because she would really get mad."

"Grandma Friedman, how did she get that way?"

"Well, it's a long story. But I guess, simply put, she rebelled against us like I rebelled against my parents. I tried to raise her with my values, and she bolted in the other direction."

"Really?"

"Yeah, baby. She went to Stanford University and joined the Jewish group, there. And then one Christmas vacation, she came back and commanded me to take down the Christmas tree. 'We are Jewish! Don't you have any respect?' She yelled. You know what I said?"

"No."

"I told her that Jewish law commanded her to honor her mother and father."

"Yes, it does say that."

"But you know what? She said that it did not apply to me because I had left the Torah. Can you believe that?"

"Wow, it's hard to believe," Yahudit said. "She always tells me that I must honor my father and mother according to the Torah."

"Well, religious people tend to be hypocritical, don't they? Well, I showed her. I did not take the Christmas tree down. In fact, I brought in a nativity scene and put it right in front of my tree. I told her that if she did not like it, then she could leave."

"Really?"

"Yeah, baby. And she did. She did not talk to me for two years. She stayed right there at Stanford and worked there during summer time and did some part-time work in the winter time. I had the Yiddish mama syndrome that I did not even know that I had. But when I was about to reach out to her and relent, she came back to me. Apparently, she had fallen in love with some dark, handsome prince at Stanford. Apparently, your dadda was a family man, being Middle Eastern and all, and wanted your mama to make peace with her mama before getting married. And they got married right after graduation. It was a nice wedding. You saw the wedding pictures, right?"

"Yes, Grandma Friedman," Yahudit said.

The fact was that Carlos was not Jewish. Yahudit felt a painful knot twisting inside her stomach as she remembered this fact. She felt like throwing up.

Yahudit

Yahudit was not quite sure why she did the thing that she did. Was it because she saw through the hypocrisy of Judaism? It wasn't really hypocrisy, was it? It was the realization that Judaism was just an evil religion. Slaughtering the converts in true love. What was really sacred in Judaism? Yahudit started to question herself.

It was then that she realized that Grandma Friedman's identity crisis at Berkeley had come to her prematurely. It was like a premature birth when nothing is expected. The doctor is surprised. The husband is surprised. The mom is surprised. And the baby is surprised.

Yahudit was filled with many questions of "why?" but could not locate a single "because." She felt frustrated, lost, and alone. Whenever she sat there in her Sunday Hebrew class, she felt like a foreigner more despised than the Goy down the street. She felt like they knew what was going on inside her mind. She was sure that they hated her because they knew that she was drifting away from Torah. They knew for sure that she was doubting Judaism and the very foundation of Jewish identity that has sustained the Jewish people for two thousand years in the Diaspora.

But she felt comforted. Why? It was because she knew that there were many Jews who had treaded the path that she was about to tread or already treading. It was the path of doubt that many Jews have experienced. After all, was not even Theodore Herzl, the Father of Secular Zionism, a doubter? He did not even circumcise his son!

And of course, there was Grandma Friedman. She was the living proof that Judaism was not the way. She liked what Grandma Friedman represented far more than what her Sunday Hebrew School represented. She liked the vision of Grandma Friedman far more than the vision of her own mother, who she came to realize was a hateful person who had abandoned the mother who gave birth to her for two years.

She knew then that she was on the right path. The first "because" stemming from the memory of her conversation with

Yahudit

Grandma Friedman started a chain reaction. The concatenation of mental processes in a linear progression on a logical path led her to Carlos. He became her unchained melody.

Yahudit remembered the second "conversation" that she had with him. She walked in after the Sunday Hebrew class. She was not paying attention during class. She was resolved the night before to talk to him, so she did not get much sleep. The nervous anticipation kept her up all night. She felt like the silly girls she read about in teenage romance novels, which she secretly smuggled in from her local library to avoid her mother's Puritanical regulation.

She felt her heart racing faster than the Porsche that raced by her father's BMW, clearly in violation of California's speed laws. But the guy had a big smile on his face as he sped by. Wasn't he scared he was going to get caught? But that thought blast from the past found its answer. No, that was not what he was thinking about. And that was not what she was thinking about. It was the thrill of avoiding capture. It was the thrill of the illicit, however harmless it seemed. It's like taking a cookie from the cookie jar when told not to do so. It is the thrill of looking through someone else's private diary. The pull of taboo has taken hold of her. More and more, she became a smuggler. She smuggled teenage romance books from the library and secretly read them at night when her mother and father were asleep.

The night before the second meeting was, however, epic in comparison to those small time violations. She felt like she was going to take the mother load of all violations. It was harmless enough, wasn't it? She was merely going to start a conversation with Carlos beyond a simple "hello." And it was not like she was going to say, "Hello, is it me you're looking for?" She was not going to be that direct. In fact, she was not going to be romantic in any way. However, it felt wrong. It felt very wrong. And the elation she felt each time she smuggled a teenage romance book right under her mother's nose intensified in the ecstasy of frenzy in her heart that made her dizzy. She felt like she could faint. With the excited thoughts of ambiguous nature racing past her cognitive process, Yahudit fell asleep.

"Wake up, darling, for your Hebrew School!" Mother said softly but resolutely.

Yahudit practically jumped up. For some reason, she feared her mother. She almost felt like she was not a human being. Maybe she imagined all that. But she even speculated that her mother was snatched up by an alien and the mother before her was an alien in disguise. Maybe she was the wicked witch of the west?

The whole class was a blur. She knew that she should not daydream like Walter Mitty, but she did. But unlike Mr. Mitty who dreamt about greatness, Yahudit dreamed about violation. She wanted to violate the Torah with Carlos. For her, that was a lofty goal worth striving for. She would make up for the slaughter of Hamor and his brothers by Dana's cruel and unfair brothers. She was going to be the heroine of the story who will make everything right again. She will bring about *tikkun olam* and shine as the light unto the nations as a Jew who can love, who is not afraid to love.

"Carlos," Yahudit said.

Carlos just smiled. Wasn't he going to say anything?

"Carlos, you look nice, today," Yehudit said after not being able to fish up anything better to say.

Carlos smiled, but he looked as if he was trying to suppress his laughter. Yahudit turned red. But she was undeterred from her goal of becoming the heroine of her own life's story and redeeming all Jewish people, everywhere.

"Carlos, do you know any Hebrew?" Yehudit asked. She wanted to keep the conversation going. She was upset that Carlos was not helping, but felt that he might be a victim like Hamor and his people. Who knows what his Jewish employers were doing to him? If they were like Dana's brothers, they were probably giving him Hell on earth.

"No," Carlos said. It was the first time that Carlos looked down. Yahudit was convinced that the owners of the kosher joint were like Dana's brothers. Yahudit quickly threw the owner near her a dirty look. He seemed to just brush it off with that I-don't-give-a-fuck Eastern European stare not unlike the stare that the landlord in Spiderman movies has plastered on his face perpetually. Was he acting or is that his real expression? It is so Eastern European. Okay, stereotypically Eastern European. Yahudit made a mental note to ask her dad about that actor. Maybe he knew him, being in the movie industry and all.

"That's okay," Yahudit said. "I will teach you."

Carlos looked up with bewilderment. Where was that friendly Mexican smile?

"Ahava," Yahudit said. "That means love."

"Ahava?" Carlos said.

"Yes, that's perfect, Carlos," Yahudit said. She thought she would start with the word that typified what she was trying to do. She was going to be the light of the world on behalf of the Jews and show that Jews are not like Dana's brothers.

Carlos seemed embarrassed especially as his boss glared at him. He quickly said, "Thanks for teaching me the word."

Then, that was it. The conversation was over.

There was evening and there was morning. The second day.

And Yahudit saw that it was good. At least, good for her even if it seemed to anger every Jew in the kosher joint. That meant everyone except for Carlos. Was it good for Carlos?

Judith hated Carlos. In fact, she hated all Mexicans, legal and illegal. Yahudit reasoned that if you hate illegal Mexicans, then you would necessarily hate legal Mexicans.

"It's not true," Judith protested. "I don't hate legal Mexicans. I just hate illegal Mexicans."

"So, you do admit that you hate Mexicans," Yahudit played the prosecutor. "Yes or no?"

"Okay, I will tell you the truth," Judith retorted. "I do hate illegal Mexicans. It's just that they are here illegally."

"Why should that bother you?"

"Because this country is for Americans."

Yahudit

"Yeah, like you?" Yahudit spoke scornfully. "Do you know what happened during World War II?"

"Of course, I do," Judith said. "I am a Jew, aren't I? All Jews know."

"So, what happened?" Yahudit asked with a forced innocent look on her face.

"You can't be serious!" Judith said angrily. "Why are you patronizing me?"

"Just answer the question," Yahudit said.

"Okay," Judith said. "I will play your twisted little game. Hitler killed six million Jews."

"See, that's what all Jews say," Yahudit said. "How about the other side of the story?"

"The other side of the story?" Judith asked, puzzled.

"Yes, the other side of the story," Yahudit repeated. "Do you know the other side of the story?"

"No, not really," Judith said and looked down, either embarrassed or confused.

"This is what I call the American Story," Yahudit said.

"The American story?" Judith asked.

"Yes, it is the story of what the Americans did in the war," Yahudit said.

"But that's us," Judith said.

"Precisely," Yahudit said. "The American government turned away boat loads of Jews who successfully escaped Nazi Germany and sent them back to die in the gas chamber."

"No!" Judith exclaimed.

"Yes!" Yahudit affirmed. "The US government sent the Jews back to their death because they were illegal immigrants."

"Really?" Judith asked.

"Really," Yahudit confirmed. "You can read all about it."

"Oh, I didn't know that," Judith said.

"It was because they were illegal immigrants that they were treated worse than trash and sent to die a death that was 100% reserved for them. And you attack illegal Mexicans!"

Yahudit

"Well, that's different," Judith said. "Of course, it's important to save a life. Jews were running away from death. It wasn't about legal or illegal immigration."

"Well, for the US government, it was about illegal immigration," Yahudit said. "What would happen to law and order if you let illegals in and gave them citizenships?"

"Yahudit," Judith replied, "You are being way sensitive because you like that Carlos, the illegal Mexican."

That's when the fight broke out and the conversation stopped.

Janice fortunately walked in and stopped the fight. Both Yahudit and Judith only had minor scratch marks from the conflict.

Judith was a wealthy Jew. Her grandfather had come over from Iran. He was one of the first ones in the West Los Angeles community. He made his money in property. He was a large landowner in Iran and had dubious dealings with the government. Like most corrupt politicians in that country, he had a large Swiss bank account. When he arrived in America, he first bought land and lots of it. Then, the property prices started to skyrocket. He made millions and millions. He and his progeny did not need to work for the next 100 years. They could just live off of interest.

Yahudit wondered if Judith was spoiled or if she was just a bad person. She could not remember a single time that Judith said a nice thing about anyone. Maybe she was in a bad mood and that was coloring her vision or memory. She decided to dismiss negative thoughts and focus on positive thoughts.

"Yakutat," Janice said. "Would you help me with something?"

"Sure thing," Yahudit replied. Judith threw both of them a dirty look. Yehudit looked away.

"We'll be back, soon, Judith," Janice chirped.

"Ta, ta," Judith said with a slight smile on her lips. It was obvious that Judith was very fond of Janice.

Yahudit

Yehudit and Janice walked away. They found a bench on the street and sat down.

"So, what's up?" Yehudit asked, anxious. It seemed like there was something serious that Janice was preoccupied with.

"Well," Janice said, looking down at her shoes. Then, there was a strange silence.

Yahudit wanted to be patient, so she impatiently remained silent for her friend's sake.

"Well," Janice began again. But again she fell silent. It seemed strange that she was not looking at Yahudit. Yahudit wondered if Janice was going to chastise her for her fight with Judith. Janice liked Judith far more than she liked her. Yahudit was sure of it.

"Can you keep a promise?" Janice suddenly looked up as she spoke the words very slowly.

Yahudit looked at her with equal intensity. "Of course, Janice."

"Okay, here it goes," Janice began once again. "I have been seeing a Goy boy."

"A Goy boy?"

"A Goy boy."

"A Goy boy?"

"Is there a broken mp3 player, here, or something?"

"Sorry," Yahudit said. "Do tell."

"I am not joking," Janice protested.

"I am sorry," Yahudit apologized. "I did not want to make light of the situation."

"Okay," Janice said, satisfied. "I feel like I can confide in you because you are in love with Carlos."

"I am not in love with Carlos!"

"Okay, whatever."

"I am not," Yahudit said.

"Okay, Yahudit," Janice said. "Anyhow, I thought you might be able to understand what I was feeling."

Yahudit gave Janice a puzzled look.

Yahudit

"What I mean by that is that I felt that I can confide in you and receive some sympathy," Janice commented. "You know Judith. She won't understand."

"Oh," Yahudit said and nodded.

"Yeah, you know," Janice said and nodded in agreement. "I am in love with this Goy boy. I feel good to get that off my chest. I had kept that in my heart for a long time and couldn't tell anyone."

"Well, you can spill your guts to me, my dear Janice," Yahudit said eagerly, more out of curiosity than sympathy. "I won't tell anyone."

"I met him last summer when I went to the summer program at Phillips Exeter Academy."

"Really? Why did you not tell me before?" Yahudit said, naively.

"Because you were as enthusiastically orthodox Jewish as Judith," Janice replied. "I did not think that you would understand."

"You should have tried me!"

"And risk everything?"

"Okay, you do have a point there."

"But now," Janice said slowly, "I know that I can trust you because you feel the same way as I do. You love a Goy boy."

"He's hardly a boy," Yahudit said, defensively.

"You know what I mean," Janice said, agitated.

"Okay, you are right," Yahudit admitted. "So, what happened?"

"Wait," Janice paused for a second until an orthodox couple passed by. "You know how my dad is always interested in academics."

"Yeah, of course," Yahudit said. "After all, he's a UCLA professor. I think it goes with the territory."

"Don't be sarcastic, Yahudit," Janice said with pain showing on her face. "This is a serious topic so important to me."

Yahudit

"I wasn't being sarcastic, Janice," Yahudit said, defensively. "I was merely stating a fact."

"You want to hear the story?" Janice asked, ignoring Yahudit's comments.

"Yes, I do," Yahudit said softly.

"Okay, that's better," Janice said. "It all started on the first day of the summer school when I arrived on the beautiful campus of Phillips Exeter Academy." Janice paused for a second and reminisced as if Yahudit weren't there. "I was walking down the main walkway of the campus, and there he was."

"Who?" Yahudit interjected.

"The Goy boy," Janice said.

"Did this Goy boy have a name?" Yahudit asked with a frown.

"Yes, but I don't want to tell you," Janice replied.

"Why not?" Yahudit said, agitated.

"Because, you may know him," Janice said flatly.

"Really? I may know him?" Yahudit's eyes widened.

"Yes," Janice said. "It turns out that he lives here in Los Angeles."

"Oh, I see," Yahudit said with all-knowing glare. "So, it's still going on."

"What is?" Janice reacted.

"The love affair with the Goy boy," Yahudit said slowly, not taking her eyes off of Janice.

"Guilty as charged," Janice said and smiled.

"What are you smiling about?" Yahudit demanded.

"I am thinking about my Goy boy," Janice said.

"Awwww," Yahudit said in earnest.

Janice smiled further, and she began to tear up.

"What's wrong?" Yahudit said tenderly.

"I love him so much, Yahudit," Janice said as tears dropped down her cheeks. "The Goy boy is It boy for me!"

Yahudit suppressed her laughter and tried to look serious. "The Goy boy seems like a wonderful guy."

"Oh, the Goy boy is awesome. He's my all."

"Wow," Yahudit replied. "It seems like you are really in love, Janice."

"I am," Janice replied. "And you know how hard it was to keep this all bottled up inside?"

"Yeah, I can imagine. So, what are you going to do, now?"

Janice replied, "I don't know. I guess I have to continue leading a double life as I have for many months. Sneaking out to see my Goy boy. Holding his hand and feeling the ecstasy of his tenderness and with my other eye scoping out the scene to see if there is anyone whom I know."

"It sounds difficult," Yahudit said.

"It is, Yahudit," Janice said. "I am not going to lie to you. It's difficult."

"So, why do it?" Yahudit asked, sincerely curious. "Why stay together with him?"

"Because he is my Goy boy, whom I love more than life itself. I love my Goy boy more than my parents. I love my Goy boy more than Judaism. My Goy boy is my God."

"What?" Yahudit said, surprised. "How can you be so blasphemous?"

"You don't know the power of love until you have experienced it, Yahudit," Janice said. "The way I feel about my Goy boy is something I have never felt about anybody. It is transcendental. It is beyond transcendental. It is higher than the mysticism of Kabala. It is divine essence. It is God. My Goy boy is God."

"Stop it!" Yahudit said. "You are scaring me."

"Sorry, Yahudit," Janice said. "I can't help it. Now that I have released my passions to you, I cannot seem to control myself in expressing how I feel about him."

"Yeah," Yahudit replied. "But there is a limit to everything."

Yahudit

"Oh, you silly girl," Janice said. "You don't know a thing about love. You haven't experienced love. You tell me that after you have really experienced love with Carlos."

"What do you mean?" Yahudit said, angry but not quite sure at what.

"I can't say any more than that," Janice said.

"Wait a minute, Janice," Yahudit said as clairvoyance struck her like a baseball bat hitting a ball that was to bring all the runners to the home plate.

"Yahudit," Janice interjected with fear in her face. "Let's go back. Judith is waiting."

"Wait," Yahudit said. But Janice already stood up and started to rush back.

"Wait," Yahudit said a second time. But by then, the conversation was lost, and Yahudit was rushing to chase down Janice.

That night, Yahudit thought about what Janice had said. She wondered and wondered. And she felt a bit jealous. She did not really know why, but she felt like Janice had something that she did not but needed. Janice had something that she could not understand, but Yahudit felt convinced in her own mind that it was the "treasure" that she had been searching for all her life. She felt hot and bothered about the whole issue. There were so many question marks. There were so many unknowns. There were so many mysteries. And before her was the enthusiastic image of Janice calling her Goy boy "God." What could all this mean? Yahudit wrestled with herself and fell asleep without self-awareness.

2

Yahudit waited a whole week for the next Hebrew school. She did not know what she was expecting, but she knew that something momentous was going to happen. The week seemed to go by so slowly that Yahudit could not stand it. She wished it would hurry up so that she would be at Hebrew school again. So that she would be at the kosher place. Near Carlos.

During the week, she employed various methods to speed up her time. Once, she tried reading the Bible. She looked up the order of creation and noticed that on the third day, God separated the dry land from the sea. She wondered what it would have been like to separate the land from the sea. Does that mean that before the third day, there was water everywhere? It seemed to be that way, didn't it?

Yahudit felt like that was a metaphor for her life. Her life was a big watered-covered land. There was nothing really special. All was homogeneous. There was water everywhere. There was no land in sight. Yahudit began to interpret the metaphor for water as it applied to her. Water was like Judaism that permeated every aspect of her life. Jewishness was the pervasive flood that covered the whole land. What is Yahudit was hidden underneath the water. The water was so deep that nothing could be seen underneath the water.

Yahudit

Yahudit remembered riding on her family yacht in the Pacific Ocean. It was one of her father's hobbies. He loved his yacht. He bought it when his last movie hit number one in the movie charts. He named the ship, "S. S. Say-Rhet." For some reason, Yahudit felt that her mother did not like the name. But she liked it. For some reason, Yahudit felt that the name was perfect for the yacht, which her father bought amidst the protestations of her mother.

Yahudit's mother was afraid that the yacht would take Yahudit's father away from synagogue worship services. It could be the source of temptation for all kinds of sins. She did not like it at all. But Yahudit's father was able to persuade her. It was the only time that her father stood his ground against her mother that Yahudit could remember. And Yahudit was glad that he did.

Yahudit loved those yacht rides in the Pacific Ocean. They would sail and sail, and there was only the blueness of the ocean before them. There were occasional fish that jumped up. She had spotted dolphins and whales, too. Sometimes, seagulls would fly by or even land on the yacht, wanting to pilfer some leftover roast beef sandwich.

Yahudit loved the brush of the wind against her hair, making them fly. She felt like Medusa, but a kinder-gentler one, without any curses, but only blessings. She enjoyed the wind blowing her shirt against her body, flapping it and making a rhythmic sound that seemed to be ethereal. She loved the way the wind tightly squeezed her loose-fitting linen pants, making it hard against her body and pressing against it as if it were as hard as a piece of wood. She loved the saltiness of the air and the sweet aroma that filled her whole nose cavity. She enjoyed the sound of the slushing water, breaking as the yacht strode through it in patterned movement.

Throughout all those pleasurable rides, Yahudit wondered about one thing. Why couldn't she see the land below the water? And at those moments when she came to realize how far away from land she was, Yahudit feared. She feared for her life. She feared for her existence. And all seemed to recede into the background. Yahudit remembered that fear now, as she read the Book of Genesis.

The third day was the day when such frightening water was separated away from the land. It was after dry ground and the sea were separated that the earth could produce vegetation and trees of all kinds. It was then, that earth saw fruit. Juicy, tasty, succulent fruit. This all happened on the third day.

Yahudit felt like she was the dry, potentially fertile land, buried under the vast depth of the sea. She felt like she needed to emerge as the dry land separated from the oppressive shackles of Judaism and Jewishness. For some reason, her Jewishness became a burden to her. Yahudit wondered if the conversation with Janice confirmed in her mind that Judaism was indeed a chain that kept people bound and locked up.

Yahudit wanted to break free and experience the epiphany that Janice had experienced. She realized that the route would be similar. Her own Goy boy would lead her to the true path. Yahudit was convinced of it.

Thus, without knowing exactly what to do, Yahudit resolved to move things along with Carlos. Yahudit desired to enter into relationship with Carlos the way Janice had done so with her Goy boy. Who was this Goy boy after all? Janice still remained secretive. In fact, Janice did not trust her. This thought pained Yahudit a bit. She wondered why Janice could not trust her. Why did she decide not to trust her? Was she not trustworthy? Yahudit became a bit morose.

Then, she was comforted in her thought that she did not really confide in Janice, either. In a sense, Yahudit was being a Janice. She knew that she was keeping her deepest, inner feelings from not only Janice, but also from everyone she knew. It was one secret that has been brewing in her own fertile mind, and no one was privy to it. The thought that it was her secret that no one else in the world knew excited her and made her a bit dizzy. Could she keep the secret for long? She had denied that she loved Carlos even when people asked. Can she go on denying the raging tidal waves of heart?

Yahudit felt that she could because the temptation to let it all out was tendered by her overarching fascination and excitement at her own secret. She liked having this secret, and she was going to keep it deep inside her woman's heart.

Despite the resolove, Yahudit knew that dividing the land from the sea was not an easy task. She wondered if it were possible. How could she deny her essential identity that has marked her whole existence so far? How could she deny her Jewishness and continue to subsist? Wouldn't her whole world just fall apart?

Then, Yahudit remembered that Janice had found her divinity in her Goy boy. Carlos would be the divinity in her life. Carlos would be God, and the relationship will be the new religion. It will be her new identity around which she would order her whole life, thoroughly and completely.

Why couldn't it be done? After all, it was possible to maintain a type of Jewish identity in the Gentile world. She did not relinquish her core identity while negotiating through the superficiality of the outside world. It was superficial but very real. In fact, her living in the Gentile world was practically her whole life.

If she could pull it off with the pervasive Gentile world, why could she not go in the reverse? Why couldn't she maintain her new deity, Carlos, and her new religion, the relationship with Carlos, and negotiate through the "superficiality" of the Jewish world, where she was to repeat the patterns day in and day out. She could do it. After all, she was experienced. She might not have been experienced in the matters of the heart and of love and of relationships, but she was experienced in negotiating through the superficiality of the "outside" world. She knew she could do it. She was firmly convinced of it.

Yahudit played out several scenarios in her mind of how she would initiate her relationship with Carlos. It was a minefield, to be sure. First of all, there was the turf problem.

Yahudit

The whole area was a big booby-trapped enemy minefield. Any sudden movement would initiate a mine blow-up. She could imagine making a romantic gesture to Carlos and the whole restaurant imploding with her and Carlos in it. She would be branded and shunned by the community. She was sure that she would no longer be able to continue in her Hebrew school if she took active steps to start her relationship with Carlos. The first explosion would kill her and Carlos off and along with it, all the dreams of a new religion and a new deity. It was a fragile setting. The turf was thoroughly Jewish, and the Jews of the area prided themselves in having taken active, strategic steps to build the thoroughly Jewish turf.

Besides the turf problem, there was the problem of individual Jewish agents. Janice was right; no one was trustworthy when it came to Goy boy love. Janice had hidden it from her for so long. It amazed Yahudit how such a big mouth could keep a secret so long. And Judith still did not know. This secrecy was needed because every Jew was a potential spy. There was an unspoken understanding among all Jews that whenever Jewishness is threatened, that every Jew does his or her part to curb the tide of attrition. What could be more deadly than a nice, little Hebrew school Jewish girl making a play for an illegal immigrant Goy boy who was a helping hand and a degenerative Sabbath Goy, at that? It would undermine the very fabric of the Jewish world as they all knew it. In such a potentially explosive situation, no one could be trusted. Yahudit knew, then, that even Janice could not be trusted. Yes, Janice had her Goy boy. But that did not mean that she would not rat her out to protect herself. In fact, Janice was more a threat to her than Judith was, in a sense. Janice had something to protect. She had her new religion and her new deity to protect. She would go to any length to protect it. After all, she had turned her back on her whole known world for the new religion. What Judith could overlook as a faithful member of the Old Order, who had nothing to fear from it, was something that Janice could not, if she were under duress. Yahudit was sure of it. Of course,

Yahudit

Yahudit was not going to tell Judith, either. Judith would probably tattletale just to spite her. Judith was a spoiled, rich JAP. She would not think about the consequences of her action, although she might regret it after the deed.

Beside the turf and Jewish agent factors, there was the problem of the Jewish network. Yahudit was deathly afraid of the news reaching her mother. As soon as something happened, Yahudit knew that the Jews in the turf will send a missive out to her dear old mother. Then, all hell would break loose at home. She knew the resolve of her mother who had temporarily disowned her parents during her Stanford days. Yahudit knew the resolve of her mother who was able, with a single stare, to reduce her father, a big powered executive to jello pudding puff. Although she had never admitted before consciously, Yahudit was afraid of her mother; she was deathly afraid of her mother's anger at finding out about her relationship to Carlos.

Yahudit knew that she would not get any sympathy from her mother. Her mother was firmly entrenched in the Jewish faith. It was for this Jewish faith that her mother had separated herself from her parents. Her parents and their secularism were the sea that had covered her own self-will for Jewish identity and religiosity. Her fertile land was discovered only after the active act of division of the dry ground from the sea. And on the fertile ground of Jewish religious identity grew plants and trees of all kinds. And she, Yahudit, was one of the fruits grown on this fertile ground of her mother.

What Yahudit was about to do represented the fall. It was the taking of the forbidden fruit. It was the act of tainting her mother's fertile dry land. It was an act that would permanently mar her mother's paradise. It was an act, Yahudit was sure, that would cast her out of the perfect garden of her mother's love. She would, henceforth, no longer be called Beloved, but rather Rejected.

Yet, despite all the reasons for why she should not, Yahudit wanted to. Yahudit wanted to create her religion and her own golden calf. In those days, they all did what was right in their eyes. And to Yahudit's eyes, embracing the Goy boy, her Goy boy, was the right thing to do. It was going to be the creation of a new world order where she would fit in perfectly, where she would belong. So, although the fear of her mother pervaded, she was going to go through with it. She was going to live her own life.

Yahudit remembered the conversation she had had with her mother.

"Yahudit, you know that we must preserve ourselves," her mother said.

"Preserve ourselves?"

"Yes, it is important that we survive," her mother rephrased her philosophy.

"But, mother, we are doing just fine!" Yahudit retorted.

"Silence, child," Yahudit's mother said. "Don't forget the holocaust. The Goyim will try to wipe us out. It is only with the intuitive intelligence and survival skills gained through hard work that will preserve us."

Yahudit remembered thinking how ridiculous her mother sounded. Perhaps, she was being unfair to her mother. Maybe she had some point to make, and maybe she was ultimately right. But Yahudit remembered how she wanted to rebel after that conversation. She felt like her mother was putting an invisible iron bar around her life. Yahudit felt that her mother was teaching her hatred of Goyim, just because they are Gentiles, and not Jewish. Yahudit wanted so much to prove her mother wrong. She wanted to show her mother that love was the way. She wanted to tap into hope and what was possible through hope and acceptance. But most of all, Yahudit wanted to rebel.

Yahudit wanted to rebel against all that her mother stood for. In Yahudit's eyes, her mother was a hater of mankind. Since there were only 12 million Jews in the world, hating Gentiles constituted a hatred of the whole world. "The whole world is against us, the Jews." Her mother's often recited words seem to ring again and again in her delicate conscience. Her mother stood for hatred. She stood for a world where there is a permanent division between the Jews and the Gentiles. She, despite her education, had embraced ignorance and intolerance. Stanford had provided her with intellectual weapons to hate the Goyim, rather than teaching her to be accepting of all humankind. How could her mother be so intolerant? She was so different from her parents. They seemed to embrace love and acceptance. They seem to find redemption through love. But her mother was out to get all the Gentiles. And she was enlisting her, Yahudit, as a little soldier to accomplish her mission of hatred.

Soon, Yahudit identified her mother as the brothers of Dana who wanted to slaughter Dana's love. They hated the Gentiles, just as much as her mother hated the Gentiles. Yes, she never used the word hatred, but Yahudit was convinced that her mother hated them. Yahudit was further convinced that she would be hated because she loved a Goy boy.

Who would have thought in a million years that a hater-mother who sent her little princess to become a Goy-hater would end up being a Goy-lover? The sheer irony of the matter brought a devious smile to her face. Yahudit began to exult in her devious plan. It was an intelligent design that her mother surely could never have predicted in a million years. It was totally brilliant.

Yahudit began to smile more widely as she thought about the new power that she yielded over the whole situation. Yahudit had felt helpless before as one locked into the inevitable. Yahudit had believed that her life would become a carbon copy of her mother's. There was to be no change, no progress. But Fate had other things planned for her. She was going to break out of the rut. She was not going to be locked down. She was going to fly and soar like an eagle. And she felt the power of a young eagle ready to take his first flight and claim his place as the master of the heavens. Yahudit could not wait to execute her plans.

Yahudit thought and thought about how she was going to start a relationship with her Goy boy. Yahudit had never been in a relationship with a guy before, so it made it difficult to act from experience. However, she had smuggled in those teenage romance stories and had read them with a voracity of an experienced and incorrigible junkie. She had read enough about romance to simulate it. It was a time to enact the models of romance she had read about. Fail or succeed, Yahudit was facing her moment of truth. Yahudit was going to find out what she was really made of. Was she going to buckle under pressure? Was she going to come through and exert herself?

Yahudit became exceedingly optimistic as she pondered her fate. She felt a serene calm as if she had found peace within herself. She reasoned that she could not possibly be in the wrong, since she was fighting for love. Wasn't love the most important value in the world? Love conquers all! How could she lose? Even if she did lose, she would have won, because she had fought for love. Love was truth. Love was the ideal. Love was her oxygen. How could she live without it?

Yahudit knew that her mother was in the wrong. Like Dana's brothers, she stood for hatred. How could anyone live for hatred? How could anyone fight for hatred? How could anyone subsist on hatred? Even if they could, their whole existence was in error, Yahudit was convinced. It was love and love only that was worth living for. Love was the only thing that was worth fighting for. As far as Yahudit was concerned, her mother's life and fight had no real meaning. In fact, her mother's life was sad.

Thus, Yahudit knew that she had won the war even before the battles began. She knew that she was in the right and her mother and her kind were in the wrong. Thus, with serene calmness she closed her eyes. And in a moment, she fell asleep.

It was strange that she had a dream because she almost never had dreams. But in the short moment of repose, she was stricken with a dream that she did not want. Like a movie in a big movie theater, her dream unfolded, interrupting her sleep. It was a scene from the movie, *Schindler's List*. Before her was a trainload of people being carted off to a concentration camp.

Yahudit

And their faces were white as people with leprosy. There was no hope in their expressions. There was no joy. Not a single person had a smile. And she looked at them, like an audience member in a movie theatre. Then, somehow, she entered the movie that she was watching. She was a part of the movie. She was now looking out at the audience. They were watching her. They had that pitiable expression on their faces. She looked at her clothes. They seemed like the similar type of clothes that people in the train were wearing. She focused on her immediate surroundings. She was in the train! She was being carted off to the concentration camp. She was one of those Jews being sent off to the concentration camp to die.

And then, a little girl said to her, "Where's your mama?"
Yahudit replied, "In California."
"California?"
"Don't you know California?"
"No, I am German. I am a German Jew, like yourself."
Yahudit responded, "I am not a German Jew. I am an American."
"You are a Jew!"
"No, I am not! Or ... I don't want to be, anymore!"
"It's too late. You are a Jew, and you are going to die like all of us."
Yahudit said, "No! This can't be happening!"
And then, Yahudit woke up.

Yahudit was a bit unnerved by the dream. It was a short dream, but it felt so real. She actually felt like she was riding on a train. She could almost smell the people around her. They smelled like the farm areas of California which smelled of animal manure. Yahudit remembered the expressions of the Jews being carted off to the concentration camp. She still heard ringing in her ears the shouts of the little girl.

But Yahudit realized that she was not in a movie. She was not in a dream. She surely was not in a train bound for a concentration camp. Soon, Yahudit dismissed her dream as just a nightmare. Wasn't it a common experience of all human beings to have a nightmare? They were not real. But everyone had to experience it to be a part of the human race.

Yahudit was undeterred in her resolve to create her own religion and her own deity that was focused on love and not on hatred. She reasoned in her mind that it was the hatred of Judaism that brought down the Jews of Germany. She became sure of it. She saw how her mother hated the Gentiles. If the Gentiles had two cents about them, they could see the hatred, and they would hate back. That's probably what happened in Germany. All the Goy hatred and Goy bashing resulted in a reaction. The holocaust was merely a reaction against the hatred of Jews against Gentiles that came first. What came first? The chicken or the egg? In Yahudit's mind, she felt she discovered the cause.

Thus, Yahudit's dream had an ironic effect. Instead of encouraging her to be more Jewish, she felt more averse to Jewishness and all that entailed. She wondered how many Jewish youths felt like her after watching holocaust movies. The dream was more real than watching a movie.

With a renewed vigor, Yahudit began to strategize about getting Carlos. She wanted him more than ever. All this thinking about Carlos and her mother had a strange effect of exponentially growing her interest in her project. To her, it seemed more important than anything that she had done in her whole life. Already, it was becoming her religion. Soon, Carlos would be enthroned as the deity of this religion.

Yahudit considered a few possibilities. She could whisper to Carlos and communicate to him that she wanted to go out with him. This option seemed like the ideal since he would clearly get the message, and a relationship could be built on honesty and truth. She liked the idea of combining her religion of love with ideals of truth and honesty. But Yahudit realized that this was not going to be possible. First of all, the kosher dive was a small place, so everyone nearby probably could hear what was being said. Second of all, even if they did not hear what was said, they would consider it extremely strange that she was whispering to a Gentile man. Prolonged conversation could arouse all kinds of suspicions.

After deciding on the third option to write a note and give it to Carlos, Yahudit pondered what she would write on the important piece of paper. She decided to write, "Ahava," along with her phone number. She hoped that he would remember the Hebrew word for "love" that she had taught him. She was going to write the English transliteration of the Hebrew word, since Carlos could not read Hebrew.

Another possibility was to wink and give a subtle signal to Carlos and hope that he would respond. But Yahudit felt impatient about this option. What if he did not understand her intent or misread it? It would create all kinds of unnecessary misunderstanding. What if he starts to talk to his Jewish co-workers about it? That would kill off any possibility for a relationship before it began. They would probably fire him, and there would be no chance for them to get in contact. This second option seemed fraught with problems, so Yahudit decided to discard it.

The third option seemed to be the best option. She would write something on a piece of paper that would relay what she wanted Carlos to know. And she would surreptitiously hand it over to him. He would read it. Voila! The relationship can start.

After deciding on the third option to write a note and give it to Carlos, Yahudit pondered what she would write on the important piece of paper. She decided to write, "Ahava," along with her phone number. She hoped that he would remember the Hebrew word for "love" that she had taught him. She was going to write the English transliteration of the Hebrew word, since Carlos could not read Hebrew.

Yahudit was quite relieved to have a definite plan at hand. She now could take bold steps toward her destiny. Maybe she was more like her father, Yahudit thought. She certainly looked more like him than her mother. She looked Sephardic.

Yahudit's father was, like many Iranian Jews, self-assured and self-confident. There is a reason why Iranian Jews seemed to have so much pride. They say that they are the heirs of the Babylonian Talmud. From them came tomes of erudition that is the foundation for modern Jewish faith. Furthermore, many Iranian Jews think that their lineage can be traced all the way back to the period of the Exile, when the brightest of Israel were exiled to Babylon after the destruction of the first

Jerusalem Temple. Yahudit's father surely had this Iranian self-confidence.

It was surely this Iranian Jewish pride that had helped him to procure Yahudit's mother's hand in marriage, Yahudit believed. Although he was her own father, Yahudit noticed traits that could easily win women's hearts. Although she did not want to confine her dad to a type, Yahudit was proud to know that her father was "cool."

Yahudit imagined herself to be more like her father than her mother. She was going to be the bold one. Just as her father had pursued her mother and won her hand in marriage, Yahudit was going to pursue Carlos and get him.

Not only was she going to get him, she was going to marry him. She would run away with him and create her own *axis mundi*. They would be in a whole new world, a world that was beautiful, one that was full of love.

She longed for Carlos. The more she thought about him, the more her heart ached for him. She knew that she could not live without him. Somehow, she has made a chemical bond with him that seemed stronger than any bond that she had felt ever before.

She wanted to be near Carlos. She wanted to feel his presence near her. She wanted to roast in the warmth of his body heat that she would feel because she was so close to him. She would turn bright red, not with shame or embarrassment but because she would be so hot from the heat emanating from him. She would be so close to him.

Yahudit allowed herself to think further. Why just be close to him? Why just be so close to him as to be feeling his body heat? Yahudit wanted to be touching him. She wanted the physical touch to warm their bodies. She wanted the natural electricity of her body to electrify his body. She wanted to feel his life electricity generating her body's electricity. She wanted to hold his hand.

Yahudit thought to herself how she would hold his hand. The palms of their hands would unite like a chemical bond between oxygen and carbon to form a carbon monoxide. It would be a strong bond, a powerful bond. She imagined her fingers pressing against the top of his hands. She imagined herself pressing harder and harder into his flesh, making her finger prints on his skin.

Yahudit then thought about gently caressing his hand with her fingers while their hands were joined in an intricate tangle. She would move her pointing finger gently side to side and feel the texture of his skin. She would move her index fingers gently over his skin, feeling the hairs that protruded from his skin. She would use her pinky finger to gently stroke the outlines of his hand to show how much she adored his form. Yahudit closed her eyes to picture how she would hold Carlos' hand in hers.

Then, Yahudit dared herself to go further. She allowed herself to imagine her fingers gently caressing his fingers. Each finger of hers lined up against each finger of his. They would stand facing each other, and she would press her right hand against his left hand. In an upright, standing position, their hands would stand pressed against each other. And then, she would gently bend her fingers one by one and start caressing his fingers with her fingers. First, she would use her index finger to caress his index finger. She would do this with every one of her fingers as their hands stood horizontal against each other, pressing into each other in a gentle rhythmic manner. His fingers, sensitive to her touch, would respond by gently caressing her fingers. Each finger would soon be intertwined in ecstatic entanglement, going from orderly and slow caress to frenzied holding onto each other. Their fingers would wrap around as the whites of their knuckles would show against the redness of pressured flesh. Soon, their fingers would start to sweat and their flesh would be mixed in the slippery passion of grabbing. The chaos would bring a strange order to their wild passions that ran deep in their fractured hearts, marred by what was taboo. Goy boy with a Jewess.

Yahudit

Yahudit kept her eyes closed and sighed deeply. In fact, she took a few deep breaths because all the imagination has taken the wind out of her. What seemed like a harmless holding of hands has turned into a hot and heavy entanglement of her heart and mind. She was utterly speechless. And she felt a slight pain with a strange pleasure running through her spine and then down her thighs to her legs. She took a deep breath, and then opened her eyes.

Her room looked different. She did not know why, but it seemed like her room had changed.

3

There was still almost a week remaining. Her Carlos was nowhere to be seen. She had to await almost a week. Why couldn't time just fly by? Why did it seem like this week was going more slowly than previous weeks? Yahudit longed for Carlos. Yahudit longed for the day when the beginning of her new life would begin. But the more she longed for that day, slower the week seemed to go.

She thought about the time that she took a trip to Israel. The week seemed to go so slowly by. Especially as the day of the departure for Tel Aviv neared, time seemed to stand still. She looked at her watch over and over to see if time was moving. She even pressed her watch against her ear to hear the tick tock. But she heard only the silence. She had forgotten that it was a digital watch.

Before this moment in life, the greatest moment in her life was the trip to Israel. She knew it was going to be special even before she embarked on the plane, bound for Israel. All that she felt and experienced were special throughout the whole trip. And even now, as Yahudit looked back at her trip to Israel, she could honestly say that it was the most perfect time in her whole life. Of course, until now.

Israel has always held a special place for Yahudit. Ever since she was a child, her mother had told stories about Israel. It was the Jewish state. It was the Jewish homeland. It was the place which belonged to the Jews. Until the founding of the state of Israel, there were Jews in the Diaspora, wandering through other people's lands. Jews did not feel accepted or welcome. Gentiles all hated Jews. Jews were persecuted. Jews were beaten. Jews were killed. All of this because Jews did not have a homeland to call their own. But it was all different now. Jews had a homeland. Jews were rescued because of the Jewish homeland. Jews around the world could stand tall because they had a country that they could call their own. Most importantly, Jews had a homeland so that they could always return there whenever there was trouble. No future holocaust was going to wipe out the Jews.

For Yahudit, Israel was a kind of a magic land. It was the place where there was only happiness. It was a heaven-on-earth for Jews. All Jews were accepted there. There was no crying there. It was a place where all the sad Jews could have their tears wiped. Israel was better than Disneyland. After all, was not Mickey Mouse a Goy mouse? It was a Goy kingdom. But Israel was a Jewish kingdom. Israel was a place where no Jew would be turned away. Yahudit could be sure that she was accepted there. That's what Yahudit believed all throughout her childhood years. So, it was no surprise that when Yahudit had an opportunity to visit Israel, she thought she was going to a place just below heavenly paradise.

The night before the trip, Yahudit could not sleep. The minutes stood still. Yahudit wondered if she could make time move. Yahudit wanted so badly to be in Israel. She was only a day away. Why wouldn't time move? Why? Why?

With complaints filling her mind and lips pouting from anticipation not satisfied, Yahudit eventually fell asleep. And the sleep whizzed the delayed time through the morning. When Yahudit opened her eyes, she saw her mother standing over her, telling her to wake up or they would miss the plane.

"Wake up! We are going to miss the plane!" her mother yelled. It seemed like she was yelling, but then, Yahudit was half asleep. Yahudit remembered the scene well because it was the worst awakening she had ever had. But then, it was filled with ecstasy. She was now headed to Israel! Yippie!

Of course, they flew El Al. Was there any other airline than the "official" Israeli airline to fly to the Jewish homeland? The plane was practically a flying Israeli flag. The flight was long. That's what Yahudit remembered. The fight was very long. It actually took almost a whole day from Los Angeles to Tel Aviv.

When Yahudit arrived in Tel Aviv, she was half-asleep, tired, and grouchy from the long flight. However, there was vitalization of spirits that was jolted by the realization that she was finally in the Jewish state. She was only eight years old, but she knew that it was a momentous period in her life.

What she remembered most poignantly from the trip was all the guns and weapons that were so visibly public, everywhere. When she got on the bus with her father and mother, she noticed people sitting down with a handgun strapped to their waist. There were soldiers in soldier uniform clutching a machine gun. What was all the brouhaha? Why all the violence? Symbols of war?

Then, Yahudit realized something. The Jewish state was not a paradise at all. In fact, it was a fearful place with all the violence to which she had never been exposed to before. Had she ever seen a real gun in real life?

But all the guns and the uniforms were only a footnote in her wonderful trip to Israel. Maybe it was because she had pictured Israel as a paradise for so long that she convinced herself, contrary to all evidence, that it was a paradise. Maybe she was too young to understand what guns represented. Maybe she was in blissful ignorance because of her innocence. Whatever the reason, Yahudit managed to salvage her ideal world of Israel. Thus, the trip was a fantasy-come-true. It was worth all the expectation and anticipation. Israel was paradise.

Yahudit remembered the blue waters of Bat Yam. The daughter of the sea. That's the English translation for the name of the city near Tel Aviv, where she and her parents had stayed during their time in Israel. Mom and dad had rented an apartment for a week, right in front of the ocean. They say that the Mediterranean Sea is the warmest sea. Yahudit had no doubt after her stay in Israel. It was sure warmer than the Pacific Ocean by far.

Every day, Yahudit woke up early and was overjoyed to see the bright sun shining above in the cloudless sky. She would peer out the open window and take a deep breath. She could smell the salty air that soothed her. She could hear the birds of the air flying and crying, yearning for their loved ones far out away from land. She could watch Israelis of all ages running about, playing beach pad-ball and yelling in Hebrew. Every morning seemed to be new. Every morning seemed to invite. Every morning she was eager to go out.

And every day she went out, Yahudit was not disappointed. Yahudit jolted her mom and dad out of their slumber. She ate her breakfast quickly and cajoled her mom and dad to go out to the beach as soon as possible. Dad carried the beach parasol, and mom held firmly onto a basket, full of snacks and soft drinks. They were a perfect family in the perfect land of Israel. They were at home.

Yahudit made some friends. Maybe it was because everybody was so friendly that she easily made friends. It might have been that her mom and dad were always reading a book at the beach that Yahudit felt a need for some companionship, camaraderie for beach play. Beach friends were not hard to find. There were moms and dads all over the beach. And there were little kids playing. Soon, Yahudit found a set of friends her age, and they built sand castles together, jumped the waves together, and played beach pad-ball together.

The week just flew by, and before they knew it, they were already returning home. All the Israeli friends complained and demanded to know why they were leaving so soon. Mom and dad made some polite excuses. However, Yahudit agreed with them. She felt that she was leaving her paradise way too soon.

Maybe it was because the trip was so short that it all seemed hazy in her mind. Yahudit remembered sketches of that trip. It seemed like something out of the remote past. It seemed almost like a dream that never really took place in the real world.

Yahudit bit her lips as she remembered the trip. Why did they not go back to Israel? It was still a mystery to her. They never went back after that first trip, and mom and dad never talked about going back to the Jewish homeland since then. In fact, the magic of Israel seemed to die at her home.

Yahudit decided to get to the bottom of this. So, she marched downstairs to where her mother was. She was sitting down and reading the newspaper. She hated to disturb her mother, but she was curious and felt entitled to know.

"Mom?" Yahudit ventured.

"Yes, dear?" her mom replied.

"Why did we never go back to Israel?" Yahudit demanded.

"What kind of question is that?" her mother responded defensively.

"Well?" Yahudit was persistent.

Yahudit's mother eyed her daughter pensively. Here she was, all grown up at the age of seventeen. Her mother was impressed by the way her daughter demanded something of her. Yahudit's mother had always imagined her daughter as too timid and unable to assert her own will. But here she was. Yahudit was demanding to know from her mother even though her mother was obviously reluctant to let her know. Yahudit's mother felt a sense of pride at her daughter's self-confidence and assertiveness, especially since it was the first time she was being so pushy. Yahudit's mother suppressed a smile and tried to look serious.

"I really need to know because Israel has been such an important part of my life. I don't understand why we have not gone back," Yahudit ventured.

Yahudit

Yahudit's mother kept looking at her daughter. She remained silent. Surprisingly, Yahudit remained silent as well. And it was as if there were a battle of two wills. Yahudit's mother caved in, first.

"Okay, Yahudit, I will explain to you," Yahudit's mother said.

"And please tell me the truth," Yahudit interjected.

"Would I tell you anything else," Yahudit's mother feigned anger. Yahudit just returned a stern look.

"The simple fact of the matter is," Yahudit's mother continued, "that we have been too busy."

Yahudit looked at her in amazement. She knew that her mother was lying.

"We have been way too busy to get back to Israel," her mother repeated to convince Yahudit.

"But, mom, we have gone on other vacations," Yahudit objected.

"Yes, that is true," Yahudit's mother said to buy time. "But you see, we have gone to new places where we have never been. Life is too short not to discover new and exciting place, isn't it?"

"Yes," Yahudit said, "but if Israel is paradise, then why would we go anywhere else?"

"Israel is no paradise!" Yahudit's mother said quickly.

Yahudit looked at her mother. There was obviously pain in her face. She wondered why her mother looked pained. What made her mother think that Israel was no paradise? What made her mother not want to go back to the paradise? There must be something there that is more than meets the eyes. What was it? What happened there?

"But mother, you said yourself that Israel was a paradise!" Yahudit objected.

"Yes, but that was a long time ago," Yahudit's mother defended her position. "Of course, Israel is very special, but it is no paradise." Yahudit's mother tried to mitigate her first reaction.

Yahudit

"But you have always said that Israel is a paradise for all Jews because it is the Jewish homeland. It is the Jewish state," Yahudit tried her best to mimic her mother's way of talking.

"Now, young lady, don't get fresh with me!" Yahudit's mother spoke sternly.

Yahudit returned a big pout as her response.

Yahudit's mother continued, "Yes, you are right. Israel is the Jewish state. It is the Jewish homeland so that any Jew who wants to go home can, but not all Jews want to go home. Some Jews are happy in the Diaspora."

Yahudit stared at her mother. She couldn't believe her eyes. If she were not mistaken, her mother was elevating the Diaspora above Israel. This was such a change. Yes, Jews lived in the Diaspora, but somehow they were supposed to be ashamed of it. Or in the least, they should act as if they were ashamed of it. But here she was, her mother, who had no guilt about stating that the Diaspora was better than the Jewish homeland. What? Some do not want to go home? What is that all about?

"Okay, mother," Yahudit retreated. She was so shocked by her mother's about-face response that she did not know what else to say. She was completely and utterly shocked. The Jewish homeland was a place where her mother did not want to go back to.

"Wait!" Yahudit's mother said, as Yahudit walked away.

Yahudit turned around to see her mother's horrified face. She must have realized what she had said and what it meant. Yahudit saw her mother fishing for words. She looked absolutely pathetic. Yahudit felt disgusted and ashamed. She did not know what to do. She felt tears welling up in her eyes. Here she was, her staunch wall, her mother, breaking down. She was perhaps the only person she feared in the world. Really feared. And here she was, just breaking down. That was when she realized that her mother was human. She was a mortal. And not only that, she was a pathetic one at that.

"Mom, I have to do some homework. Can we talk later?" Yahudit came to the rescue.

Yahudit

"Okay, dear," Yahudit's mother said. She looked relieved to be let off the hook.

As Yahudit walked up to her room, she realized that her relationship with her mother had changed forever. In a way, it was her wake up call. Or rather, it was a wake up call that let her know that she, Yahudit, was now a fully grown adult capable of standing her own ground. Yahudit was a woman who was actually stronger than her mother. Her mother needed to be rescued. Her own mother!

Yahudit did not know what to think. It was all too much for her. It seemed like she lost something very dear. It seemed like she was becoming someone new and entering into a whole new world. She did not know what to think. She walked quickly toward her room as tears began to stream down her face. She could not stop the stream of tears that flowed down like the cascading waterfalls of Niagara Falls.

Yahudit pushed open the door and tried her best to close the door quietly. She did not want her mother coming up to her room to see what was wrong. She just wanted to be alone. She wanted to be left alone to cry. Cry out all the waterfalls of tears until there was no more to cry out.

She collapsed on her bed and kept sobbing. And she tried to keep her sobbing noise quiet. She did not want to disturb. She did not want to disturb her mom who could not help her. She wanted to be alone. She wanted to deal with this alone.

Then, she felt a strong sense of loneliness overwhelm her. She felt utterly alone in the world. Here was her mother, who had changed. She no longer loved Israel. She kept all that change inside of her as if it were a big secret which she did not want her own daughter in on. In Yahudit's mind, her mother had left her first. And she did not even know when her mother left her. She had left secretly. Yes, she was there in body, but her spirit was somewhere completely different. Her mom had obviously changed inwardly in ways that she could not really begin to fathom at this point of self-pity. Her mom was gone. She was gone forever. Now, there were two women in the house; an older woman and a younger woman, but both women were women in every sense of the term.

Yahudit began to feel betrayed. She felt betrayed by her mother who had evolved secretly apart from her. While living under the same roof, her mother had left her behind without telling her. How could she do that? How could she do that to someone she loves? Did she not at least owe it to her to tell the truth? Why did she lie? She lied about Israel. What else did she lie about? How could they have a deep and close relationship, if it were not built on truth. Obviously, if her mother had lied about this, she could have lied about anything. Everything.

Yahudit started to tremble in her loneliness. She wanted somebody to hold her tight and tell her that she was loved. She felt so unloved. She felt so alone. She needed Carlos. Carlos was going to be her God, and their love would be the new religion. Yahudit would find a new identity in the love of Carlos. Their love will defy Judaism and the Jewish state. She now only had Carlos. She did not even have her mother.

Yahudit's mother sat in her living room, pensive. She regretted becoming so emotional, but she felt that she had every reason for it. But still, she could not shake off the look of disappointment and shock that was plastered on her daughter's face. She had disappointed her beyond repair. What was her daughter thinking now?

Yahudit's mother could not stand it. Each second seemed to pass by with a thump. She could even hear the digital second hand turning. The silence was too much. Then, she heard the sobbing. Her daughter was sobbing. It was so heartbreaking. She wanted to do something to help. She wanted to go up and hug her and tell her that everything will be okay. But she could not. For she caught the contagious virus of self-pity. Those sobs hooked her in ways that where debilitating.

Julia Kashiri put both her hands on her face and felt the wetness of the tears that had already begun to flow. She thought of the waterfalls of Ein Gedi, and remembered the poems of David. Then, she began to remember the poems of penitence when David had committed adultery with Bethsheba. She cried even more. She cried the tears of David, the tender poet, who was utterly remorseful. She cried the tears of a mother who knew that she had let her daughter down. She cried the tears of a woman who knew deep inside that she had lost her daughter, forever. Their relationship was going to be different, forever. And it was all because of it.

Before Julia Kashiri could continue indulging in her thoughts, she received a telephone call.

"Hello?" Julia said, trying to sound as normal as possible.

"Julia? Have you been crying?"

"Mama, is that you?" Julia asked.

"Yes, child. It's me. What's wrong?"

"Everything. I can't talk, now. I will call you back." Julia said, remembering that her daughter was just upstairs and could hear the conversation.

Julia took the car keys and went outside. She started her car. She noticed how smoothly the engine roared. She had never paid attention to the engine before. But for some reason, she paid attention to the engine, now. Julia felt like it was her only friend. And she sobbed aloud inside her car.

After a few bursts of loud sobs, Julia wiped her eyes with tissues she kept in her car. She took out a handkerchief she always kept in her purse but never used. She blew her nose, looked at her puffy eyes in the rearview mirror, and opened the garage door.

It was dark outside. It looked darker than usual. She remembered that her husband was not going to come home until late that night, if at all. They were working on an important movie right now, and he was spending all his time at the Studio. Julia wondered what her husband was doing, now.

For the first time in many years, Julia wanted to call her husband. She longed to hear his voice. But most of all, she wanted to hear him tell her that he loved her. Even if he did not mean it, she did not care. She just wanted to hear those words. She needed to hear those words.

But Julia did not call her husband. She did not want to impose. She did not think that she had the right to impose. After all, she knew that he did not impose on her. He did not think that he had the right to impose on her.

Julia then left the house. She drove off not knowing where she was going.

Yahudit heard her mother's car drive away. She felt like an abandoned baby in the cold, cold world, so she sobbed loudly. And as she sobbed and sobbed, she felt weaker and weaker. She felt tired. She felt very tired. And she fell asleep.

Yahudit had a dream. She had a dream about being back in Israel. There she was with her mom and dad, all happy. It was a trip that she was looking forward to all year, and the flight was wonderful. It whizzed by without any discomfort. In fact, the plane ride was fun. Yahudit was all smiles as she walked through customs with her parents. And they were so happy together. They were smiling and looking at each other amorously. They were such a happy family. Yahudit could not be happier.

And they rented the same apartment that they had many years ago. They were right in front of the ocean. Just like before, Yahudit would run up to the open window and take a whiff of the salty sea air. It seemed to clear up her sinuses and her lungs. She felt rejuvenated and refreshed.

Just like the first visit to Israel, Yahudit tried to rush her parents to the beach. There was the beautiful Mediterranean Sea waiting for them, warmed by the sun floating in the cloudless skies. How could they even waste a second?

After all three of them went down the escalator and across the street to the beach, Yahudit saw a man not too far off. He had his back turned, but somehow she knew that he was the one. Her dream continued.

Yahudit

She tried to lead her mom and dad toward the mysterious man. They walked. Her father and mother looked at each other because they were walking diagonally.

"Yahudit, where are you going?" Julia Kashiri asked.

"Mom, I need to visit the restroom," Yahudit replied. "She couldn't tell her the truth."

"You should have thought about that before coming down," Yahudit's mother said.

"Yes, mother," Yahudit said, "I will catch up with you. You and father go ahead."

"Okay. See you soon," Julia Kashiri said.

As was usual, Mr. Kashiri just smiled and did as his wife bade him.

Yahudit saw her father and mother walk off. When she thought they were at a safe distance, she walked towards the mysterious man. He was talking with someone in Hebrew. It sounded like the flawless Hebrew that her Hebrew school teachers spoke. It had a Sephardic accent. It sounded like Iranian accent! Yahudit was overjoyed. It was destiny that she meet this mysterious man. This man was going to make her happy. He would be like her father to her mother. He would create *tikkun olam*. All will be okay with the world.

Yahudit accidentally crashed into him. It really was no accident at all. The man turned around.

"I am so sorry," Yahudit said, and then looked up at his face. It was Carlos!

"That's okay," the mysterious man resembling Carlos said in perfect Hebrew. "You are not from around here are you?"

"No, I am not," Yahudit said. "I am from the United States. And you?"

"I am from here. I live in Bat Yam."

"Where?" Yahudit said excited.

"Over there," the mysterious Israeli man said, pointing his finger in a direction away from the sea. "You can't see it. It's quite far inland."

Yahudit

"Oh," Yahudit said. "I am a tourist, so I don't know this area really well."

"So, how do you like Israel?" the mysterious man asked.

"I really like it," Yahudit replied. "I have been here before when I was eight years old. This is the second time I am here."

"So, do you find that things are different?"

"No, it seems the same."

"Is that a bad thing?"

"No, not at all," Yahudit responded. "It's just as splendid as before."

"That's fine. Mighty fine."

"What's your name?" Yahudit asked.

"My name is Dodi," the Iranian Jew replied.

"Dodi?" Yahudit said, a bit disappointed.

"Yes, Dodi," the Iranian Jew replied. "Why? Don't you like my name? You look so disappointed."

"Oh, I am sorry," Yahudit apologized. "I thought you would have a different name."

"Like?" Dodi asked, looking curious.

"I don't know," Yahudit lied. "But that's okay. I like you the way you are."

She knew she was too upfront and said too much. But Yahudit felt that she had to compensate. It was amazing how perspicuously she was thinking in her dream.

"Okay, what's your name?" Dodi asked.

"It's Yahudit."

"That's an Israeli name!"

"Yah, I know. My mom's gungho about Israel."

"Really?" Dodi said excitedly.

"Wow, you are excited!"

"Yes, I am. I love this country. It's my homeland." Dodi responded with a light glare in his eyes.

"Wow, it's impressive how much you love Israel," Yahudit said in her dream.

"Don't you?" Dodi asked.

Yahudit

"Well, maybe I will love Israel as much as you love Israel," Yahudit responded honestly.

"Ahava," Dodi said.

Yahudit woke up in shock. She was sweating. She did not know why, but she was drenched in sweat. Maybe it was because her dream of the Mediterranean Sea was so real that she actually "felt" the heat of the Middle Eastern sun. Maybe she actually responded physically to the neurological responses in the dream. She was drooling over Dodi, who looked like Carlos, in her dream, and she was sweating in her real life. Maybe it was because the word "ahava" triggered her memory about Carlos and reminded her how much she was anticipating seeing him after the Hebrew school.

Yahudit felt cold. Yahudit felt alone. Yahudit realized that her house was empty. No one was home. Not a single soul. Where was her mother anyway?

Yahudit picked up the phone and called her father. She did not feel like calling her mother.

The phone did not pick up. There was only the answering service. Yahudit did not want to leave a message, so she just hung up.

Yahudit then called Grandma Friedman. She picked up the phone.

"Hi, grandma!" Yahudit said excitedly.

"Hi, baby," Grandma Friedman said. "How are you?"

"Not doing so well, grandma," Yahudit replied. Surprisingly, tears were welling up again in her eyes. She had thought that she had cried herself out thoroughly, but she was wrong.

"Oh, honey, what's wrong?" Grandma Friedman asked, genuinely concerned.

"Mama and I had a fight," Yahudit said.

"Oh, that's okay, baby. Moms and daughters always have fights," Grandma Friedman said.

"But, grandma, it's different this time," Yahudit said.

"What's wrong, baby?"

Yahudit

"Mom took off," Yahudit said, sobbing.

"What do you mean?" Grandma Friedman asked.

"She drove off, and she is not back, yet," Yahudit said.

"And she did not tell you where she was going?" Grandma Friedman asked.

"No, grandma, she didn't."

"She did not leave a note or anything?" Grandma Friedman asked.

"I was at home, grandma," Yahudit said, half-yelling.

"Okay, baby, don't get upset.," Grandma Friedman said. "Why don't you go check if there is a note. And I will try to reach your mom, okay?"

"Okay," Yahudit said, comforted.

Yahudit rushed downstairs and checked everywhere. There was no note.

Yahudit sat down on the sofa and deliberated within herself to decide whether she should call her mom on her cellphone. She decided against it. Grandma Friedman was probably calling her, right now. She would just wait for Grandma Friedman's phone call.

The wait seemed to be long although the clock on the wall showed that time has moved only a little bit. It was strange to Yahudit how waiting for something wonderful resembled waiting for something worrisome in a negative way. Time seemed to stand still.

She thought about the time that her mother had a car accident. It was about three years ago. Julia Kashiri was driving along the Santa Monica Pier, and a drunk driver rammed her car into hers. It was broad daylight. It was later found out that the driver had been abandoned by her lover and she was drinking herself senseless to get over the pain in the heart.

Her mother was rendered unconscious by the hit, although she suffered minor physical injuries. She did not come out of the coma for a week. She remembered how terrible that week was. What kind of thoughts went through her mind? What if she never comes out of the coma? What if she dies?

Yahudit

She realized for the first time in her life that she could lose someone she loves to death at any time. There was no time schedule for death. And it was not up to you. You can die because some distraught drunk driver drives into you.

Yahudit Kashiri realized during that week how much her father loved her mother. He came every day and sat beside her. He spent hours holding her hand and caressing her arms as if that would wake her up. Of course, her mother, being in a state of coma, did not realize that he was there and was being so tender with her. But Yahudit knew, and that meant the world to her. It was one time that she felt safe and reassured.

David Kashiri was not an unaffectionate man. In fact, he was very affectionate. They say that it is in the Iranian blood. David Kashiri was Iranian through and through and was actually more affectionate than the average Iranian. Yahudit never felt unloved by her father. He was always fussing over her. But Yahudit's father was never around. David Kashiri seemed to be closer to his work than his family.

Perhaps, it was because he wanted to impress the Ashkenazi princess with whom he had fallen in love with and never felt quite equal to that drove David Kashiri to seek success. Stanford University was a long time ago, and Julia Kashiri was becoming more and more demanding. And in social functions, they stood out, Mr. and Mrs. David Kashiri. Everyone looked at how dark he looked and how light she looked. He was an Iranian Jew, and she was a Polish, Germanic Jew. They were the yin-and-yang of the Jewish world; they were from the opposite color spectrum. Their cultures, one Iranian Jewish and the other Ashkenazi through and through, were diametrically opposed. Although David Kashiri did not exhibit the Iran-ness of his parents, he did not always pass through complexities of the Ashkenazi world without some faux pas.

It irked him every time. But worse, it made David Kashiri feel that he was not quite good enough for Julia, the love of his life. As David felt the weight of his inadequacy heavily pressing down against him, he became more and more

Yahudit

withdrawn, even when he was at home. It seemed to affect him in serious ways. He was still quite cheerful by Ashkenazi standards, but he was visibly withdrawn in the eyes of those who knew him for a long time.

"David, what's wrong?" David Kashiri's mother would always say when she was around.

Yahudit's father would always respond by saying, "Mama, I am happy. Very happy, indeed."

But somehow Sarah Kashiri did not seem convinced.

Yahudit often wondered if her father was truly happy. He smiled a lot, but they were smiles of affectation rather than those produced via spontaneous combustion. Sometimes, Yahudit could swear that she saw a tense, forced muscle around the edges of his smiles. Yahudit wondered why he was so unhappy.

David Kashiri struggled all his life to make it in the world. There were so many trials and tribulations facing a dark-skinned boy in those days. People thought he was black.

"Nigger, what cha doin' in these part of the woods?" a neighbor would ask.

San Diego, his hometown, was not the most friendly part of California. There were a lot of rednecks out there according to Yahudit's father. Like most Iranian, David Kashiri was quite talkative. His verbosity and the elegance of it were what captured most women and held them in enthrall. Yahudit was always mesmerized by her father's eloquence. And she supposed that it was why her mother had fallen in love with him. David Kashiri was especially loquacious when it came to describing the anti-Semitism of the residents of San Diego.

"They would say, 'Nigger-boy, what cha doin' here? Shoo, Shoo!' Could you believe it?" David Kashiri said once. Yahudit could not believe it. There were no racists in California. Why does her dad keep talking about anti-Semitism? Although Yahudit did not believe half of the stories told by her father, she loved his anecdotes and always craved for more. They were so entertaining.

Yahudit

Sometimes, Yahudit thought that her father was over-sensitive. Yahudit did not encounter any racism or anti-Semitism personally. There was nobody who was out to get her and her kind. What was her father talking about? She lived in privilege, and so did all the Iranian Jews she knew. They lived in big houses. They lived in bigger houses than most non-Jewish people they knew. They lived in nice neighborhoods. There were Jewish politicians, businessmen, movie producers, doctors, professors, and so on. How could her father think that there was discrimination against Jews?

Yahudit believed that it was all a myth. None of her Gentile friends in school ever made an issue about her being Jewish. In fact, they always happily celebrated with her on Jewish holidays. When she invited her Gentile friends for Hanukah and Purim, they came and loved it. Most of the attendees in her Bat Mitzvah celebration were Gentiles. Yahudit simply could not believe that Jews were discriminated against. It was a big lie. At least from her own personal experience, there was no discrimination against Jews.

But it was one unalterable axiom for her father. David Kashiri lived his life with the scarecrow driving him. It was the same apparition that seemed to cause his despondency whenever he was with his beautiful wife in social settings where he represented the night and she the day. Some say that in the pecking order of the Jewish world, Germanic Jews were at the top and the Iranian Jews were at the bottom. So, in a sense, Julia was the head and David Kashiri was the smelly feet of their togetherness.

Yahudit had no doubt that her mother loved her father. Julia was not Iranian, so her affections were not so outrageous or overt. She shunned showing affection in public. She even avoided expressing her emotions in private. Yahudit could imagine how this could eat away at her father. She realized more and more as she grew older how her mother's Ashkenazi ways were a form of a torture system for her father. They were from a different world. Their bond, previously held together by the passionate love and hormones of youth, was now hanging on by a thread. There was misunderstanding. There is what the one wants, which the other didn't seem to be able to give because of the divergence in cultural backgrounds. There were perceptions about the world, about social settings, that clashed and impeded on the bond. Although David and Julia tried to show that all was okay, Yahudit knew that there was something wrong. But Yahudit tried to ignore this reality. It wasn't the world she wanted to explore. She wanted a happy family, and she was going to have a happy family. Even if she had to push all doubts out of her mind, she was going to do it for the sake of her present and future happiness.

David Kashiri had a different formula for happiness. He felt that he could maintain or create happiness through hard work. It is the American way. Nothing is impossible with hard work. Hard work would make him successful, and then he could give Julia, his love, all the things she wants. Julia would be proud of him. She would be proud to be with him. She would be happy. Thus, David Kashiri toiled and toiled away at work. And he was less and less at home.

Yahudit did not really think about her mother's state of happiness. Like all children, Yahudit assumed that their mother was a staunch fortress. But Julia Kashiri was unhappy. She has been unhappy for a long time.

It was then that the telephone rang. It was Grandma Friedman.

"Grandma? Do you have news?" Yahudit Kashiri asked.

"Yes, baby," Grandma Friedman said. "Your mama is on her way to see her mama."

"What? She's driving all the way to San Francisco?"

"Yes, baby," Grandma Friedman said in a soothing soft voice. "It seems like she has some things to talk over with her mama. Don't worry. I will fix her, and she will be good as new. You will have a new and improved mama when I'm done with her. But you got to take care of yourself for a few days, okay?"

Yahudit

"No problem, I can do that. I'm seventeen, you know," Yahudit said confidently. "But what's wrong with mom?"

"Nothing's wrong, baby," Grandma Friedman said. Yahudit thought her grandma's voice was becoming a bit more husky and thought that strange. "Nothing's wrong. I make everything all right."

"Okay, grandma," Yahudit said. She always trusted Grandma Friedman.

For some reason, Yahudit did not feel like she wanted to call her dad to tell him what happened. She was a bit afraid since it was an argument that they had that precipitated this journey on the part of her mother. But more importantly, Yahudit was not sure about her father's role in this surprising flight of her mother. So, Yahudit decided to fix herself dinner. She did some school work. Then, she fell asleep.

It was a day before the Hebrew Sunday School, and her mother was still not back from San Francisco. For some reason, Yahudit did not feel like her mother was not there. Maybe it was the fact that it's been a while since Yahudit has done thing on her own in her own space that she did not miss her mother being in the house. Even when they were together, each did her own thing in her own little world.

It is also possible that Yahudit did not miss her mother's presence because she was mature enough to know that her mother was human with a need to be left alone to figure some things out. Obviously, there was something more than meets the eye. Maybe her mother had been repressing trials and tribulations for a long time. She's earned a little time to herself to work things out for herself. Yahudit felt she had been selfish when it came to her mother. Her mother needed time alone. It's possible that this was the reason.

Of course, it was possible that the inevitable had occurred. Maybe Yahudit did not love her mother as much as she did before. They say mother's love is different from a child's love. Mother loves her child unconditionally, but the child does not. Maybe it is because the mother carried her child

65

in her womb for so long that the child is a part of her. There is a psychosomatic bond that the mother is conscious of; after all, the mother was an adult when she had her baby. The baby was unconscious or not really self-aware in a cognitive way. Thus, the child, although subconsciously remembering the bonded time in the subconscious state, cannot really recall how the period was like. It's possible, therefore, that the psychosomatic bond exists in the child but only on the subconscious or the unconscious level. Thus, it is easy to find that a mother loves unconditionally, but the child cannot. Maybe this is the reason why so many of the children abandon their parents to Old Folks Homes, although a mom is reluctant to abandon her baby. Even when Britney Spears is in a frenzied state of mind or under duress, self-imposed or otherwise, she seeks to fight for her kids; she wants her kids near. This explains the whole custody fight initiated by many mothers. They are her children. They are a part of her being, her essence. It may be that Yahudit did not have the love of a mother for her child, and that is why Yahudit loved her mother less than before. Was this possible? Is it because she loved her mother less that she missed her less?

It may be the case that Yahudit was not so bothered about her mother's absence from home because she had so much in her mind. This was the week that her new world will be created. This new world will replace all the things from the old world. Yahudit was a bit afraid, but she was also excited that she could create something amazing, something altogether revolutionary, all by herself as she bonds with Carlos, her new God and Supreme Being. Through Carlos the whole world will receive meaning in her eyes. Her existence will have a value that could not have been imagined before or without him. This week was when that was all going to happen. Tomorrow, in fact, was when the creative process would start. The world will be recreated. She will be recreated. And all will be new.

It was not that she loved her mother less. Yahudit was convinced of it. The fact is that she was so focused on something else or something more central that everything else just fell into the background. Tomorrow, the dry land will be divided from the sea. And plantation will grow on the dry land. Her life will be fruitful and multiply. Yahudit longed for the day to arrive. It was less than 24 hours away.

Yahudit dedicated her whole day to preparation. Her mother was in San Francisco, and her father was away filming something or other, so Yahudit had the whole house to herself. She skipped all the synagogue programs for that day. She avoided meeting up with her friends. She just stayed in her house and tried to reflect and to prepare.

She made herself some cappuccino and placed herself on the living room sofa. She sipped her cappuccino and thought about the best cappuccino she ever had.

It was the cappuccino she had drunk with her father in Italy. The family had taken a family vacation to Italy, the previous summer, because her mother loved Italy.

"Oh, I love Italy, and I know you will love it, too," Julia Kashiri had said. Surprisingly enough, her mother was right. Yahudit absolutely loved Italy.

They flew into Rome and spent a few days in Rome. They did the touristy stuff, like visiting the Coliseum by day and by night. It was absolutely beautiful to see the ancient building all lit up at night. Yahudit imagined all the gladiatorial races. Men fighting to the death. Lions and tigers battling it out with some hapless slave. She wondered if she would have cheered or turned away. Maybe she would have boycotted the gladiatorial races because they were so bloody and inhumane.

They visited several pizza places in Rome. Yahudit was surprised to find that they were quite different from those found in the United States. Pizza crust was thinner and there were more creative toppings. When they were in Italy, their mother knew that they could not find any kosher places, so they all went vegetarian. As long as meat and milk were not mixed, Julia reasoned, pizzas were kosher in spirit, although they might have been prepared with utensils that touched both milk and meat products.

Yahudit

"Of course, dear, the Talmud and the Sages would have agreed with you that you are keeping the spirit of the kosher laws," David Kashiri said and winked at his daughter when his wife was not looking.

At first, the pizzas tasted a bit funny, Yahudit thought. The sauces tasted like nothing she had before. And the cheese was different. But soon, she fell in love with her personal vegetable pizza with exotic toppings like artichoke and spinach. Soon, she looked forward to lunch and dinner times because she could order her own vegetable pizza.

It was too hot during the summer to spend much time inside museums. There were many to be sure, but Italians did not seem to understand the American concept of generous airconditioning during the summer time. All three of them hated to be icky and sweaty, so they avoided prolonged stays inside stuffy old buildings.

But of course, they had to visit the Vatican. How could anyone avoid the Vatican when in Rome. They took the guided tour after a long-line wait outside. But it was all worth it because it was just amazing inside. Yahudit was surprised to find swastikas imbedded on the floor of the Vatican. Her mother explained that they were symbols of peace and harmony in India and in Buddhism. Her father emphasized that the Vatican hated Jews and wanted to kill them all off. He was probably half-kidding, but Yahudit felt uncomfortable. Her father was going on one of those rants again! And in Rome.

Yahudit was looking forward to their visit to Florence. She was going to meet a pen-pal. As tacky as it was, she had kept up a pen-pal relationship with a guy from 7th grade. It was rare because everyone did the email, instant message, net-calling thing. But Yahudit remained true to the spirit of the pen-pal experience and just wrote snail mail after snail mail. Her pen-pal reciprocated, and Yahudit received quite a number of letters with beautiful Italian stationeries.

They had written to each other for almost six years! That's over a third of her life. Yahudit felt closer to her pen-pal the closer her train came to Florence. They were to meet in a famous café, the next day. Alfonso Giovani gave very detailed instruction to the place. They couldn't miss.

Her father, mother, and she settled in at a nice hotel in Florence. Most of the hotels in Florence apparently did not have airconditioners. Apparently, Italians were cold-blooded and did not need them, many Americans complained whenever they met other Americans. But their hotel was nicely airconditioned. In fact, after her father was through with the control, a penguin could have been happy inside their room.

David Kashiri said, "You can always put more blankets on, but there is only so much you can take off. It's better to be cold rather than too hot."

Yahudit understood her father's sense of humor. Her mother seemed amused at times, but she looked more annoyed than amused most of the time.

The next day, her father and Yahudit decided to go to the place to meet her pen-pal. Yahudit's mother was not feeling well. Maybe it was the swastika sightings that cast an evil eye on her, but whatever the reason, Julia Kashiri decided to stay in and take a sleeper.

It was rare for Yahudit to be walking alone with her father. She did not remember when the last time was. Her father was always making the movies, and when he managed to get away, they always did things as a family. Mother was never absent. So, today was special.

They were at the café an hour early. Yahudit was embarrassed, but her father laughed the situation off with a typical Iranian sense of humor.

"My darling, we can have coffee together and catch up on things," David Kashiri said enthusiastically.

He made her feel much better.

"Two cappuccinos, please," David Kashiri ordered the waiter.

"Pronto," the waiter said and tried to act like the Italian waiters in American movies.

Yahudit

David smiled and shook his head. Yahudit joined in smiling.

"It's good that we are able to chat like this," David said.

"Yeah, I am glad, daddy," Yahudit said.

"So, tell me about your friend," David said.

"Okay, what do you want to know?" Yahudit asked.

"Whatever you tell me will be fine with me," David responded.

"Okay, daddy," Yahudit said, trying to figure out what information to reveal and what information to dissemble. "Alfonso Giovani is fond of Latin."

"Latin?" David Kashiri said.

"Yes, daddy, Latin," Yahudit repeated. "I know you may be surprised because there are not many people in America who study Latin, but in Europe, all the students study Latin."

"Really?" David seemed surprised.

"Yes, daddy," Yahudit was feeling self-content at knowing something her father did not know. This made her loquacious. "Daddy, Alfonso wrote me that he started learning Latin in fourth grade and has become very good at it. Now, he can write in Latin and read texts written in Latin by Cicero and Tacitus."

"Wow, impressive," David said.

"Isn't it?" Yahudit said.

"But don't sell yourself too short, honey," David said to his daughter. "You are one impressive young lady. You speak Hebrew, and you are the brightest in your class."

"Yeah, but I can't read Hebrew written by some famous author," Yahudit said.

"Come on, darling. You read the Bible. Ha-Shem wrote that thing, so you do read Hebrew written by a famous author. Who can be more famous than Ha-Shem?" David nudged his daughter.

"Awwww, dady, you are so sweet," Yahudit said and hugged his arm. He seemed to like that, so Yahudit hugged his arm tighter. But soon she released his arm when she felt like a little puppy holding onto a lamp-stand in the living room.

"So, do you like him?" David asked in a fatherly way.

"Of course, I do, daddy," Yahudit chirped. "He's my pen-pal."

"But do you like him, like him?" David asked.

"Daddy!" Yahudit said and turned bright red. "You know I have never had a boyfriend. I don't like boys that way."

"Really?" David said, incredulous. "But I bet all the boys are after you!"

Yahudit looked down at her cappuccino that had mysteriously been set in front of her without her noticing. Maybe the waiter put it there during the sensitive moments of clinging when she had her eyes closed for a second. She took the cappuccino and began to sip it.

"Oh, this cappuccino is sooooo good!" Yahudit said genuinely. It's the best cappuccino that she has ever had.

"Let me try," David said and started to sip his cappuccino. He closed his eyes and looked like he was floating on clouds.

"Darling, that is marvelous!" David said. "Your boyfriend knows his café's."

"Oh, daddy!" Yahudit said and gave a soft punch on her father's arm.

"Ouch," David said. "Darling, you don't know your own strength. I think I have a bruise there."

Yahudit felt sorry, so she looked up at her dad. He was looking at her with gentleness. She felt moved.

"Daddy?" Yahudit said.

"Yes, darling?" David responded.

"I am not as liked by boys as you think I am," Yahudit said, feeling like she was at a confession, like in the movies. "Boys don't like me too much."

"I don't believe that, Yahudit!" David said firmly.

"It's true, daddy," Yahudit replied.

Yahudit

"Well, those boys in America are all stupid," David said. "You see, this Italian boy, Antonio...."

"Alfonso!" Yahudit interjected.

"Sorry," David said and gave his daughter a nod. "Alfonso Giovani knows what is good."

"But he hasn't even really seen me," Yahudit objected.

"A person is more than how she appears," David said. "Alfonso is smart enough to know that."

Yahudit was appeased. "I guess you are right, daddy."

David said, "Father knows best." And he gave a big grin.

"Daddy?" Yahudit asked.

"Yes, darling?" David replied.

"Can I ask you something?" Yahudit asked.

"Of course, dear," David said tenderly.

"Why do you think mom thinks I am too young to have a boyfriend?" Yahudit asked, point-blank.

"Oh, because she's a mother," David said.

"But other mothers want their daughters to have a boyfriend," Yahudit said.

David quickly looked away for a second. Then, David looked at his daughter and said, "She's just trying to protect you, darling. The world is a crazy place. Not everyone is nice or genuine."

"Oh, you think that's what it is?" Yahudit asked, genuinely wanting to know.

"Yes, darling," David said. "But I think it is about time you started dating."

"Really?" Yahudit asked excitedly.

"Of course!" David replied. "Your mom was not much older than you when I romanced her on Stanford campus."

"Yeah, you are right!" Yahudit said.

"You are going to Stanford, too, right?" David said.

"I was thinking more about Harvard," Yahudit said to tease her father.

Yahudit

"Oh, you traitor, you!" David said. "A child of two Stanford alums. Of course, you are going to carry on the Stanford legacy!" And David laughed.

Yahudit joined in the laughter.

They sipped their cappuccino in silence for a few seconds, getting over their laughter. It was such a good cappuccino. Simply amazing!

Their celestial silence was interrupted by a tall, nicely dressed young man.

"Hello!" the dark, handsome stranger said.

Yahudit instantly recognized the face from the photo. Her legs when numb, and her tongue became tied. She could not really say anything.

"Are you Yahudit?" the stranger asked.

Yahudit nodded and then managed to let out, "Yes."

"I am Alfonso Giovani."

Alfonso introduced himself with such a flair that all American men whom Yahudit had known before seemed to be mere boys compared to Alfonso. He looked majestic in person. And he talked with an air about him that was simply magical. Yahudit did not know what to do and lost herself in his gaze, so that she started to giggle.

Yahudit's father eyeballed her daughter because he had never seen her act that way before. For the first time in his life, David Kashiri found himself speechless. David looked at her daughter and then looked at her daughter's pen-pal.

"How nice to meet you!" Alfonso let the words roll out of his mouth like sweet-scented honey. "You must be Mr. Kashiri." Alfonso Giovani turned to Yahudit's father and gave a slight bow. What grace! Yahudit had heard about the graces of Italian men, and here he was, the quintessential Italian Adonis.

"Yup, that I am and proud to be," Yahudit's father regained his equilibrium out of necessity than anything else because he did not want his daughter to think that he was a dork.

"I am very honored to meet you," Alfonso said in a slightly more serious tone.

Yahudit

"Likewise," David Kashiri said.

"Why don't you sit down," David said.

"Oh, yes," Yahudit chimed in the invitation.

"I would be glad to," Alfonso said and sat down.

"It is so good to finally see you," Yahudit said after regaining her composure.

"You know, you look far more beautiful in real life than in the picture?" Alfonso said. The man did not waste any time! Yahudit wondered if he was as fast with women as Italian men were reputed to be. She felt tingly as she felt an advance from the Italian Adonis.

"Thank you," Yahudit said and smiled.

"Yes, she is our sweety pie," David Kashiri said defensively.

"Dad!" Yahudit was embarrassed because her father was babying her in front of the Italian Adonis. "You are embarrassing me."

"I am sorry, honey-puff!" David said with a tone. The tone angered Yahudit, but soon she realized that he was being over-protective. Fathers! Yahudit shook her head.

"What's wrong, honey?" David asked.

"I am just glad to see Alfonso," Yahudit said. Alfonso smiled, but David did not.

"He's a good-looking fella," David said with sarcasm in his voice. Yahudit caught it, but it did not seem like Alfonso did. Maybe he did, but he was being polite. Yahudit liked him even more for his composure.

"How do you like my country?" Alfonso asked.

"It is absolutely marvelous!" Yahudit exclaimed.

"We are enjoying your country tremendously," David said.

Alfonso ordered a cappuccino, and David Kashiri ordered two more cappuccinos for himself and his daughter.

"I am glad that you love my country," Alfonso said.

"Well, I don't know about 'love'...." David was being negative.

Yahudit

"Oh, dad!" Yahudit said. She did not like the fact that her dad was playing the protective father. What's gotten into him? Yahudit gave her dad a dirty look, covering the view from Alfonso with her coffee mug.

"Isn't it nice that Alfonso came all the way from Pavia to see us?" Yahudit said, trying to put her dad in line.

"Well, we came all the way from Rome," David said. Yahudit kicked her dad on the leg.

"Oooh," Alfonso said. Apparently, Yahudit had kicked the wrong leg.

"Oh, I am sorry, Alfonso," Yahudit said. "I don't know what's gotten into me. It must be the jetlag."

"That's okay, Yahudit," Alfonso said so earnestly that Yahudit wanted to squeeze both of his cheeks. "You have my permission to kick me any time and as often as you want."

"I don't want to kick you," Yahudit protested.

"You can do whatever you want to me," Alfonso said, smiling. David cleared his throat in a cacophonous way. Yahudit reacted with squints. Alfonso looked down for a second.

"I have a wonderful program planned for us, Yahudit," Alfonso said.

"Dad, didn't you have something you needed to do, today?" Yahudit said. She was surprised at herself for taking such an initiative to get rid of her dad.

"No, darling," David said in a hurt tone. "I am all yours for today."

"Mom's sick and she needs you by her side," Yahudit said. She had checkmated her dad. He could not stay after that comment.

"Maybe you are right, darling," David said, defeated. "I will go and see if your mom's okay."

Victory! Yahudit did somersaults in her heart. For some reason, she felt happy. Genuinely happy.

"Do you think you can find your way back?" David asked.

Yahudit

"Dad, I am not a child any more," Yahudit said. David looked alarmed. "Dad, I am sure Alfonso will get me there fine."

"Yes, sir," Alfonso said. "I will escort your beautiful daughter to the hotel. No problem."

"That's what I am worried about," David said softly enough for Yahudit to hear. Yahudit shook her head.

"Excuse me, sir?" Alfonso asked. Apparently, he could not catch what David had said.

"Nothing," David said. "I was just bidding my daughter goodbye."

"Goodbye, dad!" Yahudit exclaimed.

David walked away with slow, dejected steps. It was as if he had lost something precious.

Yahudit thought for a second, but lost her train of thought. She looked at Alfonso.

"I am so glad that you came down from Pavia to meet me," Yahudit said.

Alfonso edged closer to the table. "Me, too."

Yahudit blushed and looked down at the table for a moment.

Alfonso broke the uncomfortable silence, "You know what I like about you?"

Yahudit looked at him and tried to conceal the powerful curiosity that was gripping her. "No."

"Yahudit, I like the fact that you are faithful in writing me for all these years. I always thought of Americans as superficial. But you are a deep person. You are a persevering person. You are like a European."

"Oh," Yahudit said, a little disappointed. She had thought that he was going to compliment her on personal things, perhaps about her pulchritude or her attractive manners.

"I find it very sexy," Alfonso said. He seemed to read her mind, and Yahudit was a little freaked out by his omniscience.

"You know what I like about you?" Yahudit said.

Yahudit

"No?" Alfonso said, fully showing his curiosity.

"You are nice and good looking," Yahudit said directly.

"Wow, thank you!" Alfonso said, losing his composure. Yahudit felt self-satisfied that she had broken his equilibrium. He seemed so self-assured and self-confident that she was a bit afraid to approach him emotionally. The directness worked, however, and she felt comfortable. Besides, she reasoned in her mind, Alfonso now knew that she liked him. Sometimes, it is good to let the other know.

"Yahudit," Alfonso said. "Are you done with your coffee?"

"Yes," Yahudit said, taking the last sip of the cappuccino as if it were a jello-shot.

"Okay, then," Alfonso said, a bit nonplused. "Let us go and explore the city."

"Sounds good to me," Yahudit chirped.

Alfonso gave her his hand to hold as she stood up. No one had ever done that for her before. In fact, Yahudit had never seen something like that in America. She was amused and felt special. Yahudit instinctively took his hand without thinking. And hand-in-hand, they walked out of the café into the beautiful city of Florence.

Yahudit did not care that there was a beautiful city before her, however. She was thrilled to be with Alfonso. He was a gentleman and a very good looking one at that. She was melting as he held her hand and would not let her go. Of course, the intensity of the sun was adding to the melting pot. As intensely hot as she was, Yahudit did not want to let Alfonso's hand go, so she held on. She squeezed it once and looked at Alfonso. He gave her a soft, gentle smile.

"Like old friends," Yahudit said, "we are walking down the street."

Alfonso did not like that comment at all, as it was evident from his brushing off the comment. Alfonso did not give her a gentle smile. In fact, he looked away into the other direction. Yahudit was puzzled, but delighted. He did not think of her as merely a friend!

Like all women, Yahudit liked to be adored. She found this fact out for the first time in the streets of Florence. She felt flattered that Alfonso wanted her as more than a friend. Perhaps a lover? Perhaps as a wife? Perhaps as a soul-mate? Whatever it was, it wasn't as a mere friend.

Yahudit smiled as she walked. She threw a glance at Alfonso and he seemed to be plunging deeper into despondency. He looked amazingly mysterious and celestial the more he became depressed. Yahudit's heart jumped a beat as she beheld the Italian Adonis becoming more vulnerable and vulnerable in her hands. She felt the power of holding someone's heart in her hand. She enjoyed the charm that she was apparently casting over Alfonso. She felt wanted. She felt needed. She felt like a goddess.

"We are not really old friends, you know," Alfonso finally objected.

"Oh?" Yahudit feigned ignorance. "So, Mr. Giovani, what do you suppose we are?" Yahudit was confident and playful. This seemed to unnerve Alfonso.

"Well, Miss Kashiri," Alfonso tried to imitate Rhett from *Gone with the Wind*, "frankly dear, I don't give a damn." Alfonso squeezed her hand and smiled.

Yahudit did not like the joke and let go of his hand. He could have said something nice. Why did he have to go the other direction and be flippant like that? He could have told her that they were "secret lovers" or something romantic like that. Even jokes can be romantic. But no, Alfonso went in the other direction. Yahudit felt mad and embarrassed. She let go of his hand. Actually, it was more like she cast his hand away from her presence. After all, should not a goddess express anger at her worshipper when he does not worship her and adore her in the way she needs to be?

"Oh, Yahudit," Alfonso said, "you know I am just kidding." Then, he started to laugh. This infuriated Yahudit even more. She literally began to stomp away from Alfonso. Alfonso did not stop laughing, although it seemed like he was trying to suppress his laughter.

"Yahudit, I do give a damn," Alfonso said and started to laugh out loud again.

"I can't believe this!" Yahudit said, now very mad. "I can't believe this!" Yahudit did not know what else to say.

"I am sorry, Yahudit," Alfonso said as he rushed toward Yahudit. "I did not mean to anger you, my precious."

Yahudit looked at Alfonso, who was now in front of her, practically kneeling in front of her. He looked so small in the kneeling position.

"Precious?" Yahudit said, still angry. But the moment that the word came out, Yahudit could not refrain from laughing.

"What's wrong, my precious?" Alfonso said, not knowing how to react to her reaction to his apology.

"Precious!" Yahudit said. "That's funny!"

"Why is it funny?" Alfonso asked.

"You know the movie, *The Lord of the Rings*?" Yahudit asked.

"Yes?" Alfonso said. He still did not seem to get it.

"Did you see the movie?" Yahudit asked, a bit puzzled.

"Yes," Alfonso responded.

"You know the ring."

"Yes?"

"That's what Gollum calls the ring. My precious!" Yahudit explained.

"Oh, really?" Alfonso said. "I watched the movie dubbed in Italian, and so I did not catch that."

"Oh," Yahudit said and realized that she was in a foreign country with a foreigner whose culture and language was completely different.

Both stopped laughing. And an uncomfortable silence descended upon their little space within the vast space of Florence.

"Will you forgive me?" Alfonso asked.

Yahudit

"Of course, I will," Yahudit said.

"Thank you!" Alfonso immediately got up from the ground and hugged Yahudit. And then he kissed her.

She took a step back. It was completely unexpected. She was mad, but she was also glad. His kissing her showed her that he found her irresistible. He wanted to be near her. She felt flattered by it.

She smiled and let Alfonso off the hook.

"Shall we continue?" Alfonso said in his usual majestic way.

"Yes, my precious," Yahudit said, smiling.

"I don't know if that's a good thing," Alfonso said and smiled.

"Precious. Precious." Yahudit said to tease Alfonso and tried to give it her best imitation of Gollum.

"You know," Alfonso said. "You are quite good. You should go into movies."

"Nah," Yahudit said. "One person in the family in the movie business is plenty."

"You have someone who is in the movie business?"

"Yes," Yahudit said. "My father."

"Really?" Alfonso said. "Why didn't you tell me about it?"

"I wanted you to like me for me, rather than because my father is a big shot."

"Oh, I understand."

"But now, you know," Yahudit said.

"Yes, I do." Alfonso. Then, he had a pensive look for awhile. But he said nothing. He just held her hand, and they started to walk down the street together hand-in-hand.

"Wow, Florence is so beautiful!" Yahudit said. "I think it's the most pretty city that I have ever been to."

"Really?" Alfonso asked. "You like it more than Rome?"

Yahudit

"Oh, yes," Yahudit responded. "Rome is too big and too crowded. Florence is a piece of art. It's crowded with all the tourists, but you get the feeling that the city is not filled up."

"Yes, I see what you mean."

"And the architecture. It's amazing. You can see that each building has been carefully crafted. It's not like America, where all the buildings look exactly alike. If you go to downtown of any city, it's easy to get lost because there is no architectural imagination in America. All the buildings are functional. They are there to provide work space for businesses. Business is king in America, you know. Art does not matter. But in Europe, it is clear that art is more important than business. People live to appreciate beauty and art. It's not a functional life that people live here. It is the art of living that people are engaged in rather than the business of living."

"Wow, you get that all from looking at the buildings in the city?" Alfonso said, amazed.

"Something like that," Yahudit said. "And having a gorgeous Italian man by my side does change my perspective on things."

"You are too kind, madam," Alfonso said and bowed slightly.

"Shall we sit here by the bench for a while?" Yahudit suggested.

"Sounds good to me," Alfonso relinquished his remote control of the tour.

"It is just beautiful by the river," Yahudit said and closed her eyes.

"Yes, I am very proud to be a part of this beauty," Alfonso said.

Yahudit opened her eyes and looked at Alfonso. "Do you see how the water mirrors the beauty of the buildings on the other side?"

"Oh, yes," Alfonso said, showing his enthusiasm.

"It gives you the feeling that you are sitting in the sky," Yahudit imagined.

"Yes, I see what you mean," Alfonso said. "It's like we are riding on the clouds."

"You have captured the essence of what we are feeling," Yahudit said. "We are on clouds."

"So, what do you imagine us to be?" Yahudit remembered that she did not get the answer.

"At this point, we are more than friends, but less than lovers," Alfonso said.

"That is quite poetic, Alfonso," Yahudit said and smiled.

Alfonso looked at Yahudit and remained silent for a while.

Yahudit felt that silence was perfect for such a moment as this. So, she remained quiet as well. They both looked ahead to the beautifully colored buildings in front of them and regarded the way they were reflected on the water. As the water moved in a wave motion, so did the buildings. Yahudit thought about the ephemeral nature of life. Alfonso thought about the possibilities every motion brought.

"Yahudit," Alfonso began.

"Yes?" Yahudit looked in his direction.

"We can be lovers, you know," Alfonso said.

Yahudit was taken aback by such a sudden proposal. She stood up.

"We have known each other for so long," Alfonso began again.

"But we have known each other through letters only," Yahudit interrupted.

"Don't you know that letters are the reflection of one's soul?" Alfonso said. "My letters reflect the intense, pure love that I have for you."

"But you never wrote about love," Yahudit protested. She did not know why she was being so belligerent.

"If you reread your letters, you can see that I have intoned my love for you with every word," Alfonso said.

"I can't decipher some European code," Yahudit said rudely.

"What are you saying?" Alfonso said, his male pride hurt.

"We can't be lovers," Yahudit said. "It's too soon."

"Six years is not too soon," Alfonso said, trying to persuade her.

"But this is the first time I saw you," Yahudit.

"The soul is unseen, but it is even more real than what is seen. My love for you is real, and it is strong."

Yahudit looked worried, "I don't feel the same way about you, Alfonso. I am sorry. We can only be friends."

"How could you be so cruel, Yahudit?" Alfonso said. "Why are you trying to hide the truth that lies deep in your heart? Why are you not being honest with your feelings?"

"Do you want me to be honest?" Yahudit said, a bit peeved.

"Yes," Alfonso said, imploringly.

"This is the truth, and it's going to hurt," Yahudit said.

"I don't care. I want the truth," Alfonso said defiantly.

"I am a Jew."

"I know that."

"I don't think you understand," Yahudit protested. "I am an orthodox Jew. Okay, modern orthodox Jew."

"So?"

"So, that means that I can only marry a Jew."

"I am not talking about marriage," Alfonso said abruptly. Then, he caught himself, "I mean, at least not yet."

"For modern orthodox Jews, marriage is the most important, and dating is for marriage. And Jews must only marry Jews."

"Now, that's stupid," Alfonso said flatly.

"What do you mean? Do you really want to insult my religion?"

"I am sorry, but *amore*, that's what it's all about. Any religion that impinges on *amore* is evil, evil, evil!"

Yahudit

"I think you need to stop it right there, Alfonso," Yahudit said. "I am a modern orthodox Jew. And you have to respect my religion."

Alfonso said, "Are you telling me that the only reason why you would not be with me is because of my religion? I am not even religious. I don't have a religion, to be frank."

"No, that's not all," Yahudit said. "We haven't known each other long, and I don't feel love for you. I am sorry."

"I can wait."

"You will have to wait until I change my religion," Yahudit said firmly. "And that's never going to happen."

"I swear on my great, grandmother's grave that you will change your religion."

"Alfonso! That's awfully selfish of you! You want me to change my religion just for your love?"

"That's not selfish! That's *amore!*"

"I am sorry, but I have to go," Yahudit said.

"No, stop," Alfonso cried and Yahudit started to run.

Alfonso started to run, but soon, Yahudit entered a crowd of tourists and was lost in the crowd.

That's the last time Yahudit saw Alfonso. She hasn't seen him since, but as she sipped her cup of cappuccino at her house, she realized how much she regretted that day. She may have lost the love of her life. There was instant electricity. There was instant connection. He adored her. She admired his beauty. They had six years of history together. Maybe letters are reflections of the soul. Yahudit had just destroyed that reflection.

Yahudit was not going to make another mistake like that. Tomorrow, Yahudit will bring about her happiness with her Goy boy. She knew that this is the destiny that was meant for her. She knew that she would be together with Carlos. Unlike in Florence, she was not going to let a girl's fear preclude the realization of her dream and destiny. She was going to deify Carlos. She was going to create a new religion. She was going to bring about *tikkun olam.*

Yahudit

She turned on the TV and noticed that there was *An Affair to Remember* playing on the movie channel. She watched it a little over a half way through. She felt so tired that she went upstairs to her room and fell asleep.

The day finally arrived. This was the day that she was going to recreate her world with Carlos. Her mother was nowhere in sight; neither was her father. Yahudit checked the answering message and found that her mother had left a message for her. She told her to take the car to go to Hebrew School or just stay home and relax. Yahudit was not going to skip out on Hebrew school. She had waited a whole week for this day.

Yahudit took one of her father's cars. He loved cars and kept many cars in the garage. He sometimes drove a different car to work every day of the week. He explained that it was a weakness that all men had; cars were symbols of the male ego. It seemed a bit strange to Yahudit that her dad put so much stock in cars. But Yahudit could not complain, now, since there was a surfeit of cars to choose from.

Yahudit took out a red Porsche. She loved the way the German-engine purred inside the finely crafted piece of art. Yahudit did not consider most cars as pieces of art, but she believed that this particular red Porsche did. Her father had done special modification work on it, so that it was one-of-its-kind in the world. He loved this Porsche, and so did she.

This was the first time she droved the red Porsche. Her father never allowed her to drive it. And if he knew that she was driving it now, he would flip. For some strange reason, this brought a smile to Yahudit's face. Yahudit wondered if she had an evil streak in her. Maybe there was bad blood from the days of the Middle Ages. After all, she did not really know where she came from. Jews moved around so much. What was her origin? At least, the Chinese know where they are from. The Germans know too. But how about her? Her past is an undecipherable mystery. She was a woman without roots, a woman without the past. And now, she was a woman without a country. The Jewish state has somehow melted in the breakdown of her mother. Israel no longer represented something wonderful, but rather, it was the cause of her family's destabilization. What's to happen next?

Yahudit knew that one thing was for certain. Reality as she knew it was a sham. There was no happy family that she had imagined herself to be a part of. There was no strong mother who could weather all difficulties. There was no Jewish state which was a paradise for Jews. Nothing was sacred. All was mere shadows of something real, which she could not access.

Yahudit knew for certain that she wanted to create her own reality. This way, she would not be chasing after shadows. She would know what the reality is because she would create it and she would be in complete control of it.

As Yahudit sat through her Hebrew class, she could not focus on the lesson at hand. There was a race going through her mind. Different cars were racing at speeds faster than light. She was driving her red Porsche and was going the fastest she could. She was afraid that she was going to crash. However, that did not preclude her striving to be number one.

Yahudit knew that the race was against everyone she knew. She was racing against her father, who would never let her drive his red Porsche, which was more precious to him than she. Her father was all about his movie business. Who was he kidding? He only pretended to love his family. If he really loved his family, he would be home to comfort her, his only daughter, rather than gallivanting around with movie stars at a time of a family crisis. He has often said that he was working hard for the sake of the family, but that was all a lie. He did not like his family. He was finding excuses to avoid family time. That's what it was all about. Yahudit was racing his car against him, whose selfishness has become the undoing of her happy family.

But her mother was no angel. She drove that family BMW up to her parents in San Francisco, neglecting her duties as a mother. How dare she imagine herself to be a Yiddish mama? She was none of the kind. She only ordered her around like a despot whose head was deemed to be worthy of decapitation during the French Revolution. Was she not a human being, with flesh and blood? Did she not have a need for nurture? Why was her mother being so selfish in abandoning her only daughter? Yeah, she's human too, but it's her duty as the mother to take care of her young. How could she abandon her at such a time as this? Did she not know that the senior year was the most important year? Senior year decides a person's fate. What college a senior goes to locks her into the place for four years. It will dictate her social relationships, her learning environment, ability to acquire the necessary skills to survive until she dies, and a set of very important experiences. How could her mother abandon her at this critically important time of her life, which was hanging by a thread? Her mother accomplished what she wanted out of life. She had already achieved what she had set out to do. Even if she had not, it was too late for her, now. But she could make sure that her daughter has the greatest opportunities. Why was she abandoning her obligations as a mother? She was being a negligent mother. Yahudit was racing against her mother, who apparently did not have her interests at heart.

Not only was Yahudit racing against her mom and dad, she was racing against her friends. Yahudit was racing against Judith, who obvious was a fake friend. She did not care for her or her needs. Judith was only interested in making fun of her and how she loved a Goy boy. Judith was only into criticizing her. Would a true friend only criticize? Should not a true friend be supportive even if she did not agree with her and her decisions? Why was Judith all critical? Why couldn't Judith lend a helping hand? Judith did not want to support Yahudit because she was fake. She was fake like all the money that her grandfather made on property inflation. Judith was fake like the long nails she put on her fingers. Judith was fake like the humus at the kosher café. Judith was a fake friend. True friends are supportive. True friends spend time to help out. True friends want their friends to succeed. Judith was a fake. She was jealous that Yahudit found someone she loves and connected with. Judith was only interested in destroying her future relationship with Carlos. That is why Judith kept talking about Carlos' negative attributes. Judith did not want Yahudit to be happy. Judith was out to destroy all that would make Yahudit's world a perfect world. Judith was no true friend; she was a fake friend. Yahudit was racing her red Porsche against her so-called friend Judith.

Janice was not on her side as well. Yahudit knew she could not trust her. Why? Because even though she knew that Yahudit loved Carlos, a Goy boy, she did not tell her about her Goy boy, right away. Yahudit was a bit hurt that Janice did not tell her right away, but in a way, Yahudit understood. Janice could not have been sure that Yahudit would have sympathized. From Janice's perspective, she could have been worried that her friend would have reported her relationship to the authorities, such as her parents or teachers. Maybe Yahudit rubbed off as a bit of a super-duper Jew. So, Yahudit understood why Janice might have felt a need for caution. But after Yahuidt's vituperative rant against Judaism and against Dana's brothers, Janice should have known that she could trust her. Janice should have told her right then and there. But the fact that she decided to hide her liaisons with the Goy boy even after that was evidence that Janice did not really trust Yahudit. Even now, Janice did not trust Yahudit. She would not share his name! And Janice knows that Yahudit likes Carlos. Yahudit was resolute that she would not share the details of her plan for a relationship with Carlos. Yahudit would mistrust Janice because that is how Janice had wanted to define her relationship with her. Yahudit was racing against Janice, her supposed friend who could not put her faith in her.

Yahudit realized that her race was more monumental than that. It was not merely against her negligent family and untrustworthy friends that she was racing against. Yahudit was racing against the whole Jewish world. Yes, she was born a Jew, but that did not mean that she had to remain a Jew. Hitler was one-eighth Jewish, wasn't it? Didn't the nephew of the famous Jewish philosopher Philo decimate the Jewish population of Alexandria on behalf of the Roman Empire? Yahudit was not going to do any killing, but she was resolved that there were probable cause that dictated a necessary conflict with the Jewish religion. Yahudit wanted to recreate her world. Central to this new axis mundi was a religious system which would centralize her relationship with Carlos. Yes, Yahudit was racing against the whole Jewish world. It was the only way she could find her happiness.

Yahudit wondered if she were the only Jew to have gone against the world at age 17. After all both Hitler and Philo's nephew were much older and they were men. Yahudit's grandparents did not count because as much as Grandma Friedman spoke of her iconoclastic stance vis-à-vis Judaism, she was proud to be a Jew. Yahudit was different. She did not want to be a Jew. She wanted to renounce her Jewish religion and her Jewish identity with it. Yahudit wanted to be Yahudit, and that's it. She wanted to be Yahudit the individual. She wanted to be Yahudit who loves Carlos and is loved by Carlos. She wanted to be who she was, and not what her Jewish world expected of her. She wanted to be free. She wanted to break free. So, in her mind, she drove her red Porsche as fast as she could.

The lunch time finally arrived. It seemed like entering the winner's circle. Yahudit was ready to take her prize, to hold her trophy in her arms, and to live out her days as a champion.

Yahudit

Her trophy was waiting for her in the person of Carlos. Oh, sweet Carlos! Yahudit could not but melt in her remembrance of her dream Goy boy.

Yahudit walked nervously as she walked along with Judith and Janice. She could not feel her legs because they had gone into automation mode. It was the keeping of synchronicity that allowed for her motion; for, her head was elsewhere, suspended in a form of oblivion. But soon, Yahudit snapped out of her reverie, perhaps induced by her nervousness. There, they were at the kosher café!

As soon as Yahudit saw Carlos, her heart jumped a beat. For some reason, Carlos looked different. He glowed under the iridescent light. He stood out among the crowd. He was the alpha male. Yahudit was convinced of it. There was Carlos, a giant among men. He was there, waiting to be crowned. He was like a prince who had taken the form of a pauper. He had traded his place. Now was the time to set things right. It was the time to re-establish the place, the rightful place.

And it was Yahudit who would do the crowning, enthroning, and deification. Carlos would be crowned king and God. All will be right with the world. Yahudit would be the one to usher in the Messianic Age. She would be the one who would bring about tikkun olam. The *tikkun olam*. It seemed so simple. A piece of paper would initiate the process of correcting all that was wrong with her world.

Yahudit handed a piece of paper to Carlos. She had written it before she had started the fast ride with her daddy's red Porsche. On this piece of paper, personally delivered, was written: "Carlos, please meet me in front of the café at 3 PM. It is of uttermost importance. Yours truly…." For some reason, Yahudit could not get herself to sign it. In the midst of all the bravery, there lay a frail heart, perhaps. But Yahudit reasoned that since she was delivering the note in person in full view of her friends, she was being brave.

Carlos took the folded note and put it into his shirt pocket. It seemed like he was used to receiving folded notes, and this unnerved Yahudit a bit. She did not know what she was expecting, but she certainly did not expect Carlos to merely put the note into his shirt pocket, unread. It was disappointing. It was like rejecting. Yahudit felt that the whole plan was going to fail. She felt like nothing will work out. She felt herself to be a complete failure. It seemed so perfect when she conceived it in her mind. How could it be that it was so different from how she imagined it to be? She imagined that it would go something like Carlos reading the note, offering a broad smile, and saying, "See you later, alligator." Or something like that. But no, he put the note in his shirt pocket, unread! How humiliating! Yahudit just wanted to cry.

Surprisingly enough, Carlos gave Yahudit a quick wink. Yahudit clearly caught it. And Carlos also smiled when he realized she received the message. It happened in a fraction of a second, but Yahudit knew as true as the earth is round that she was going to see Carlos at 3:00 PM. She was thrilled. There was a rush of jolt in her being that was nothing like what she had felt before.

Yahudit was beaming. She tried to hide it. She quickly looked at her friends. They were looking at each other and saying something to each other. It was clear that they did not catch what Carlos did in the way of a wink and a smile. They were hung up on Yahudit offering a note. They surmised that it was a love note. It was then that Yahudit realized that she was wise not to have trusted Janice. Janice had a Goy boy of her own, but she was saying all kinds of horrible stuff to Judith. Hello! Yahudit was right there. How are you doing?

Janice and Judith looked at each other with a discerning look and started to walk away from Yahudit. So, that was it? A silent treatment? Yahudit was upset, but she felt relieved. She feared that Janice and Judith would make a scene in front of all other Jews. It would have been embarrassing enough to have two of her friends ball her out, but all the Jews in the room. Has anyone seen a Jew-Attack? That's when all the Jews ball a single Jew out for an infraction that affects the whole community. It is not pretty. At least, Yahudit was spared of that. Bar-youk-ha-Shem!

It didn't seem like anyone else noticed. The kosher joint gets quite crowded during lunch time, so it was not surprising. All the Jewish workers behind the counter are busy cooking, making stuff, taking orders, taking cash, and all other kinds of business-related activity related to running an efficient, money-making fast food place. And all the Jews on the other side of the counter were busy releasing their pent-up loquacity, so that they were completely focused on their conversation partners. There was no room for interference. As many words as possible had to be rattled off without being incomprehensible to their intended audience. If others heard what they were saying, that was collateral benefit. But their measured talk was meant to elicit responses from their intended. Yahudit was relieved that Jews took their lunch time talk seriously. Basically, the whole environment functioned mysteriously to camouflage her initiation of affair with Carlos.

Strangely enough, Carlos seemed to know how the whole environment functioned. It was like a supremely well-timed set of events initiated by Carlos. How did he know? How did he understand? Then, Yahudit remembered that Carlos was God-in-waiting. Of course, he would know. He is going to be the God of the new religion! Why should that be surprising? Yahudit repented of her lack of faith in her new deity and in the new religion. She was so bad. So, so bad. She felt like she needed to do some penance. Maybe the new God will assign her something to do to allay her guilty conscience?

Yahudit took the food she ordered and walked outside. She felt like she wanted to be alone. Her friends have already gone to their table without waiting for her. Although she was walking alone, this time she felt a lightness of her feet. Yahudit was energized. She was filled with happiness. She knew that her offering had been accepted by her God. And she was merely waiting for divine blessing and reward. 3:00 PM. That was the precise hour of the reward. These Christians do not know what they are missing. No one knows the time or the hour? What kind of divine blessing is that? Yahudit was glad that her religion, her new religion, was one of certainty and not of unfulfilled promises and mysteries that amounted to a lack of blessings.

Yahudit was certain that Carlos was her God. Yahudit knew that her religion was true. Yahudit was sure that she had found the truth to all things. Yahudit has found the truth, and it will set her free. She was going to be freed from the oppressive constraints of Jewish religion to which she had been imprisoned for so many years. Judaism represented shackles and chains; Carlos represented freedom and happiness.

Yahudit quickly ate her lunch and went back to Hebrew school. There was still a couple of hours to go until 3:00 PM. It was going to be a turning point of her life. Yahudit did not know what would happen after that. For all she knew, the whole world will change, at least for her little world. She may not be able to attend Hebrew school ever again. Who knew what changes were in store for her?

Not knowing the future and the changes that were in store for her, Yahudit made a point of savoring her last few hours in Hebrew school for that day. Judith and Janice ignored her throughout the last remaining hours of that day's Hebrew school. It was certain that it was at the instigation of Judith who seemed to exert a hold over Janice. Certainly, Janice was the weaker one. Judith overpowered her. Here was a Goy boy dater, who was ignoring another who hasn't even started dating a Goy boy. To a certain extent, Janice had something to hide. To hide it well, she had to pretend like she was a super Jew. And that's the route she took. Sure, it was probably out of fear more than anything else, but Yahudit understood why Janice took that route. It did not mitigate the disgust Yahudit felt for Janice. In fact, it increased it. Yahudit returned their favor and remained aloof throughout the Hebrew class.

Realizing that it could be the last few hours of the Hebrew school, Yahudit particularly paid attention. It seemed as if every word came to her in a pronounced way. She could distinguish every intonation, every stress, every inflection, every crescendo, every depression. She noticed the difference in accents of the students who spoke up in class. She, in essence, became hyperaware. It was funny that it was after that she decided to leave the world of the Hebrew school and join the world to be created with Carlos that she became the most attentive in Hebrew school.

3:00 PM finally arrived. Yahudit walked softly out of the classroom, ignoring her friends who were ignoring her. Yahudit wanted to rush out, but she restrained herself. She knew that that wouldn't be prudent. Since most of the students went toward the Hebrew school parking lot or in front of the building, they were headed in a different direction. Yahudit tried to make it seem natural that she was walking in the opposite direction. As soon as she left the Hebrew school building, she headed towards CVS Pharmacy store, just in case anyone was following or watching. She wanted everything to look natural.

When she had dawdled for five or ten minutes in the store and was sure that she was not being followed by anyone, she picked up a mint, paid for it at the cash register's, and walked out of the store. Yahudit was headed to her goal, her final destination, to meet up with Carlos. It was going to be the beginning of a new beginning, a pure and wonderful world.

Yahudit knew that she was a bit late. Fear gripped her as she pondered the possibility that Carlos left without waiting for her. After all, what was he to expect? It was a nebulous note. Yahudit rushed her steps because she did not want to miss her new world due to tardiness. She walked so fast that she was out of breath when she reached the appointed spot.

Carlos was there. And he had that broad smile that is so characteristic of Mexicans whom Yahudit knew. Yahudit realized that all was well with the world. She was going to get her wish. The new world was going to be created and Carlos was going to be the new God.

"Hi, Carlos," Yahudit panted out his name.

"Are you okay?" Carlos said with a smile.

"Of course," Yahudit said. "I am glad that you came."

"Me, too." Carlos beamed. Yahudit was so happy that Carlos was excited.

"Carlos, we can't talk here," Yahudit said. "Come with me."

"Okay," Carlos said and quickly followed Yahudit.

Yahudit spoke as she rushed alongside Carlos, "Is it okay with your work?"

"Yes," Carlos said. "Don't you worry about that."

"It's okay if you don't go back to work, today?" Yahudit asked. Immediately after the words were uttered, Yahudit regretted it. She did not want to get off to a bad start with Carlos. She knew she was sounding neurotic and resented her mother, who gave her the Jewish neurosis, in her mind.

Carlos looked at Yahudit for a second and smiled. He seemed to enjoy the neurosis, and that made Yahudit a bit uncomfortable. "It's okay."

"Fine," Yahudit said, trying to sound nonchalant. "Great. Let's continue on, then."

They walked side by side, and Yahudit led Carlos toward her red Porsche. She had claimed it as her own, and now it was a part of her.

"Would you like to get into my car?" Yahudit asked nervously. She did not know why, but she was worried that something would go wrong.

"Of course," Carlos said, seeming to sense her fear. He quickly got in and that made Yahudit feel better.

Once both of them were inside, Yahudit said, "Here we go." And the red Porsche began to drive away from the Iranian Jewish part of Los Angeles.

"Where are we going?" Carlos asked.

"We are going to Venice Beach," Yahudit said.

"I haven't been there in a while," Carlos commented.

"Neither have I," Yahudit said.

Yahudit

It wasn't a long drive. Yahudit did not think that it was a good idea to broach the heavy topic of why she had called him to herself. But somehow, Yahudit felt that Carlos knew.

"Thanks for inviting me," Carlos said.

"It's my pleasure," Yahudit said.

"I am sure we'll have a great time in Venice Beacch," Carlos said.

Yahudit realized that Carlos wanted to get the conversation rolling. "Me, too. I like Venice Beach because there is something going on every day of the year."

"You can say that, again," Carlos said. "There is always a constant flow of tourists from all over the world."

Yahudit remarked, "It's amazing how many languages you hear walking down the walkway. Isn't it?"

"Yeah, it's like United Nations on bikini."

Yahudit laughed. "Can you imagine all those serious United Nations leaders in their swimwear?"

"No," Carlos said. "And I don't want to."

"Ha, ha," Yahudit laughed. "I know what you mean."

"But I bet you would look fabulous in a bikini," Carlos said sneakily.

"I would never wear a bikini," Yahudit protested.

"Why not?" Carlos said with a genuine curiosity on his face. Yahudit felt flattered.

"Because I do not have the body for it," Yahudit sad just to see what Carlos would say.

"You must be crazy, girl!" Carlos yelled. "You are so fine. You would look great in a bikini."

"Really?" Yahudit asked and giggled.

"Yeah. You would be mighty fine, girlfriend," Carlos said with a high-pitched tone.

"You are so funny," Yahudit said and giggled some more. "But I wouldn't wear a bikini. I would be too embarrassed."

"Oh, come on," Carlos said. "You are depriving the world of your beauty."

"Well, the world can go on without my beauty," Yahudit said.

"Yeah, but I can't," Carlos said. "You have to wear a bikini for me."

Yahudit was a bit surprised by Carlos' aggressiveness, but she liked it. "Nope, not even for you, Carlos."

"You will come around," Carlos said. "I can wait."

"Well, Carlos, you will have to wait a long time," Yahudit said. "Like until the world comes to an end."

"Come on, girlfriend!" Carlos said and threw her a quick glance.

"So, tell me, Carlos, what's your favorite type of food," Yahudit wanted to change the subject.

"Favorite type of food?" Carlos asked puzzled.

"I want to know more about you," Yahudit explained.

"Oh," Carlos responded. "I like Chinese food the best."

"Me, too!" Yahudit exclaimed. She was happy that they had something in common. Carlos laughed at her enthusiasm and joined in the laughter.

"What's your favorite dish?" Yahudit asked.

"I like Sweet-and-Sour Pork," Carlos said.

"Oh," Yahudit said, a bit disappointed. She wondered if he was telling the truth or if he was testing her. She wondered also if he was teasing her. After all, he worked in a kosher kitchen. He should know better than spring a non-kosher dish on her.

"What's your favorite Chinese food?" Carlos asked.

"I like Wonton Soup," Yahudit said.

"Yeah, those are good, too," Carlos said. "Can you eat Chinese food?"

"Of course," Yahudit said. "Why do you ask?"

"Well, because I thought you kept kosher," Carlos answered. So, he was sensitive to the kosher thing!

"There are kosher Chinese restaurants," Yahudit said, a bit coldly.

Yahudit

"Oh, yeah," Carlos jumped in. "There is one a few stores away from where I work."

"And there are some in other parts of Los Angeles," Yahudit said.

"Would you ever eat non-kosher?" Carlos asked.

Yahudit marveled at the question. Would she eat non-kosher? It hadn't struck her what the implications of what she was doing were. What was her new religion going to be? Was she to turn her back on everything? Including kosher foods? She had never eaten anything non-kosher.

Carlos watched as Yahudit wallowed in her own silence.

"I don't know," Yahudit said honestly. "I honestly don't know." Yahudit sounded very serious.

"I don't know what I would do if there was something that I was not allowed to eat," Carlos said. "I guess it's one of the good things of not being a chosen people."

"You are making fun of me," Yahudit said sensitively.

"No, I am not," Carlos said. "I am just saying that it must be hard being a Jew and keeping kosher and all."

"You don't know the half of it," Yahudit said as tears welled up in her eyes. She was thinking about her fight with her mom. The Jewish state had crumbled in her imagination. Her family seemed to be breaking apart. No one was at home. It did not seem like she was creating a new world for herself, but rather that she was being pushed out of her old world.

"I am sorry," Carlos apologized. "I didn't mean to upset you."

"No, don't apologize," Yahudit said. "It's not your fault. It's me. I am dealing with some issues."

"Do you want to talk about it?" Carlos asked.

"No, I don't," Yahudit said.

"Okay," Carlos said. "You don't have to talk about it if you don't want to."

"No, it's not that," Yahudit said. "I kinda want to talk about it. But I shouldn't."

"Okay," Carlos said. "If you think that you should not, that's okay."

"But I want to talk about it," Yahudit said.

"Okay," Carlos said. "If you want to talk about it, I am all ears."

Yahudit hesitated for a moment. She was not sure what to do. Carlos remained silent and was looking ahead, although he was throwing a sideway glance, now and then.

"Here it goes," Yahudit said.

"Okay," Carlos encouraged her.

"It seems like everything is fine one moment," Yahudit began. "And then everything goes wrong. Do you know what I mean?"

"Yeah," Carlos interjected one-word encouragement.

"Things were so fine in our home," Yahudit said. "We were like a perfect family. And now, everything seems to be wrong. Mom is off to San Francisco. Dad is who-knows-where. The big house is empty. And it seems like the whole world is broken."

"I see," Carlos said.

"It's horrible," Yahudit said. Tears were trickling down her cheeks. She tried to keep one hand on her wheel and wiped her tears with the other one.

Carlos put his hand on her leg. "It's going to be okay."

His gentle words made Yahudit feel more sad and depressed. She started to cry.

"There, there," Carlos said. "You are going to be okay."

"No, I am not," Yahudit said.

"Of course, you are," Carlos said. He spoke with firmness that surprised Yahudit. She felt a ray of happiness enter her heart.

"Really?" Yahudit asked.

"Sure," Carlos said. "You will be okay."

"I don't know," Yahudit expressed her doubt.

"Don't you worry, girlfriend," Carlos said. "Everything's going to be okay."

Yahudit

Yahudit realized how nice it was to hear Carlos say "girlfriend" as if they had been dating for a while. She knew that it was just an expression, but she still desired what was a platitude. She wanted to claim it for herself. She wanted to claim Carlos for herself. She wanted to own Carlos and be owned by him.

"Carlos?" Yahudit said, wanting to pronounce his name with her lips.

"Yeah?" Carlos responded.

"Why don't you call me by my name?" Yahudit asked.

"Do you want me to?" Carlos asked.

"Yes, of course," Yahudit said. "Don't you think my name is pretty?"

"Of course, I do," Carlos said.

"I know it sounds very foreign," Yahudit said. "And I can understand it, if you don't like it."

"No, of course not," Carlos said. "What could be more foreign-sounding than Carlos?"

"Come on, Carlos," Yahudit said. "Yahudit sounds far worse than Carlos."

"Yahudit," Carlos said. "You have a beautiful name."

Yahudit smiled. In the moment of silence, she realized that Carlos' hand was still on her leg. She felt self-conscious because she was afraid he noticed her blushing.

"Do you know where we are?" Yahudit asked.

"No, I don't," Carlos said. "I generally don't drive."

"Really?" Yahudit asked. "How do you get to the Iranian Jewish area?"

"I take," Carlos started to say, but he stopped himself for a second. "Someone drives me."

"Who?" Yahudit asked.

"Do you really want to know?" Carlos asked. For some reason, he wanted to put all his cards on the table.

"Yes," Yahudit said, apprehensively. She was afraid that he was going to say, "Girlfriend."

"My wife," Carlos said.

"Your wife?" Yahudit shouted.

"Wow, that's loud," Carlos said.

"Your wife?" Yahudit asked more quietly.

"Yes," Carlos said.

"Ex-wife?" Yahudit asked.

"No, my wife," Carlos said.

"You are married?" Yahudit asked.

"Yes," Carlos said. "Don't you know that we Mexicans marry very young?"

"You must be kidding me!" Yahudit exclaimed.

"Can you please speak a little softer, please," Carlos said.

"I can't believe that you are lying to me," Yahudit said.

"Lying to you?" Carlos protested. "This is the first time you have asked me."

"Oh," Yahudit said and realized that she had thought many things in her mind, but she had not really spoken to Carlos until that moment.

"I am not going to lie to you, Yahudit," Carlos said softly.

"So, where are we?" Yahudit asked.

"We are near Venice Beach, I believe," Carlos said, trying to be funny. Yahudit was not laughing.

"You know what I mean, Carlos," Yahudit said.

"I don't know," Carlos said. "You tell me. What do you want?"

"I don't know what I want," Yahudit said.

"No, you know what you want," Carlos objected.

"Okay, I know what I want," Yahudit agreed. "But I did not expect this."

"Does that change things?" Carlos asked.

"Of course, it does," Yahudit said.

"I am sorry to hear that," Carlos said.

"Unless," Yahudit interjected.

"Unless what?" Carlos said.

Yahudit

"Unless you are willing to do what I am willing to do," Yahudit said.

"And that is?"

"Leave your whole world behind," Yahudit said.

"Leave my whole world behind?" Carlos said, puzzled. "For what?"

"For me," Yahudit said boldly. "And for us."

"For us?" Carlos said, puzzled.

"For us and what we can be together," Yahudit said. Now, she was going into a familiar territory. She had talked to herself in her mind about a new world with Carlos. Now was the moment of truth. New world could be created. It was within reach.

Yahudit continued, "We can create a life together, you and I. We can be to each other what the world cannot be for either one of us. We can leave behind the world of hatred and rejection. We can embrace the world of acceptance and togetherness."

"But my wife accepts me. My children accept me. I am loved in my home. And I love them."

"But they cannot give you what I can give you."

"And what is that?" Carlos asked, curious.

"Me," Yahudit said. "They cannot give you me."

"You?"

"Yes, me."

Carlos remained silent for a second. He took his hand back from her leg and put it on his leg. He was thinking. He looked genuinely lost. He looked like he was losing his control. He looked like he was hesitating in his dedication to his family, to his world.

Yahudit felt a self-satisfied sense of victory. Carlos was falling into her spell. Would a man deeply in love with his wife hesitate? Would he look so lost in his indecision? Who was he kidding? His world was not perfect. It was a mirage. It was fake just like her world was fake. He had managed to ignore its spurious nature until now. But the Anointed One has come to show him the truth, the way, and the life.

It was like all salvation. Carlos had to realize that he was in a state of the shadows. Reality was out there somewhere, but he could not see it. He was chained down like everyone in the world and forced to stare at a two dimensional wall where shadows were being flashed through an artificial medium. Carlos was living in the shadows of fictive reality that was not reality at all.

It was Yahudit the Savior who came to set him free from his state of being lost in the world of the shadows. She was the messiah for Carlos. Salvation is personal. Messiah is personal. For Carlos, Yahudit was the personal savior who was to bring unimaginable, unconditional love into his life. Yahudit was specially anointed for Carlos. Carlos did not realize it. But he was being effectively called, directly by his savior.

Carlos still looked lost. Yahudit looked upon Carlos and felt compassion for him. She knew more than ever that this was meant to be. It was predestination. It was his predestination. It was her predestination. This was the intelligent design of the Supremeness of All That Is Good.

"Come," Yahudit said. "You are heavy-laden with the pressures of the world. Come to me, and I will give you rest."

"Huh?" Carlos said as his silence was broken.

"I offer myself to you, Carlos," Yahudit said. "Partake and eat. For, I am the bread of heaven, and you will never go hungry. Drink and you will never be thirsty."

"Huh?" Carlos looked a bit worried.

Yahudit had imagined the creation of her new world, her new religion. She had practiced in her mind all the sacred things she was going to say. She had read books after books on religion in anticipation of a new religion. She had visited internet site after internet site that dealt with religion. She was going to be a part of a new world order based on new religion. It was serious business.

Yahudit

"I will give you rest," Yahudit said. "Deny yourself and follow me."

"Follow you?" Carlos said.

"Bring me into your heart," Yahudit said. "And you will be born again into new life. Old will pass away and behold new will come."

"Are you for real?" Carlos said, surprised. "This sounds like mass."

"You are troubled, are you not?" Yahudit said.

"No," Carlos said. "Well, maybe. Okay, I am."

"Well, you need a new life," Yahudit said. "And I can give it to you. We can hold onto it, together. We can be Us, Togetherness, Reconciliation, Togetherness, *tikkun olam.*"

"Tikkun olam?" Carlos asked.

"Healing of the world," Yahudit said. "Fixing of what is wrong. Making all things right. Perfection itself."

"Oh," Carlos said. "We can be that?"

"Yes, Carlos," Yahudit said with an affected voice. "We can be."

"And all I have to do is leave my wife and children?"

"Renounce thy name and thy house," Yahudit said. "Take upon yourself me, myself, and I."

"Renounce my name?"

"Turn your back on the past," Yahudit said. "Turn to the future. I am your future."

"You?"

"Me."

"You will give yourself to me completely?"

"Completely, truly, madly, and deeply."

"And what do you get?" Carlos said suspiciously.

"I get you, Carlos," Yahudit said. "You are going to be my God."

"Your God?"

"My God."

"My God!" Carlos exclaimed. "You are mad!"

Yahudit

"I am mad for you," Yahudit said. "I am crazy for you. I am crazy about what we can have together. I am crazy for the future world we will create together for ourselves."

"You are absolutely crazy," Carlos said in a softer tone.

"And shall we be crazy together," Yahudit said.

"Crazy together," Carlos repeated.

"Yes, crazy together," Yahudit said.

"Yes," Carlos gave in. "Yes."

"Yes," Yahudit said. "Now, you have thrown away the old jug of wine. Behold, you have a new jug of wine which will last forever."

"What should I say to that?" Carlos asked, mystified.

"Amen."

"Amen."

At that moment, Yahudit pulled into a parking spot near Venice Beach.

"Here, we are," Yahudit said, beaming with smiles.

"Yes, we are," Carlos was not really smiling, although Yahudit could see that Carlos was trying to force a smile.

As soon as both of them got out of the car, Yahudit gave Carlos a big hug. Carlos's hands hung limply from the sides.

"I am so happy," Yahudit said.

The tightness with which Yahudit held Carlos made him feel wanted and needed. Carlos began to feel happiness in his heart.

"Shall we go and explore the beach?" Carlos asked.

"Yes, let's do it," Yahudit said.

Both of them went onto the walkway of Venice Beach, hand-in-hand. They walked for a bit and looked at predominantly empty shops along the walkway.

"Should we go towards the sea?" Carlos asked.

"Yes, let's do it," Yahudit said.

They walked on the sand and sat down looking at the sea. They could hear the seagulls flying about and singing. They could hear the water pushing against the sand with occasional violent thumps. They could see the sea shining high above in the sky, providing light unto the world.

Yahudit leaned her head against Carlos' shoulders. Carlos began to stroke Yahudit's hair. Yahudit held tighter onto Carlos's arm. Carlos kissed Yahudit on the head. Yahudit looked up at Carlos and looked into his eyes. Carlos looked into Yahudit's eyes. Carlos drew closer to Yahudit. Yahudit lifted herself up to draw closer to Carlos. And their lips met. Yahudit pushed slightly against the lips of Carlos. After a few seconds, Yahudit pulled back.

Carlos seemed startled.

"Carlos, that was perfect," Yahudit said and leaned her head against the shoulder of Carlos. Yahudit looked ahead into the Pacific Ocean. She tried to trace where the sky was separated from the sea. As hard as she tried, it seemed impossible to know where the sea ended and the sky began. Then, she looked at the beach in front of her. She noticed the tide coming in. Undulating waves kept coming without fail. She noticed where the sea ended and the land began. Although the delineation seemed to change with every tide, the demarcation was clear. She thought about the endless possibilities as she looked ahead towards the sea. She felt the ground beneath her and Carlos next to her. She felt like a tree planted by the streams of waters. She knew that the land would produce vegetation. She knew that her tree will bear fruit. Lots of it.

There was morning and there was evening, the third day.

6

The kiss was so perfect that Yahudit did not want to ruin it with any other memory. She wanted to preserve the sacred moment, the sacred place, and the sacred time. After a few moments of savoring the moment, Yahudit rushed Carlos back to the red Porsche. Her red Porsche. Their red Porsche.

As soon as they got into the car, Yahudit called her dad's cell phone. As usual, he did not pick up. She left a message. "Dad, I have the red Porsche and am enjoying it with a friend. Don't worry about me. I am okay."

Yahudit knew that she had to leave that message. It wasn't that she was worried her dad would be worried sick about her. He was not home often enough to notice that she was missing. But she feared that he may pop in home or have someone check the situation out at home, especially his garage, to see if everything was okay. If there were a report that his favorite red Porsche was missing, then the world would break apart. Her dad would probably report a theft, and thing could get messy. Everyone at home know that it was his favorite car. No one was supposed to touch it.

Yahudit started to drive the car.

Yahudit

"Where are we going?" Carlos asked.

"We are going to our promised land," Yahudit said mysteriously. "And we have to drive through the vast wilderness to get there."

"What do you mean?" Carlos asked, more confused.

"Shall we make a covenant between each other?" Yahudit said in the way of an answer.

"A covenant?" Carlos responded with a question.

"Yes, a covenant like the one made between God and Abraham."

"You must be kidding!" Carlos said.

"Do I look like I am kidding?" Yahudit asked.

"No," Carlos said.

"Yes, Carlos, my dear," Yahudit said, softening her voice. "I am quite serious right now because we are talking about our destiny."

"Okay," Carlos said slowly. "Tell me what the covenant will be."

"The covenant is simple," Yahudit said. "You will be my God, and I will be your people."

"My people?" Carlos asked.

"Yes, me and my offspring through you as the collective 'I.' Do you see?"

"Yes, I see," Carlos said, befuddled. "You and our children will be the covenant partner with me. And who am I?"

"You will be my God," Yahudit said.

"Your God? Isn't that a bit extreme?"

Yahudit answered firmly, "Do you want to make this covenant or not?"

"Okay, I do. You will be my people, and I will be your God."

"No, no, no!" Yahudit said, irritated. "Don't get the order confused. Order is very important. Law can flip-flop because of errors in the order. Ask the Jewish sages of ancient times. They will tell you."

Yahudit

"Ancient times?" Carlos said. "This is the 21st century, Yahudit. We cannot communicate with the dead."

"But you, my God, can," Yahudit said beseechingly.

"Okay, okay," Carlos said. "I will be your God, and you will be my people."

"Yes, my Lord," Yahudit said. "You became my God first."

"Really?" Carlos said with smiles.

"And then, afterwards, I became your people," Yahudit said, ignoring Carlos' question.

The bright red Porsche was running fast on the 10 freeway. They say faith is free, and God's love is free. But Yahudit's God was penniless, like Jesus of Nazareth who had nowhere to lay his head. Yahudit understood why Christians believed in Jesus as God. She never understood before. How could anyone believe a pauper to be God? How could anyone believe that a child conceived by a virgin, supposedly without a man, could be God? How could such a lowly person be God? How could a carpenter's son who had no money to his name, no property or even mortgage, be God? But the stupid Christians believed that this pauper Jesus was God. This never made sense before. But it all made sense to Yahudit, now. God can be poor. God can be penniless. Jesus of Nazareth was such, and he is God to billions of people. Carlos, in the same way, was God.

Judith hated illegal immigrants. She wanted to kick out all the illegals. She saw them as less than human. She saw them as the sewage of the world. She saw them not only unfit to be Americans but human beings on the same level with her. Just like the New Englanders who wanted to create a colony for African-Americans after they emancipated them from slavery, Judith was a champagne Democrat with no convictions. She flew where the champagne poured amidst socialites and Ivy Leaguers who pretended to talk the liberal talk. But she, like the rest of them, was a bigot and a racist, who hated illegal immigrants. How quickly she had forgotten that Jews were in the same situation! After the Russian pogroms, illegal immigrants flooded into America from Russia and other Eastern European countries. During and after the Holocaust, illegal immigrants flooded in from Germany and other European countries. Now, Judith wanted to send them back? Send them back to where? To their versions of concentration camps? They may not be killed off in a gas chamber, but they will be killed off through poverty and disease and all kinds of social ills from which they cannot escape in the "Old Country."

Here he was, a Mexican. Carlos was the Every-Mexican. He was the Every-Illegal. He was the divine sheep who takes away the sins of the world. The sins of America, having turned the Jews back to face their gas chamber, the transgressions of the colonialists who decimated Indians, the trespasses of 21st century Americans who prefer to pigeonhole Mexican immigrants into an intolerable social depression with the votes that blare the epithet, "Go back to where you came from!"

Carlos was the savior of the world who takes away the sins of the world. He is the man-God who symbolizes the suffering of all illegal immigrants. Yahudit could still hear the taunts of her Jewish friends against Carlos and illegal immigration. Did not the Christian God-man say, "All ye who are heavy-laden, come, and I will give you rest?" A pauper telling others to come to him to find rest. How laughable! But how true. Yahudit knew it to be the absolute truth that it is possible for a pauper to give "rest" for Yahudit was feeling this redemptive rest in the presence of her God, Carlos the Lord.

Now, Yahudit understood the religion of following a pauper. All this pauper did was to wander around the country side, manipulating uneducated people, and to make trouble for city folk in the New York of ancient Israel; namely, Jerusalem. But he is widely believed to be God. Yahudit understood how that was possible, now that she had accepted Carlos as her God. If a religion based on one pauper's divinity was possible, why not this religion of hers based on her faith in Carlos? After all, was not Jesus of Nazareth a walking, talking, potty-using human being, just like Carlos? Did he have some special bowl system that required him not to go to the bathroom? Carlos is flesh-and-blood like Jesus of Nazareth. This religion is just as valid as the religion created by the disciples of Jesus of Nazareth after his death. Isn't that what Rabbi Kimhi said about how Christian religion came to be? A lie created by the disciples of Jesus of Nazareth after his death because they needed a social club they could belong to?

Yahudit was not about social clubs. In fact, she was abandoning her perfectly fine world where she had a secure place of belonging for her faith in Carlos the Lord. Her faith was genuine. It was not an opium for the masses. It was not a form of escapism. It was not a way to create a sense of belonging. Yahudit's religion was pure, devoid of the shackles of Christianity, which might have given something to the rejects of society but at a high price of all the rules and regulations that made a slave out of a person. Yahudit's religion was pure and simple. There was only one rule, which Yahudit called, "The Diamond Rule," which was far better than The Golden Rule. "I shall be your God, and ye shall be my people." There is no requirement for fear or love. The religion just is. The covenant just is. No need for circumcision or baptism. No need for Passover seder or the Lord's Supper. Yahudit's religion was truly free.

Carlos looked ahead. For some reason he was speechless. Maybe it was too much for him to take in one day. Maybe he was self-satisfied with his God-status. Yahudit did not know Carlos long enough to read his face. So, Yahudit concluded that he was deep in thought about many different thoughts and basically shut down his body for a moment. He had his eyes open, but they were blankly staring out into the open road.

Yahudit had some thinking of her own to do. What was to become of her? Although she played out the scenario in her mind over and over again about how this day would go, she realized that she was not quite ready for it. She thought she was, but she wasn't. Was she really ready to leave her world behind? Was she ready to abandon her father and mother? Was she ready to embrace the life of a wandering charismatic? Would it last? Really, would it last? Would Carlos keep the one rule that was a part of the religion? Would he always be her God, and she his people?

Silence seemed to be the appropriate response to the gravitas of the moment. Carlos seemed to be holding his breath in terms of conversation. Yahudit managed to keep her mouth shut as she drove, although there were so many things that she wanted to tell Carlos.

Soon, the open freeways of route 10 East signaled a change to the freeway for Las Vegas. I-15 North would lead them to Las Vegas, and that was the freeway they were going to take. The shift from 10 to 15 seemed symbolic to Yahudit. She could not quite put her fingers on it, but there was significance of epic proportions. She wondered what that significance was.

Yahudit had studied a little Gemetria. She knew that the first letter of her name written in Hebrew was "*yod*," and it had a numeric value of 10. The second letter of her name written in Hebrew was "*heh*," and had the numerical value of 5. Going from 10 to 15 on the freeway system was like starting to complete the writing of her name. It was like after writing the first letter of her name in Hebrew, she was writing the second letter of her name. She was completing her name, which was like she was fulfilling what she, symbolized in her name, was meant to fulfill.

This was the sign that she was looking for! She was on the right track! How could she have doubted her destiny? How could she have doubted herself? But most importantly, how could she have doubted Carlos the Lord? Yahudit prayed in her heart that she would be forgiven for her lack of faith. Carlos the Lord, give me faith!

As she drove on and on, she felt lighter and lighter. She looked at the open road, becoming scarcer and scarcer with cars. She was driving toward her fulfillment. As the letters in her name began to be fulfilled, she was on her way to her destined happiness and bliss. She started to giggle at the thought.

Carlos threw a quick glance at Yahudit, but reverted to his old position of staring ahead. Yahudit found this a bit odd, so she looked at him for a while. Carlos tried to pretend that she was not looking. Yahudit noticed something very interesting. Every time that there was a sign post, Carlos followed it. He looked like he was trying to read every sign post on the road. Yahudit was not sure if that was his usual habit or if he were trying to focus on something to ignore Yahudit. What was bothering him?

Yahudit wanted to ask, but she decided against it. She decided to give Carlos his free space, and she just focused on the road. The car was moving at a tremendous speed. She was driving faster than usual to see if she could elicit a response from Carlos. Nada.

As Yahudit drove on, she fell into a reverie. Yahudit began to hearken back to the good old days of her youth. She thought about the mystery she found in Jewish practices. She had felt that everything performed was special. She thought that the fact that she kept kosher meant that she was special. She believed every word of her parents when they told her that she was a part of the chosen race, which was a light unto the nations. She remembered how she always looked forward to Shabbat meals and all the traditions associated with them. She remembered how Halah bread was her favorite bread. She thought about all the fun activities during Purim. She enjoyed watching her mother clean the house with the maid during Passover. She enjoyed the grandiose meals after the ritual fast on Yom Kippur days. She loved receiving gifts during Hanukah and bragged that Jewish kids were luckier because they received so many more gifts than Christian children during the holiday season. Those were good old days, Yahudit thought. Now, she did not find any mystery in Judaism and Jewish customs.

She wondered what it was that led to her denial of Judaism. Yahudit knew that it was a gradual process and not a spontaneous thing, although it may appear so at a superficial glance. When she tried to pinpoint all the causes for her losing her religion, Yahudit became more and more confused. She did not like the feeling of confusion. She wanted order in her life. Yahudit began to forget the Jewish religion wholesale and not dwell on what-might-have-been's. Yahudit again reaffirmed her desire for Carlos and the New Religion.

Yahudit looked at Carlos. Carlos was still staring ahead with a singular intensity.

"I am so happy to be here with you," Yahudit said with a slight rasp in her voice. She felt that her throat was dry.

Carlos looked at her for a while, like he was looking for something. What was he looking for?

"Are you happy to be here with me?" Yahudit asked slowly.

"Do you want the truth?" Carlos asked point-blankly.

"You can't handle the truth," Yahudit quoted a line from a movie and laughed. Carlos was not smiling. Maybe he hadn't seen the movie. Yahudit added in a more serious tone, "Sorry about that."

"That's okay," Carlos said with a softer tone.

"Yes, I want the truth," Yahudit said.

"The truth is that I am scared," Carlos said. "Fear has gripped me and desensitized my every other emotion. I cannot feel anything but fear."

Yahudit was taken aback by these words. She did not know what to think about the situation. Her God filled with fear? Fear? Fear of all things? Was she to believe in this frail God?

Then, Yahudit remembered that Jesus of Nazareth was a frail God. He was a pauper without a home. Nobody accepted him. Even the Gospels written by his own disciples show that he was not accepted. The religious establishment hated him. Scholars hated him. Politicians hated him. Even the common people hated him. After all, did they not side with the religious establishment to have him killed? Who could be weaker than that?

Clearly, this Christian God was filled with fear. Jesus of Nazareth is recorded by his own disciples as having said, "Remove this cup from me." He was afraid and did not want to go to the cross until the last moment. And this frail Jesus of Nazareth is God to billions of people. Why should Carlos not have the right to feel fear?

"Carlos," Yahudit said and gave a short bow. "You have nothing to fear except fear itself."

Carlos looked at Yahudit and smiled. He seemed to recognize the quote.

"We are going to a wonderful place," Yahudit continued. "And you are going to be filled with joy and jubilation."

"Am I now?" Carlos said in a more-or-less his usual jocular mood. Yahudit was glad to see him back.

"What can be better than Las Vegas?" Yahudit asked.

"Heaven?" Carlos ventured.

"Carlos, my God," Yahudit said. "We are in heaven."

Carlos smiled and squeezed her thigh. It was so sudden that she felt a jolt of electricity go through her.

Yahudit smiled and said, "And you know what we are going to do when we are in Las Vagas?"

"No," Carlos said. "What are you going to do?"

"We are going to get married," Yahudit said.

"That's what I was afraid you were going to say," Carlos said.

"No fear," Yahudit said, trying to feign a stern voice. "Okay?"

"Okay," Carlos said. "But you do remember that I am already married."

"No problem," Yahudit said. "We will get an Elvis Wedding, but will not fill out the paper work until your divorce is finalized with your wife. We'll live up in Las Vegas until our union is complete."

"What about your family?" Carlos asked.

Yahudit

"My family will have to understand," Yahudit said.

"What about your school?" Carlos asked.

"I'll get a GED in Las Vegas as we wait for the finalization of your divorce down south," Yahudit said.

"What about me?" Carlos asked.

"You will be happy with me," Yahudit said. "You will experience happiness like never before."

"What about money?" Carlos asked.

"I have a trust fund worth millions, and I have access to it as of my 18th birthday."

"When's your 18th birthday?"

"In 2 weeks."

"How about until then?" Carlos asked.

"I have a savings and checking accounts, and they are more than sufficient to tie us over until then," Yahudit said.

Yahudit had planned everything out. As soon as she moved to Las Vegas, she was going to withdraw all her money from her Los Angeles accounts and open up bank accounts in Las Vegas. She had already made arrangements regarding the trust fund. Yahudit had become quite resourceful and independent since he had put in her mind to start a new religion.

Carlos was impressed by all the planning that had gone into the planning process. He was not sure if he should admire her or fear her for it.

"Wow, you planned everything out," Carlos said.

"This is the beginning of the rest of our lives," Yahudit said with an echo effect. It sounded like a proclamation of the prophets of old.

"Where are we going to stay when we get to Las Vegas?" Carlos asked.

"We are going to stay in Paris Hotel until we find a more permanent arrangement."

"Oh, what the heck," Carlos said. "It sounds great to me."

Yahudit was glad to see that Carlos was fully on-board.

Yahudit

Yahudit drove faster and faster. She was not afraid that she would get a ticket. It was dark, and it was the desert. Even the scorpions were sleeping, probably. Carlos started to sing the cockroach song.

Soon, they arrived in the City of Lights. Or was it the Sin City?

Yahudit pulled the car around to the entrance way and had the valet drive the car into a lot. Yahudit and Carlos walked into the lobby and checked in. Nobody seemed to notice that they had just eloped and that they had both abandoned their families. In the case of Carlos, he had abandoned his children. But strangely, Carlos was in a good mood. Yahudit was right. He was going to be happy.

Yahudit had brought some essentials, but she had packed light. Carlos did not have anything with him. They both were quite tired from the journey so they went upstairs. Yahudit had ordered a suite with two rooms. Carlos was going to stay in one room, and Yahudit was going to stay in the other room. Yahudit wanted their consummation to be special, after the Elvis Wedding.

7

The next morning was a late morning. Both Yahudit and Carlos allowed themselves to sleep past the early morning. It was almost noon-time. They both washed up and got ready and went downstairs for a big breakfast. They had forgotten to eat dinner the day before. Both of them were so preoccupied in thought that they had completely forgotten about it.

It was the biggest breakfast that Yahudit had, and it was the first meal which was non-kosher. Yahudit tried bacon for the first time and absolutely loved it. She understood why her Gentile friends liked it so much. It seemed like Carlos loved bacon as well. Along with bacon, Yahudit had pancakes, toasted bagels, yoghurt, cereal, and various fruit items. Carlos loaded up on salmon. It was Norwegian smoked salmon. Yahudit tried one on Carlos' plate and liked it. But she was too full by then to get a serving of that.

The morning was spent on running errands. Yahudit closed out her Los Angeles accounts and opened up a Las Vegas account. After taking care of that, Yahudit and Carlos did apartment hunting. They wanted to be near enough to the city so that they could visit the city whenever they wanted. But they wanted to be far enough from the city that they would enjoy quiet suburban existence. They found an apartment in the edge of a suburban community and took it. It was not very hard to rent the place because they were willing to pay one year's rent in cash up-front. The one year lease was signed and they were set for a year. They were not sure how long they would stay in Las Vegas, but they were stuck with one-year lease because that was the minimum rental period. Yahudit was content with the arrangement, and so was Carlos. They would begin their new life in Las Vegas, and it seemed that the nice apartment in the suburb was the perfect place to do it in.

Apartment hunting took one hour, so they had plenty of time to get furniture for the apartment. Yahudit enjoyed shopping, so she was happy to go about hunting for furniture and all that they needed for the new apartment. Carlos did not like shopping so much, so they made a compromise and decided to be efficient in their shopping. Yahudit acquired a whole apartment set from a furniture store. The furniture store owner was a practical man, and he expertly made the recommendations that were suited to Yahudit's tastes. They had the living room, dining room, bedroom, and bathroom set. The furniture was going to be delivered that day in a few hours. Yahudit was amazed by the efficiency.

Yahudit and Carlos did not want to waste time waiting for the furniture, so they went to the nearby mall and purchased all the bed sheets, towels, cutlery, and other items they needed for the new house. Then, they quickly returned to their new apartment and waited for the furniture people. They arrived on time, and their apartment was nicely furnished. They needed to do some decorating, but they decided to put that off to the next day. The whole afternoon had rushed by. They had such a big breakfast that they skipped lunch. They were, however, quite hungry by late afternoon. They decided to go back to Paris Hotel and prepare for a nice dinner out in the town.

After they washed up and got dressed in their respective rooms in the hotel suite, they had to decide on a restaurant. Yahudit remembered that Carlos liked fish, so she figured that a

Yahudit

Japanese sushi restaurant was the way to go. She called up the front desk and received a good recommendation. It was a "high class" Japanese restaurant with all-you-can-eat sushi, which is beautifully arranged, so that the restaurant clientele could see what they want to eat.

"Wow, you look really great!" Carlos said when both of them met at the common space within the hotel suite.

"Well, thank you," Yahudit said. "You don't look so bad yourself."

"Thank you kindly," Carlos said with a smile.

"Nothing kindly about it," Yahudit said. "You look mighty fine!" Yahudit joked. Carlos laughed, and with smiles both of them walked out of the suite.

"You are going to like this place," Yahudit said with a smug smile.

"Which place?" Carlos asked.

"The place where we are going to eat," Yahudit said and gave no further details.

"What's the name of the restaurant?" Carlos asked.

"It's for me to know and for you to find out," Yahudit said, teasing Carlos.

"Oh, come on," Carlos said. "Just tell me."

"Patience is a virtue, my darling," Yahudit said and held his hand.

"Oh, okay," Carlos said and walked along with Yahudit, glad to be holding her hand.

"Let's take a cab," Yahudit said.

"Why?" Carlos asked.

"It's just nicer not to have to worry about driving and parking," Yahudit said. They had a packed day, and Yahudit was beginning to feel the effects of fatigue. Maybe the hot shower made her realize how tired she really was. "Besides, Las Vegas is a small city, so it's just easier to get around in a taxi."

"Okay," Carlos said. "You have convinced me."

They both got into the cab.

"So, I find out the name of the restaurant after all!" Carlos said smugly.

"Yep, that's the way the cookie crumbles," Yahudit said.

"Cookie?" Carlos said in response.

"Never mind," Yahudit said, gently dismissing Carlos' comments. She was too tired to explain the platitude. Yahudit looked at the disappointed face on Carlos and felt bad, so she gave Carlos a squeeze on his hand.

They were at the restaurant in less than five minutes.

"Voila!" Yahudit exclaimed, trying to be enthusiastic. "Here we are!"

"Hey, it's a Japanese restaurant!" Carlos said enthusiastically.

"Do you like it?" Yahudit asked.

"How did you know that I was feeling like Japanese food?" Carlos said, looking surprised.

"See," Yahudit exulted. "I know more about you on a soul-to-soul level than you think."

"I suppose so," Carlos said and shook his head.

They both walked into the Japanese restaurant and were seated by the sushi buffet spot. Carlos seemed satisfied with the seating arrangements.

"Shall we go and get 'em?" Carlos said, like a little boy.

"Okay, let's do," Yahudit said.

They walked to the sushi buffet area, hand-in-hand, but they had to release each other's hand when they grabbed their plates. Yahudit was disappointed, so she looked at Carlos to see if he was. He did not look disappointed at all. In fact, he looked enthusiastic. He was ogling at the sushi rolls. Yahudit felt like she wanted to scream. Men!

"Have you ever heard?" Yahudit said, as they walked down the sushi isle. Yahudit looked at Carlos' plate. He already had four sushi rolls on it.

"Huh?" Carlos said. He did not even look up from the sushi platters!

"Do you know what they say?" Yahudit asked.

Yahudit

"Yeah?" Carlos said in a low-reflex response mode.

"They say that the way to a man's heart is through his stomach," Yahudit said and glared at Carlos.

"Yeah," Carlos said, putting a couple more sushi items on his plate. "Of course."

"What?" Yahudit said a bit louder. "You think it's true?"

"I am just giving you the truth," Carlos said as he looked at Yahudit a bit alarmed. "I hope I did not offend you."

"No," Yahudit said. "I guess not."

Carlos just went his merry way, putting more sushi rolls on his plate. Yahudit was upset, but she realized how hungry she was, so she decided not to put on a hunger strike. She put some of her favorite items on the plate. Carlos was a few paces ahead of her, so she walked quickly to catch up to him. With full plates, they walked back to their table.

As soon as they sat down, Carlos began eating. Yahudit thought it was a bit rude, but she said nothing. She just watched Carlos eat. He looked like he had nothing to eat for days.

"Why are you watching me?" Carlos said with his mouth full.

"Didn't your mother teach you not to speak with your mouth full?" Yahudit said sarcastically.

"Is that what your mother taught you?" Carlos asked gently.

"Yes," Yahudit said. "All the time."

"So," Carlos said. "Does it offend you that I eat with my mouth full?"

"Well," Yahudit said. "Not really, come to think about it."

"Do you miss your mother?" Carlos asked.

"I don't know," Yahudit said slowly. "Honestly, I don't know."

"How could you not miss your mother?" Carlos said. "She's your mother for God's sake!"

Yahudit

"You talk to me like I were a monster," Yahudit said. "But how about you? You left your wife and children without much protest, didn't you?"

"So, you want me to go back to my children?" Carlos demanded.

"No," Yahudit said in an appeasing tone. Fear gripped her as she realized that she had said what she should not have said.

"And I did not ditch my mother," Carlos said. "I would never do that. Besides, my sister will take care of my children once she realizes that I am not coming back. We are close that way."

"How about your wife?" Yahudit asked.

"How about my wife?" Carlos said, realizing that he said too much in anger.

"Yes, your wife," Yahudit said.

"My wife is dead," Carlos said.

"Dead?" Yahudit said.

"Yes, dead," Carlos said.

"Then, why did you say you were living with your wife?" Yahudit said.

"I don't know," Carlos said. "I guess that I did not want you to get too serious. I thought maybe that I can have a fling with you and then would not be tied down. You would either abandon your efforts or if you do pursue them, you would be psychologically prepared to accept the fact that the affair has to end at some point."

"Gee," Yahudit said. "You thought about all this in that short period of time?"

"Well," Carlos said and did not answer the question fully.

"Why did you do it?" Yahudit asked. "I do not like anyone lying to me."

"I did not want you to get hurt," Carlos said. "That's all."

Yahudit

"What?" Yahudit asked. "You think that lying to me will help me? That doesn't make sense."

"And I had to worry about my children," Carlos said. "I did not want you to get any ideas about going near my children. The eldest daughter is about your age."

"Really?" Yahudit asked. "You are that old?"

"I am not old," Carlos said. "I just married young. That's all. But I still didn't want you near my children."

"And now?" Yahudit asked.

"I don't know," Carlos said. "I thought you were just one of those precocious teenagers out to have fun. I did not want my children to be collateral damage of your whims. But now, I see that you are serious. You really want a future with me. So, at this point, I don't really know what to say."

"But you are committed to going through with marriage with me?" Yahudit asked.

"Yes, I have made my decision and am committed to it," Carlos said.

"If your wife is dead, then we can get married right away," Yahudit said.

"Yes," Carlos said. "You are right on that point."

"Great!" Yahudit said enthusiastically. "Why wait? Let's do it."

"Get married?" Carlos said surprised.

"Yes, get married," Yahudit confirmed. "Let's get married, today."

"Today?" Carlos reacted.

"Yes, today," Yahudit said. "Why hesitate when it is our destiny."

"But it's already so late," Carlos said.

"This is Las Vegas," Yahudit said. "There are places where you can get an Elvis Wedding, 24 hours per day."

"Really?" Carlos said.

"Really," Yahudit said.

"Really?" Carlos repeated.

"Really!" Yahudit said more firmly.

"Okay, let's do it," Carlos said.

"Great!" Yahudit said.

Knowing that there was a wedding, her wedding, right after dinner made Yahudit a little nervous. But still, Yahudit was very hungry, so she pressed ahead with her sushi. Carlos was done with his plate and got up to get the second plate.

"Would you like me to bring you something?" Carlos said politely. It was clear that he was feeling a bit guilty about his earlier altercation.

"No, that's okay," Yahudit said. "You go ahead."

Carlos got up and went for a second serving. He quickly returned with a plate filled with sushi. He gulped them down as quickly as he did the first plate. For some reason, his great appetite endeared him to her. Yahudit watched Carlos as she slowly chewed on her sushi. Carlos was like a tiger chomping on his bits of raw meat. Yahudit wondered what it would be like to be chomped on by Carlos like that. It was clear from his eating that he was a passionate man. Yahudit could not wait for such energy, such passion to engulf her once they were married.

As Yahudit looked at Carlos, she imagined what her first passionate, desired-filled kiss would be like with Carlos. Would Carlos press his lips tightly against hers? Would he slobber all over her lips and show his affection like a large pooch? Would he try to stick his tongue into her mouth like she had read about in those romance books? Yahudit was curious how he would kiss her. She kept looking at Carlos. This time Carlos did not complain. He just kept eating his food without looking up.

Both of them were done with their meal. The moment has arrived. It was time for them to get married. Yahudit felt her heart beating as she thought about her wedding. This was the moment that she has waited for her whole life. She remembered the conversations that she had with her friends, Janice and Judith, after one Hebrew school session.

"How do you imagine your wedding to be?" Janice asked Yahudit.

"I haven't really thought about it," Yahudit said.

Yahudit

"You are lying," Judith said. "Every woman thinks about her wedding day."

"Yeah," Janice said. "I have to agree with Judith on this one."

"If that is the case," Yahudit said defiantly, "then, you tell me how your wedding will be like."

"Okay," Janice said. "I'll start."

"No," Judith said. "Let me."

"I called it, first," Janice said.

"Fine," Judith said. "You go."

"I am going to be honest," Janice said, "totally honest, not like someone around here." Janice gave Yahudit as stare. Yahudit stuck her tongue out.

"Just go on," Judith said. "We all know that Yahudit is a liar."

"Hey!" Yahudit protested.

"Just kidding," Judith said. "Just kidding."

"Okay," Yahudit relented.

"To continue with the story," Janice said, "my story, my fairytale wedding, if you will, I will start by describing the setting."

"That's a good place to start," Yahudit said to show that she was not cross with her.

"Thank you, Yahudit," Janice said. "I want my wedding to be outside in the garden. I want the birds to be singing in the air and the sun to be shining brightly over the sky."

"The sun may be shining," Yahudit said, "since it is California, but how can you ensure that the birds will sing?"

"Yeah!" Judith said. "Maybe the birds will be pooping all over you and your fiancé."

"Judith!" Yahudit yelled. "That's not nice."

"Yes," Janice said. "You are ruining my fairytale wedding."

"Apologize, Judith," Yahudit said.

"Why?" Judith said defiantly.

Yahudit

"Please apologize so I can continue with the story," Janice said.

"Okay, Janice," Judith said. "I am doing this for you and not for Yahudit. I am sorry."

"So, to continue with the story," Janice said. "I want a wedding outside where the birds will be singing and not pooping. The sun will be shining. There will be white benches made out of bronze for all to sit on. There will be a red rose at either end of the white chair rows. In the middle will be a walkway for the husband and the brushing bride."

"You sure you will be blushing?" Judith interjected.

"Judith!" Yahudit chided. "Shush yourself!"

"To continue again with my fairytale wedding," Janice said, ignoring the comments. "There will be my favorite rabbi."

"Who is that?" Yahudit said, curious.

"Rabbi Haberman," Janice said.

"Rabbi Haberman?" Judith said. "He's not your rabbi."

"Well, he is a rabbi and he works at the school," Janice said. "I am sure he can marry us."

"You should get married by your rabbi," Judith said.

"I consider him my rabbi," Janice said. "Besides, I don't like the rabbi at my synagogue."

"Let's not go there," Yahudit said. "Let's stick to the wedding."

"Okay," Janice said. "That sounds good. Is that okay with you, Judith?"

"Fine by me," Judith said nonchalantly.

"How many guests will you have?" Yahudit said to soften the atmosphere.

"I want a big wedding," Janice said.

"Outside?" Judith said.

"Yes, why not?" Janice said. "I think we can find a place that can accommodate five hundred people or so."

"Sure," Yahudit said. "You can find a place like that."

"It's going to be awfully expensive," Judith said. "You sure you can afford such a wedding."

"Oh,   I-live-off-my-grandpa's-property-investment princess," Janice said, "you are not the only wealthy person in this room."

"Gee," Judith said, "you don't need to be nasty like that."

"Nasty?" Janice said and was ready to give a speech of sorts.

Yahudit interjected, "Please, let's not fight. Can't we just all get along?"

"Okay," Janice said with a softer tone. "I am done talking about my wedding."

"How about the reception?" Yahudit asked.

"I am going to hire Shallosh Battim," Janice said.

"You must be kidding," Judith said. "They are like children's band."

"They are not like a children band," Yahudit said. "They perform at weddings, and I have heard that they are great."

"Well, I really liked their performance at my Bat Mitzvah," Janice said. "So, I am going to have them at my wedding. It's my wedding after all."

"You are right," Yahudit said. "I am sure they will be great."

"It'll be a child's wedding," Judith said.

"So, why don't you tell us what an adult wedding will be like?" Yahudit said.

"Yeah, Judith," Janice chimed in.

"Okay," Judith said. "I will talk about my wedding."

"Let's see how good it will be," Janice said.

"It'll definitely be better than your wedding," Judith said.

"Okay, okay," Yahudit jumped in before Janice could say a word. "Start the story already!"

"Here it goes," Judith said. "I want to have my wedding in the Caribbean."

"What?" Janice said. "That's so far away."

"Well," Judith said. "I only will get married once. I want it to be very special."

"And how will everyone get there."

"I thought of that too, Janice," Judith said. "I will have the wedding during the winter break, so families can have a nice get away. It can be a second honeymoon. They can have a nice winter vacation. It will be like 'Home Alone' movie, but no one will be left out of the family vacation."

"So, you expect everyone to pay their way to the wedding?" Janice demanded.

"If they can afford it," Judith said.

"Yeah, we can afford it," Janice said.

"I don't know if I can," Yahudit said.

"What are you talking about?" Judith said. "You are the richest out of us all."

"Just because my dad is in the movie business does not mean we are wealthy," Yahudit said.

"You are filthy wealthy," Janice said. "My mother told me."

"How does your mother know?" Yahudit asked, curious.

"She's friends with your father's accountant," Janice said.

"You mean, Mr. Nachtbaum?" Yahudit asked.

"Yeah, I think that's his name," Janice said. "I don't know him personally, but I think my mom went to college with him or something like that."

"So, continuing on with my wedding," Judith jumped in and cut the discussion short. "My wedding will be in St. Martin."

"Why St. Martin, particularly?" Janice asked.

"Because," Judith continued. "I had the most magical memory of the place."

"What happened?" Yahudit asked.

"I went there with my family one winter vacation on a cruise. It was a cruise stop," Judith said and took a deep breath. "It was so amazing. The island was like a primitive paradise.

People were so friendly and happy. I felt like I was in a mystical paradise. It was then that I decided that I would get married on that island."

"Really?" Yahudit asked.

"Why did you never tell us?" Janice asked.

"You never asked," Judith said. "On this island, I will rent a nice area for the wedding. We'll occupy like half the island for the wedding. We'll have the wedding ceremony. And after the wedding ceremony, there will be buggies drawn by horses to take people to a nice reception hall at a five star hotel. Then, there will be a band flown in from Israel, which will sing Yiddish and Hebrew songs to entertain us. Kosher champagne will flow from the cascading pyramid of pure crystal glasses. And there he will be, my beloved husband, who will be my soulmate, forever."

"Do you have a soulmate in mind?" Janice asked.

"No," Judith said. "It will be someone who follows the Torah and wants to raise the children Jewish. That's very important for me. I want my children to be the leaders of the American Jewish community. Preservation of Jewish identity and community is my mission in life."

"You must be kidding," Yahudit said.

"What is marriage for but to propagate the world with more Jews?" Judith said.

"Are you for real?" Janice asked.

"As real as kosher apple juice," Judith said.

"Huh?" Yahudit said.

"What about love?" Janice asked.

"What about love?" Judith said. "Love is in the heart, mind, and one's strength. Love is an act and not a childish sense of feeling and emotional turmoil."

"You must be joking, right?" Yahudit said. "Love is so important. Love is what bonds. Love is what recreates. Love is the fuel to our universe."

"Yeah, I agree with Yahudit," Janice said.

"That's because you are mere children, mere girls who are still tied to their Barbie dolls," Judith said condescendingly.

"Whatever!" Janice said.

"Talk to the hand," Yahudit said. The moment Yahudit started to push her hand toward Judith's face, all three started to crack up and laughed uncontrollably. Janice had tears in her eyes from so much laughing.

"How about you, Miss Love?" Judith said. "What is your wedding going to be like?"

"My wedding?" Yahudit said, sounding surprised.

"Yeah, have you not thought about it before?" Janice asked.

"Of course, I have," Yahudit said. "But I have never really talked about it with anyone before."

"Well, that's like us," Judith said.

"I don't believe it," Yahudit said. "You probably talked about it with your mom."

"Okay," Judith said. "You got me there."

"So, who's the liar, now?" Janice said.

"I was not lying," Judith said.

"Whatever," Janice said.

"Okay, I will tell you about my wedding," Yahudit said and tried to make peace between Judith and Janice. "I am going to have my wedding in Los Angeles. I am going to let mom arrange everything because she is good at that. I am just going to look very hard for the perfect wedding dress."

"A perfect wedding dress?" Janice asked.

"That's all I care about," Yahudit said. "I am sure my wedding will be perfect with mom's planning. I just want a wedding dress that I love to go with the husband that I love."

"Oh," Janice said. "That is so sweet!"

"Too much mush for me," Judith said.

"Here it is, folks," Janice said. "Words of a robot princess without a heart."

"Janice!" Yahudit said. "That's not nice."

Yahudit

As Yahudit sat in the taxi waiting to be delivered to the Elvis Wedding chapel, she could not help but to think about the conversation, the wedding conversation. She smiled and tried to remember her happiness. She looked at her dress. It was an elegant evening gown, but it was not a wedding dress. She missed out on the pleasure of hunting for a wedding dress. And here she was, about to get married. Tears started to stream down her cheeks.

"What's wrong, honey?" Carlos asked.

"I don't know," Yahudit said. "I guess it is tears of joy."

Taxi driver stared at them through his rearview mirror.

"Women," Carlos quipped. "They get so emotional around weddings."

Yahudit looked at the Taxi driver who was glaring at them through the mirror.

"Yeah," Yahudit said. "I am so happy to be getting married."

"Here we are, folks," the taxi driver said.

Carlos and Yahudit walked hand-in-hand toward the Elvis Wedding chapel. The outside of the building was filled with kitsch. But for some odd reason, this was comforting to Yahudit. She planned on getting married only once, and she had imagined her wedding day to be perfect. This was hardly the wedding that she had imagined. And because she had been so preoccupied with the New Religion, she had not really thought about the details of the wedding. She had been worried that Carlos would not go ahead with the Program. It was great luck he went along, and everything worked out. But everything was happening too fast. She was not able to keep up with the speed although she was the brains behind the operation. It was she who had convinced Carlos to abandon his family. It was she who had suggested a wedding in Las Vegas. It was she who had picked out an apartment and saw to its furnishings. It was she who was handling all the expenses. And even when it came to food, it was she who made the choices and took care of Carlos.

Yahudit

Yahudit had hoped for a knight in shining armor, but it felt like she was getting a helpless babe to take care of. She wondered how her religion became such a religion. A religion with a feeble God. But then, she was again comforted by thoughts of Christianity. Jesus of Nazareth, the God of Christianity, was feeble and could not feed himself. Did not the Gospels describe him as not having food, a place to sleep, and nice clothes to wear? Following this Jesus of Nazareth was like the blind following the blind, at least when it came to finances and food. No wonder that this Jesus taught his disciples not to worry about what to wear or what to eat. He was trying to make his disciples forget about the lack of daily essentials. He made a religion out of bashing the wealthy.

Did not this Jesus of Nazareth tell a pious Pharisee that he must sell all that he has and give to the poor? What kind of financial irresponsibility is that? Would God be happy if this wealthy Jew squandered all of God's blessings and followed a supposed God who could not do simple math? Did this Jesus of Nazareth, to defend his own incompetence in financial matters, bash the rich who were good stewards of their possessions, by saying that it is difficult for the rich to enter the Kingdom of Christ like a camel going through the eye of a needle? The only way the camel is going to go through the eye of the needle was by being killed and pulverized into bits. Even then, it would still be hard to push a camel through the eye of a needle. Not only did Jesus of Nazareth not know how to handle his wealth, he seemed to be incompetent in gathering a winning team around him.

Was it not one of his chosen 12 disciples who betrayed him? He would have gotten an "F" for being a bad recruiter and manager. This supposed God could not read people. And did his right hand man, the man called Peter, not betray him three times? Jesus of Nazareth was a poor pauper without any management skills or leadership, who put together a ragtag team of incompetents and traitors. Yahudit felt her New Religion was better. Carlos was a humble God like Jesus of Nazareth, but at least he had her. They made an effective team, and she was not going to betray her God, unlike Judas Iscariot or Peter. Yahudit figured that her New Religion was at least one step above Original Christianity. If Christianity can grow from such a shoddy beginning, her religion could be magnificent. She needed only to be patient. Patience is a virtue after all.

She felt better after she thought about how superior her religion was to Christianity. When both of them had gone inside the chapel, a colorful Elvis impersonator greeted them.

"Hello, nice folks," Elvis said.

"Hi," Carlos said with a stupid smile on his face.

"Hi," Yahudit said.

"So, you are here to tie the knot?" Elvis asked.

"That we are," Carlos said, visibly forcing a smile.

"Well, you have a-come to a nice place for your splendid nuptials," Elvis said. "The power of love will a-engulf you, tonight."

"That's what we are hoping," Carlos said enthusiastically.

"Do you a-believe?" Elvis asked. "Do you a-believe in the power of love?"

"Yes," Carlos said.

"Wise men say only fools a-rush in, but a-I cannot help falling in a-love with you," Elvis said.

"The Gospel according to Elvis," Elvis said. "Do you a-believe?"

"Yes," Carlos said quietly.

"Can't hear you," Elvis said. "Do you a-believe? And say, 'Amen.'"

"Amen," Carlos said.

"Amen," Yahudit said.

"So, you love birds take each other as your foolhardy but true love to hold and to caress and squeeze and smooch all the days of your life?"

"Huh?" Carlos said.

"This is where you say, 'I do.'"

"Oh," Carlos said as he looked at Elvis. "I do."

"And you?" Elvis looked at Yahudit.

"Yes, I do," Yahudit said.

"Now, I pronounce you man and wife," Elvis said and then started to sing, "Wise men say…."

Carlos went with the flow and started dancing with Yahudit. Yahudit wanted him to kiss her, but was content with being held by him. Yahudit squeezed him tightly towards her. Carlos started to squeeze tight. Without intending to, Yahudit felt herself breathing a bit heavier. She could feel Carlos' heartbeat.

"Now that you had your first dance to the sacred song of the King," Elvis said, "you may kiss each other."

Carlos looked at Yahudit and kissed her. He pressed his lips against her. She pressed back.

"Now, you love birds are married," Elvis said. "By the power vested in me by the state of Nevada, I proclaim you to be married."

"Thank you," Carlos said.

"That will be $1,000," Elvis said.

"For a five-minute wedding?" Carlos protested.

"Five minutes of magical wedding," Elvis said. "Even that King-induced kiss is worth more than a thousand!"

"He's right about that," Yahudit said and paid Elvis with ten Benjamin's.

"Thanks, Elvis," Yahudit said.

"You are the King," Carlos said.

They gathered their marriage paperwork and rushed out onto the streets. Strangely enough, Yahudit did not feel different. She had imagined that the wedding would be world-shattering. But it wasn't. She felt the same as she did before. Then, she felt the sushi coming up.

"Excuse me," Yahudit said and rushed to the corner of the building. All the sushi she had eaten that night came flooding out of her mouth. She did not feel so well.

"Are you okay, Yahudit?" Carlos asked.

"Yeah," Yahudit yelled with her back turned. "It's just that it's all so exciting."

Yahudit wiped her mouth with a tissue from a tissue pack and put a mint in her mouth.

"As good as new," Yahudit said to Carlos. "Shall we walk back to our hotel?"

"If you wish," Carlos said.

"Yes, I do," Yahudit said. "My stomach is not feeling too well, and a taxi ride would upset it again."

"Okay," Carlos said. "The hotel is not too far off, anyway."

Yahudit and Carlos began to walk towards their hotel not holding each other's hand.

Carlos walked with light steps, but Yahudit seemed like she was dragged down by her steps. Carlos turned toward Yahudit and noticed that she was crying.

"What's wrong, Yahudit?" Carlos asked, alarmed.

"I don't know," Yahudit said earnestly. "I am happy, but I am also sad."

"It is a state of profound change," Carlos said, holding her hand tighter. "It's not easy making a transition from one state to another state."

"No?" Yahudit looked up trying to wipe away her tears.

"No, it isn't easy," Carlos said and tried to wipe away her tears with his hand. Carlos held her face with both of his hands. She turned slightly and kissed one of his hands.

Carlos drew closer to Yahudit and kissed her forehead. Yahudit looked up with her large brown eyes with a look that a child would have if she were to meet a live character out of Harry Potter books. Carlos felt a heavy weight of responsibility on his shoulders, but he felt happy that a woman was depending so utterly on him. He felt he had the heart of a knight about to save a woman in a dungeon. Yes, there are risks involved. Yes, it is possible that the knight would die in the rescue effort. But he was the hero. He was the one who was to save a woman in distress. He was her only hope. Carlos felt joy flooding into his heart as he realized that he was Yahudit's hero. She depended on him. She looked to him for salvation. He was her God.

Carlos began to stroke Yahudit's hair. For the first time, Yahudit looked so frail like a new-born infant. How could she survive without him? He could not be weak because she depended on him. He had to be strong for her sake. Carlos kissed Yahudit on the head and felt the softness of her hair. Carlos felt Yahudit's arms swing around him and holding him. It seemed to get tighter and tighter. Carlos was overwhelmed by the frailty of a woman who had dictated the whole course from the beginning to now. For some reason, he was the strong one, and she was the weak one. Carlos felt his importance in the embrace of a woman whom he had lusted after for so long. She was now his wife. And he began to love her.

"You are always going to be with me, Carlos, right?" Yahudit said in a frail voice.

"Of course, dear, I will never leave you or forsake you," Carlos said. "I will be with you until the end of the age."

"You are my hope and my salvation," Yahudit said, looking up with teary eyes. "If you left me, I would die. I would simply die."

"I am not going to leave you, Yahudit," Carlos assured her and kissed her in the forehead.

"Do you promise?" Yahudit beseeched. "Do you promise that you will never leave me?"

"I promise, Yahudit," Carlos assured. "I promise with all of my heart."

"We will be together forever?" Yahudit asked again.

"Yes, we will be together forever," Carlos assured.

"Kiss me, Carlos," Yahudit begged.

Carlos reached over and kissed her on the forehead.

"No, kiss me like a man would a woman whom he loves dearly and does not want to let go," Yahudit said.

Carlos paused for a second, trying to digest the meaning of the sentence, and then he plunged in. Carlos kissed Yahudit on the lips. This time, he was not pressing against her lips like a gentleman. He was slobbering all over her lips. Yahudit felt the wetness all over her mouth. For some reason, the wetness which would have grossed her out previously seemed comforting. Yahudit slobbered back with all her energy.

Carlos started coughing. He had tasted some of her vomit, and it struck a cord with his nervous system, which kicked back in low-level reflex. Serious of cough engulfed Yahudit's face. Yahudit started to cough as well as if she had been struck by a highly contagious plague.

Both looked at each other and laughed. Yahudit did not know if the whole episode was romantic or not. She was a bit confused by all that transpired. She felt lost, but also found. She felt like she belonged in the midst of confusion. She felt like her ship had docked and that she needed not to sail the vast, heartless sea, anymore. She felt like they were husband and wife.

Carlos and Yahudit continued on their walk, hand-in-hand. The night was clear. They could see the stars in the sky. They felt the gentle desert breeze. And they realized that they were in the midst of a bright world of lights, which surrounded them. This was a city that never sleeps. It was Sin City, but for them it was the City of Redemption. The City of Salvation. The City of New Beginnings. The City of Rebirth. The world was being recreated, here.

Carlos and Yahudit continued with relative gravitas that they both felt in their hearts. They were in the midst of something great. And it was not just the marriage. Carlos had realized his self-importance, the fact that he was needed so badly. The existence of another depended on his own existence. Yahudit realized emotively the need for Carlos. It was not a mere intellectual exercise or an interesting project of an intelligent teenager, anymore. Yahudit knew in her heart that she needed Carlos. It was beyond love. It was beyond affection. It was beyond needing Carlos for the sake of love. Yahudit felt that she needed Carlos for her existence. She existed because Carlos was there. Without Carlos, she would cease to exist. She would be a walking zombie without direction or meaning, at best. At worst, she would drive to the edge of a cliff and drive her daddy's red Porsche off the cliff into the abyss below, plunging voluntarily to her death. Nay, not just voluntarily, but with alacrity and enthusiasm. Life would hold no meaning and death would be better than the pain of living. Both realized what the other meant to the self.

They walked through the streets, passing by people without noticing them. There were people in suits walking around. There were people in shorts walking around. There were depressed people walking around. There were happy people walking around. All the people whom they passed by, they did not notice. They were invisible as the two tried to comprehend the oneness of their new existence, together. They tried to understand the cosmological, existential, metaphysical realities that they were experiencing. It was like a computer programmer trying to perform complex algorithms on an outdated personal computer. The computation was slow to be processed, and without delicacy the whole system would crash. It could all come tumbling down. Thus, Carlos and Yahudit were self-absorbed. But they were selfish for a purpose that might be deemed to be of "higher order."

The self-imposed silence on the oneness of the two walking together down the street of Las Vegas was broken by their arrival in their hotel. Paris Hotel loomed large before them, and they felt like they were in Paris. It was the beginning of their honeymoon. Their conjugal union has led them to this makeshift Paris, the city of love. They both looked at each other and kissed each other gently on the lips. Then, they went up to their room.

After they were both inside, Yahudit stood by the entrance way, as if she did not know what to do. She wondered to herself if she were going to be unlucky. Her husband had not broken a glass. Then, Yahudit dismissed those thoughts as silly Jewish superstition. After all, she was here with her God and involved in a new religion.

Yahudit

Carlos also stood there, not knowing quite what to do. He felt like a new groom in his teens, who had never touched a woman. And he felt afraid. He was scared of hurting her. She seemed so frail and helpless. What if he did something and created pain for her? He could not bear the thought of hurting her in any way. He cared about her. He wanted her to be happy. He loved her. Yes, he was convinced that he was in love.

Yahudit looked at Carlos and said, "I don't know what to do." She looked down for a second as she blushed.

Carlos inched closer to her and kissed her on the cheeks. He held both of her hands in his hands. He pulled her hands up toward her breasts and pressed her hands against them. Then, Carlos kissed Yahudit in her lips. He gave one, two, three quick kisses. Then, he let her experience a lengthy kiss. She felt the wetness of his lips on hers and felt a strange sensation shoot up her leg. She felt a strange pleasure of someone experiencing light electricity permeating her being. Yahudit squeezed Carlos' hands and felt the motion of his hands on her breasts. Carlos pushed her hands into her breasts. And he felt the softness of her breasts on his hands. Yahudit's breasts moved about under the weight of the pressure, and her breasts became more exposed as they moved about inside the evening dress. Yahudit's breasts felt soft. Carlos used his pinky fingers to feel the texture of her breasts and felt her skin heat up. Yahudit's breasts heaved, and she breathed irregularly. Carlos looked at her heaving breasts, restrained himself, and kissed her on the lips. Yahudit smelled like flowers.

The beautiful scent of her perfume engulfed her being and seemed to become starker in its aroma as she visibly heat up. Carlos felt a pang of desire shoot from his brain to his thigh and to his extremities below. He felt his manhood beat with a ferocious intensity as it ascended to exert pressure on blushing new bride who was standing very close to him. He felt his male identity brush up against her evening gown and press her skin underneath and was seized with an uncontrollable desire. Carlos stuck his tongue inside Yahudit's mouth and heard a slight but highly audible shriek from his wife. Carlos let go of Yahudit's hands, which fell quickly like a man thrown off of a hotel penthouse onto the hotel swimming pool some forty floors below. With a savage-like ferocity, Carlos pressed his hands against Yahudit's breasts and cupped them in his hands. Yahudit's mouth seemed to open wider as if her brain had sent it a special message. Carlos began to suck on the lower lip as he squeezed Yahudit's breasts tighter and tighter. Carlos began to feel Yahudit's body writhe, so he put his left hand around her waste. With his right hand, he stroked the bare-skin part of her breasts, popping out of her evening gown. Then, Carlos pushed against her breasts and tried to put his hand inside the breast cup of the evening gown. Soon, his hand was being pressed between her full-sized naked breast and the soft clothing of her evening dress. Carlos pulled out her breast from its constraint and began to kiss the more rounded bottom part of her breast. Slowly, his kisses inched slowly up the curvature toward the pleasure button of her finely sculpted natural form. Carlos began to suck gently on Yahudit's nipple and heard Yahudit begin to breathe louder. Carlos freed her other breast from its constraint and began to squeeze it with his hand without taking his lips off of their tight hold on her nipple. Carlos began to squeeze his wife's other nipple with his fingers as Yahudit's breathing came to acquire a tone. Sporadic tone made a music of its own. It sounded more like the beginning of a complex symphony. Carlos became more and more excited and felt like his manhood would explode. As much as he wanted to gratify his desire, he thought of his new wife. It was her first time, and he wanted to make the occasion very special for her.

Carlos lifted up Yahudit and cradled her in his arms. He began to walk toward his room within the two bedroom suite. The walk was not a short one, but Carlos did not feel the pain of the carriage. He was busy kissing Yahudit on the lips, on the cheeks, and on the breasts as he carried her to his room. Yahudit had her eyes closed and was breathing deeply.

Yahudit

When Carlos reached his room, he gently put her down on his bed. She opened her eyes, but only slightly. She smiled when she saw him. Carlos reached down to kiss her lips once again. Yahudit closed her eyes. Carlos stroked her cheeks and began to brush her hair with his hands as he kissed her. Then, he brushed the back of his hand against her breast and felt her nipples jutting out and pressuring his hand. Carlos continued to kiss Yahudit on her lips.

Slowly, Carlos turned Yahudit over and placed her on her stomach. He caressed her hair and the exposed part of her back. He kissed her back for a minute or two. Then, Carlos began to undo her zipper. As the zipper rode down a free fall from top to bottom, the silence of the room, which was only broken by Yahudit's breathing, was disturbed by a foreign noise. Yahudit moved a bit, but then remained calm. It was not easy for Carlos to slip the dress down, but he tried to lift Yahudit gently up as he slipped the dress from her body. Soon, she was completely naked except for her panties, which was bright red in color. The red matched the red of the red Porsche.

Carlos began to kiss Yahudit's neck. Slowly, he began to allow his kisses to slip down south as she was showered with his quick kisses all over her front torso. Yahudit's breasts moved about and hit Carlos on his cheeks and head. Different sounds created added to the movement of the orchestral piece generated by the expertise of a conductor who had realized that he was giving himself completely and selflessly to a woman who had given herself completely and selflessly to him. Carlos began to slow down his kisses as he neared the bright red underwear that seemed so uncharacteristic of the blushing bride who had her eyes tightly closed. Yahudit moved slightly in a rhythmic motion, so Carlos held Yahudit by her waste. Both of his hands holding the soft curvature of her waist began their instinctive slide down and met the top ring of her underwear. Slowly, Carlos began to drag down the underwear with his two hands. He looked up at Yahudit to see if she were watching him. She wasn't. She still had her eyes closed.

Yahudit

As Carlos opened up the hidden space behind the red clothing that had concealed the intimate sanctum sanctorum of her being, he saw the harbingers of pleasure in the form of wildly arranged black hair which looked like a floral arrangement of some exquisite flower that most living souls have never seen. As Carlos slid the clothing down further and further and revealed the sculpture of magnificence that was juiced with feminine libation, he smelled the sweet aroma of scent offering prepared specially for him. It was the first fruit offering of a dedicated worshipper who had taken extreme care to grow her sacrifice without any blemish or fault of any kind. It was the whole burnt offering that is dedicated to a divinity with no reservation or hesitation. It was the sweet sacrifice that was to be consumed completely by the deity for his pleasure. As he beheld the beauty of the sacrifice and the sweet aroma of unblemished sacrifice, Carlos felt a bit dizzy. He felt dizzy with pleasure. He could feel the pain in his groin, which has not been satisfied but had been so close to satiation of the exquisite sort. Pleasure had turned into pain, but yet there was more pleasure that overwhelmed. Carlos blinked several times to focus because his head was swirling around. He could not hold himself back. He was her God after all, wasn't he? The sacrifice was for him, wasn't it? He rushed his lips against the fountain of her essence and began to lick the drink offering of feminine libation. She felt the sweet aroma of her scent engulf her and rub against his whole face. He felt the prickly plants of her fertile sacred ground stroke his face. And he heard the moans of a woman in pleasure who had not known such pleasure. Yahudit's body was moving about in a sort of gentle frenzy. Carlos tried to hold her body as he drank from her well the springs of life. He felt anew the thumping beat of his male protrusion. It was thumping in the midst of a painful strain on the sides of its shaft. He felt pleasure and pain at the same time. He could not hold back any longer, so he quickly undid his pants and his underwear. It was not even completely off of his person, when Carlos plunged deep into the abyss of Yahudit. With instant contact and the sudden penetration, Carlos felt his hands and legs go weak. With only a few rhythmic movements, Carlos quickly expressed his divine pleasure on the explosion of his being inside her body. Yahudit yelped a couple of times and was still with her eyes closed. She realized that her sacrifice was accepted by her God and that he had unloaded the blessings of his divine being in her personhood. She felt the roughness of his clothes on her naked body. She remained silent and had her eyes closed. She was breathing softer. On top of her body, Carlos gently took off his clothing, one by one, until he was lying on top of her, completely naked. Carlos held her. Yahudit held him. Yahudit opened her eyes. They both looked at each other's eyes. Then, they both closed their eyes, and they were asleep.

There was morning and there was evening, the fourth day. And all was good.

Now, Carlos and Yahudit were man and wife. The next morning, they both woke up very late. Yahudit woke up first. She felt strange, lying naked on a man's bed. But surprisingly, there was not a sense of dread. It was perhaps because she knew that they were lawfully married that she did not feel herself to be cheap or valueless. Although she had given up her Jewish religion, she valued the institution of marriage. Yahudit could not completely shrug off her value system. She still believed that family was important. She still believed that faithfulness and monogamy were ways to go. She still believed that a woman's value was tied to her chastity and her loyalty to her husband. For seventeen years of her life, she had grown up with this value system, and she embraced them. As an idealistic young woman, she wanted to live the virtues of strength as she saw them. For her, it was easier for a woman to be loose and be with many men. For her, it was easier for a woman to live with a man without getting him to commit to a marriage. Yahudit saw these as weaknesses of a woman. For Yahudit, it was not only about morality or a value system, it was about a woman's strength and power to persuade the man whom she loves to commit to her in marriage. Yahudit realized that she had lived her value system, and that made her celebrate in her heart. She felt she had nothing to be ashamed of. She felt proud of herself for her strength.

As Yahudit regarded Carlos, lying naked next to her, she felt a sense of pride invade her heart. She had succeeded. She had succeeded in the deification of Carlos. She had succeeded in making him God of her private religion. How private can a religion be than the one created by her? It was a religion of the two. After all, the Jewish religion exulted in its exclusivity. Can a religion be more exclusive than having two members? God and the worshipper? In a sense, religion is a deeply personal experience. It is a private experience. Most of the religiosity goes on in the heart, doesn't it? Yahudit reasoned with herself and stared at Carlos who was still sound asleep. As much a she was used to getting up right after waking up, Yahudit allowed herself to linger in her bed. It was now her bed as well, wasn't it?

Yahudit thought about what led to this moment. She had always been taught by her mother that a woman's virginity was her crown. Her mother was strictly Jewish and wanted her to be the perfect Jewish woman. Her mother had invested a lot of her time and energy to inculcate Jewish values in her. Yahudit tried to remember if they did anything that did not involve being Jewish. Even when they did the most mundane of activities, her mother tried to bring them around to some lessons about being Jewish. The virtuous woman was a virgin. A non-virgin before marriage could not be, by definition, virtuous. Such notions felt so odd at times to Yahudit. It differed so significantly from the value system that she was exposed to in television and in internet. Radio seemed to blare the virtues of losing virginity, and so did the movies. It seemed almost odd to be a virgin before marriage. Her sense of normalcy seemed to vacillate between the value system that her mother instilled in her and the value system that was pervasive in society. In the end, her mother won. After all, her mother's influence was constant. And her mother was focused on her vision.

Yahudit

Yahudit wondered what was going on with her mother. Did she have an emotional breakdown? Was something related to Israel? Did her mother suspect something about her? Although she was worried, Yahudit did not worry too much because she knew that her mother was in good hands. Grandma Friedman was taking good care of her, for sure. Yahudit wondered what was going on with her father. He was making a movie, like he always does. He was missing from home, like he often was. He seemed to take care of himself pretty well. But come to think about it, Yahudit decided that he was not really fathering in his behavior. Without her mother, she would have been almost an orphan. Then, Yahudit thought about how blessed her father was to have her mother. She was his anchor. She was the anchor of the family. Maybe, it was because the anchor had been lifted that Yahudit was able to set sail and travel to distant lands. Would she have left for Las Vegas had her mother been home? With her keen motherly instincts, she would have ferreted the secret plan out and stopped it before it could be executed. Fortunately for her, Yahudit's mother was hundreds of miles away. That made the plan possible. That made this possible. Yahudit looked at Carlos and tried to smile, but for some reason, she was not able to.

Yahudit felt a tear drop travel down her cheeks. For some reason, extreme sadness gripped her. She was not a virgin any more! This was the moment that her mother had been preparing her all her life. And there was no mother around. She did not even know that this has happened in her absence. For some reason, Yahudit felt like it was not her mother who was missing out, but it was she herself who was missing out. She did not know what it was. Was it her latent motherly instinct trying to assert itself on her person? Her tears flowed more plenteously, and her cheeks were covered with salty liquid. Yahudit tried to wipe away her tears with her hands. All the while, she did not take her eyes off of Carlos, who was fast asleep.

Yahudit

Maybe, this is what her mother meant when she said that all women are an island. The comment struck her as odd when she heard it because it was the first comment that did not divide Gentile women from Jewish women. All women are an island. There she was, having lost the most precious thing that a woman can own, which resulted in an actual physical change in the most private area of her body, and there he was, oblivious and with a stupid smile in his face, sleeping and sleeping away. He probably has no idea what had happened to her and in her. Yahudit was sure that no man understood. All women were an island. All women are one island.

With tears still flowing down her cheeks like the waters of Niagara Falls, Yahudit got off Carlos' bed and went towards the bathroom. Although Carlos was fast asleep, Yahudit covered her private parts with her hands and started to rush toward the bathroom. She felt a sense of shame and embarrassment. Yahudit knew in her mind that there was no reason to feel shame because she was married. She had lost her virginity to her husband. Everything had been done according to her ideal system. But still, she could not tame the sorrow that was growing in her heart. By the time she reached the Bathroom, Yahudit was shaking in fear. Fear of what? She did not know. It was the fear of the unknown. The fear itself was frightening.

Yahudit quickly turned the shower on. She made the water as hot as possible. She needed a hot shower. She felt a need to be warmed up. She was feeling cold. She was feeling alone. She was feeling miserable. She did not understand. She did not understand what was happening. She did not understand the emotions that were rushing at her. She did not understand why a small physical change, which is meant to be a natural process for a married woman who had preserved her virtue until her wedding night, was causing so much sorrow and shame. Did all women feel this way after their first time? She wanted to know. She wanted to ask her mama. She wanted to ask someone. Maybe Grandma Friedman? She would go on and on and explain everything. But no, she was alone. She was alone in a hotel room in Las Vegas with a stranger she had just met. And she had lost her virginity to him. She had given him her life. She had lost all.

Yahudit began to soap her body. But she did not stop. She kept soaping her body constantly. She thought that she could change the color of her skin from brown to white. She felt like her heart had come to match the color of her skin. She had never thought of her body and color as anything but a beautiful creation of God, but now, she felt like she was ashamed of them. She stood under the shower head, tired from all the soaping, and allowed the water to wash away all the soap. She felt good, standing below a powerful shower stream, with her arms limp at the sides. She was doing no work. The shower head was doing all the work.

After she felt the warmth of the shower stream feel too hot to handle, Yahudit turned off the shower head. She began to dry herself with a nice, fluffy hotel towel. She felt refreshed. She felt good. She looked at herself in the mirror. She thought she noticed a glow in her cheeks. She wondered if it was from all the crying. She looked closer in the mirror to see if all the tears had left a temporary damage on her delicate skin. She ran her fingers through her cheeks. She thought she felt some bumpiness, but did not notice a significant difference in the mirror. Maybe, it was a blessing that she had dark Iranian skin.

Yahudit rolled the long bath towel around her body and stepped out of the bathroom. She went toward her room. She quickly got dressed after she pulled the bath towel off of her body. She dressed in bright colors. And she made a point of wearing pants. For some reason, she did not want to wear a skirt. But she felt fine, now. There were no tears in her eyes. She felt a rush of happiness come back in her heart. She looked at herself in the mirror and liked what she saw. She was happy with herself and the way she looked in colorful clothing.

She sat down in her bedroom; then, she closed her eyes. Yahudit did not know why, but she wanted to remember. She wanted to remember what went on the previous night. With her eyes closed, Yahudit remembered the sensations that she had felt. She felt the pangs of pleasure rush into her body. She felt the tingly ecstasy she had felt in every inch of her body as she was caressed by her husband. There was no doubt that he desired her. The fact that he desired her excited her. The fact that she was so wanted made her happy. The fact that he wanted to be closer and closer to her made her feel like she belonged. The fact that he could not contain his excitement and allowed his manhood to explode in her body so abruptly made her smile. She was wanted. She was desired. They had shared a special moment. It was the right way to start off the marriage. It was a magical way to start the conjugal union that was to last a life time. It was the right way to start the New World, the New Religion.

The New Religion had actually begun. Yahudit was different, now. Carlos was different, now. Like Romeo and Juliet, they had abandoned their worlds, for the sake of love, for the sake of a higher calling. But unlike the hapless Juliet and her Romeo, Yahudit was in conjugal bliss with her Carlos. Everything was going to be fine. Everything was going to work out. All was going to be okay. With her eyes closed, Yahudit fell into sleep.

When Yahudit woke up, she saw Carlos staring at her. Carlos was fully dressed and groomed. He had a big smile on his face. It looked like the smile he had when he was asleep, but it was much bigger. He was absolutely radiant.

"Good morning, beautiful!" Carlos chirped.

"Hi," Yahudit responded. "What time is it?"

"Can you imagine," Carlos started to answer, "it is already 1 PM?"

"1 PM!" Yahudit said. "No wonder I am hungry."

"Me, too!" Carlos said.

"Well, honey," Yahudit said, endearingly, "shall we go get some lunch?"

"Yes, my wife," Carlos said and smiled.

Yahudit

Yahudit felt a knot in her stomach when she heard Carlos address her as his wife.

"Yes, my husband," Yahudit responded after a slight pause.

Carlos beamed even more as he heard Yahudit call him her husband. They were really married. This was really happening. And happiness all around! That was the look on Carlos' face. But then, Yahudit wondered if she was imagining it all. Carlos did always have a Mexican smile plastered on his face. Maybe, that's what it was. Maybe, she was imagining that it was a special smile. Maybe, he was smiling like he always does, and she was imagining things.

"So, what should we eat?" Carlos asked.

"What do you want to eat?" Yahudit asked.

"I feel like Chinese," Carlos said. "Some Kung-Pao Chicken would do me good."

"Yeah, me, too," Yahudit chimed in.

Both Yahudit and Carlos were in no mood to move fast, so they walked slower than usual. And they were somewhat silent. They felt revived, yet fatigued. It seemed like tiredness that had built up had suddenly been unleashed. Despite all the rest, it was not enough. But they knew that they were both hungry, so they moved like zombies toward their final destination of food.

They got into the taxi and asked to be delivered to the best Chinese restaurant in town. Once they arrived, they walked to the main entrance way. They were seated in a nice seat. In their laziness, they decided to order the specials of the day. They were Panda Beef and Sweet and Pungent Shrimp. They decided against Kung-Pao Chicken.

Yahudit did not care about keeping kosher any more. She had tried bacon and liked it. And she assumed that she would like the shrimp dish. She was experiencing new things in Las Vegas, and she was not too displeased with herself as she looked at the shrimp rolls that came out. There was red sweet sauce. Yahudit dipped a shrimp roll in the dish and tasted the non-kosher morsel. It was heavenly. Absolutely delightful.

Soon, their wanton soup arrived. There were thin strips of pork swimming inside. It was definitely non-kosher, like the appetizer. Yahudit took a spoonful of wanton and consumed it. The meat inside was pork to be sure. It tasted great. What was transgression to one was heaven to another. Yahudit thought about all the non-kosher food that she had avoided all her life and wondered what else she had missed out on.

Next, the two main entrees arrived. Panda Beef was nothing like anything that Yahudit had seen before, either in real life or in television. It seemed like beef had been deep fried in some kind of batter, and then was dipped in some special sauce. They looked strange. But Yahudit decided to try that first. Once she took a bite, Yahudit realized what falling in love with food meant. Yahudit absolutely loved it. She could not help but to have another one. Then, another one. Then, another one. She kept eating the weird beef strips with avarice that seemed to surprise even Carlos. She gave him a smile and continued to eat like a hungry wolf.

Sweet and Pungent Shrimp was sitting right there, waiting to be consumed. Yahudit did not disappoint. She plunged into the dish like a tiger jumping on its hapless victims. After the first bite, which confirmed the culinary ecstasy attached to the food item, Yahudit consumed little shrimp morsels with shameless abandon. Yahudit was not consuming for her hunger anymore; she was consuming to satiate her desire that had been triggered.

Finally, Yahudit finished her wanton consumption. She looked up to see Carlos, who was chewing slowly and looking at Yahudit with a look that can only be described as fear. Yahudit could not but burst out in laughter.

"What?" Carlos asked, showing irritation.

"You look absolutely frightened," Yahudit said between her laughter fits.

"Yeah," Carlos said, "Why don't you sit where I am and tell me you would not be afraid."

"Be afraid," Yahudit said, laughing, "Be very afraid."

"I think I passed that phase in Venice Beach," Carlos said, somewhat serious.

"Wow," Yahudit said, "Can you believe that that was only a few days ago?"

"It's hard to believe," Carlos responded.

"But it seems like ages ago," Yahudit said. "Like in a different life-time."

"I guess you are right about that," Carlos concurred. "It was a whole life-time ago, because we are starting a new life."

"Isn't that the truth," Yahudit said. "It's a new life for you and for me. Old things have gone, and behold, new things are come."

"It's a new life, alright," Carlos said.

"Is that why you are afraid?" Yahudit asked.

"Do you want the truth?" Carlos asked.

"Yes, I want the truth," Yahudit said.

"The truth is that I guess I have to admit that I am a bit afraid of the new beginning," Carlos said, looking at Yahudit. "But I am more afraid of how fast you ate."

"Oh, Carlos," Yahudit said and laughed.

During the rest of their meal, they talked about what they were going to do that day. Both of them were eager to move into their new apartment. It was hard work, getting it all perfect for the move-in. And it seemed like it would be a real married life to move into their apartment together. After the meal, they were going back to their hotel to get everything packed for the move out. Yahudit felt lighter about moving in with Carlos in their new apartment. A real marriage was beginning, and she would be the woman in the house.

The move was uneventful. Both of them packed whatever they had, which was not much and moved them to the new apartment. They noticed how small their personal belongings were and decided to go on a shopping spree. Yahudit wanted to dress her new husband in the way she thought he would look best. She felt that Carlos would look good in Polo outfits. He might have worked in a kosher kitchen as a help, but Yahudit was going to make him great by being the helpmate who knew how to make him great. Yahudit was more concerned about Carlos than herself.

Carlos looked absolutely marvelous in his new outfits. Yahudit was feeling self-satisfied that she had made him a great dresser. It restored her confidence in herself as a woman of good taste. She needed a pat on the back as someone who can do great things in her new marriage, and it seemed that dressing Carlos up was one step in the right direction.

Then, they went shopping for Yahudit. She picked out some casual wear, since she felt that she was going to go casual for a while. But she also bought a semi-formal outfit for occasions that might call for such an outfit. She felt like she was really married and was being a good wife.

She thought about having a family of her own, and that excited her. She thought about what name to give her first child. It seemed like everything was happening so fast, and it pleased her that things were going so smoothly, given so many obstacles.

She thought about a conversation that she had with her mother.

"Yahudit," Julia Kashiri said.

"Yes, mother," Yahudit Kashiri responded.

"You know that I am the proudest of you out of all that I have," Julia said.

"Really?" Yahudit said, surprised by her mother's comments.

"Yes, dear," Julia said.

"So, you are more proud of me than going to Stanford?" Yahudit asked.

"Yes, of course," Julia said. "It goes without saying."

"Really?" Yahudit said, amazed. "It can't be! It's Stanford."

"No, really," Julia said in a serious tone. "I am the most proud of you."

"You are just saying that because it wasn't Harvard," Yahudit said.

"No, I am not," Julia said. "I am more proud of having you than having studied at Stanford. Even if I had studied at Harvard, I would consider you a more proud accomplishment. Having you was my dream come true."

"So, what am I studying for?" Yahudit responded. "Maybe I should just have a child."

"Hush!" Julia said. "Don't even joke about such things. Good education makes a good mother."

"Yes, mother," Julia relented because she knew that arguing would get her nowhere.

"Can I ask you a question?" Yahudit asked her mother.

"Sure," Julia responded.

"Is the highest achievement of a woman having a child?" Yahudit asked.

"A woman should consider it her highest achievement," Julia said. "Why? Does that trouble you?"

"A little," Yahudit said, throwing her mother a furtive glance. "I always thought a woman can be whatever she wanted to be and that she should strive to be the greatest in her field."

"Well, Yahudit," Julia said. "That's probably the feminist message. But those feminists are all Goyim or Jews who do not know they are Jews. Being a mother is the greatest achievement of a woman."

"So, are you saying that if you had to choose between Stanford and me," Yahudit said. "You would have chosen having me to going to Stanford?"

"Of course," Julia said with a confidence that shocked her daughter.

Yahudit did not remember when she had this conversation with her mother, but it had made a big impact on her. And she recalled it as she was driving back with Carlos to their apartment, loaded with all the shopping goodies for him and for her, husband and wife.

Yahudit smiled as she realized that she has chosen what was better over what was inferior. Her mother had taught her well. Now, she will have her crown achievement in the bearing of a child, whom she can proudly say is the proudest in her life, just like her mama.

"Carlos," Yahudit said.

"Yes?" Carlos said.

"You know," Yahudit continued, "I am very happy."

"Me, too," Carlos concurred.

"You know why?" Yahudit asked.

"No, darling," Carlos said.

"It is because I have you," Yahudit said. "And because we are starting a family."

"Me, too," Carlos said in a low-reflex response.

"Do you love me?" Yahudit asked.

"Of course, I do," Carlos responded.

"How can you, if you had known me for such a short time?" Yahudit asked, playing the devil's advocate.

"I fell in love with you the first time I saw you," Carlos said.

"Really?" Yahudit asked with glee.

"Yes," Carlos said. "I saw you walking in with those friends of yours, and I said to myself, 'There is an amazingly beautiful woman!'"

"You think I am beautiful?" Yahudit asked.

"That can't be a serious question," Carlos said in a feigned serious tone. "Everyone who sees you will have to admit that you are absolutely beautiful."

"Everyone?" Yahudit asked.

"The fact is," Carlos continued, "I am the lucky bastard who got you."

"That's the sweetest thing that anyone has ever said to me," Yahudit said.

"So, you think that you are lucky?" Yahudit asked.

Yahudit

"Damned lucky!" Carlos said emphatically.

"Me, too," Yahudit said. "I feel that, too."

"Now, can I ask you a question?" Carlos asked. "Why did you choose me? A girl like you can have anybody. Why me? Why not an Adonis your own age? Why an old geezer like me?"

"You are not old, Carlos!" Yahudit chastised him.

"I am probably old enough to be your father," Carlos said.

"I don't know about that," Yahudit said. "And you are young at heart. And you are young. I cannot think of you as old. It has never crossed my mind."

"Really?" Carlos said, smiling. "So, why did you fall in love with me?"

"I don't know," Yahudit said. "It just happened."

"Just happened?" Carlos said, puzzled.

"Yes," Yahudit said. "I saw you, and the moment I saw you, I felt your kind heart shining through you."

"Kind heart shining through me?" Carlos repeated.

"Yes, that's it," Yahudit said as in an epiphany, "Your kind heart has captured me, and I became yours even before you knew it."

"Wow," Carlos said. "That's amazing."

"Isn't it great that we now have a married life?" Yahudit asked.

"Yes, definitely," Carlos responded. "Do you not have any worries, Yahudit?"

"No, not really," Yahudit said. "My parents can take care of themselves, and I am truly happy, here."

"Yes, we are making a new life over here," Carlos said.

"You sound like you have some worries," Yahudit said.

"You want the truth?" Carlos asked.

"Yes, always," Yahudit responded.

"Okay, here it goes," Carlos said. "I have to confess that I am a bit worried about my children."

Yahudit

"But you said that your sister will take care of them, didn't you?"

"Yeah, but I still worry," Carlos said.

"I am glad that you are a good father," Yahudit said. "I know that you will be a good father to our children."

"Why?" Carlos jumped. "Do you know something?"

"Don't be silly, Carlos," Yahudit said dismissively. "We just got married, yesterday."

"That's right," Carlos said and smiled.

Soon, they arrived in their new apartment. They brought all their goodies upstairs. And they decided to go out to a magic show for the evening. They both wore something new that they purchased that day. After taking a shower, grooming himself, Carlos emerged as a radiant gentleman with all his Polo wear. Yahudit was also satisfied to see that she appeared sophisticated, yet playful. Carlos smiled as if he was exceedingly pleased.

They decided to go for Italian food in the evening. For some reason, both of them were feeling like pasta. They chose an Italian restaurant near the magic show. Carlos has never been to Las Vegas before so he was enjoying every minute of his honeymoon. Apparently, he has never seen a magic show before either, so Carlos was like a little child before Christmas day wanting to open his presents sooner than the scheduled time.

Yahudit had been to Las Vegas before with her parents, so Las Vegas was nothing new to her. However, the experience she was having with Carlos was altogether new and something that reached beyond her previous expectations. Yahudit felt like she was experiencing Las Vegas for the first time. It certainly felt like what a wonderful honeymoon should be. Yahudit was all smiles as they entered the Italian restaurant.

Carlos ordered the sea food linguini plate, and Yahudit joined him. Yahudit was beyond kosher observance. In fact, she has, for some reason, fallen in love with non-kosher food items. Thus, Yahudit was actually eagerly expecting her non-kosher dish as she and Carlos were getting ready to consume their French Onion Soup. Yahudit had ordered the French Onion

159

Yahudit

Soup just because she remembered eating it in Israel. It was nostalgia that directed her appetizer order. Carlos had never had French Onion Soup before, so he wanted to try something new. Interestingly enough, French Onion Soup was just like the one they had in Israel. The soup was dark brownish with onion strips filling the soup. On top of the soup was Mozzarella cheese melted and almost covering the coup like a jar lid. Yahudit was absolutely thrilled.

"This is absolutely wonderful!" Yahudit exclaimed.

"What is?" Carlos asked, curious.

"This French Onion Soup is just like the one I had in Israel," Yahudit said.

"You have been to Israel?" Carlos asked.

"Yes, just once," Yahudit said.

"Did you like it?" Carlos asked.

"Well, not as much as I thought I would," Yahudit said. "You know, Israel is like the Jewish Homeland, and all the Jews are supposed to be loyal to it. I grew up being led to believe that it was a paradise on earth. But it really wasn't."

"So, you did not like it?" Carlos asked.

"I guess, you can say that I was a bit disappointed by it," Yahudit said. "Come to think about it, that's precisely the way to describe it. Disappointment. I had high expectations, but was not properly prepared for the harsh realities."

"Do you think that our marriage is something like that?" Carlos asked.

"Absolutely, not," Yahudit said. "After the Israel experience, I have learned not to put too much expectation into anything. I had hopes that it would be great and that all would work out, but I did not have any expectations."

"You know," Carlos said, "You are more mature than me even though you are only seventeen."

"You know what they say," Yahudit said in the way of an answer, "Women mature far faster than men."

"They must be right about that," Carlos said. "I am glad that I have married a very mature and very wise woman."

Yahudit

"Well, thank you, dear," Yahudit said to lighten the gravity of the conversation. "Do you like your soup?"

"Yes," Carlos said, "Very much so."

"I am glad," Yahudit declared. "I am now looking forward to my seafood linguini dish," Yahudit said. "It's going to be so good."

"You are bad," Carlos said.

"Why?" Yahudit asked, surprised.

"You are intentionally exulting in the consumption of non-kosher foods," Carlos said.

"What's so bad about it?" Yahudit said defiantly.

"Don't you think that it's disrespectful to the Jewish religion?" Carlos asked. "After all, it's your religion. It's the religion of your parents. It's the religion of your ancestors?"

"I don't know about it being the religion of my ancestors," Yahudit said. "There have been many conversions throughout the period of human history, so I don't know if my ancestors were converts to Judaism or not. I cannot even tell you if my great, great parents converted to Judaism. I just don't know. I just don't have the proof of my lineage to back that up."

"Yeah, but you know what I mean," Carlos said, feeling stupid.

"I'm sorry, Carlos," Yahudit said. "I did not mean to rag on you like that. It's just that I guess I am more sensitive about the issue than I had thought I was."

"That's okay," Carlos said, still sulking somewhat.

"I guess, what I am trying to say is that," Yahudit continued, "I don't really have any regrets about abandoning Judaism. I believe that a person should be free to choose her own religion. And I choose to leave Judaism and embrace a new religion."

"Christianity?" Carlos asked.

"No, silly!" Yahudit gently chided. "The New Religion of You and Me."

"Huh?" Carlos said in confusion.

"The New Religion where you are my God and I am your people."

"So, that was not a joke?" Carlos asked seriously.

"Of course, not!" Yahudit exclaimed. "What do you think is going on here?"

"Two people in love getting married?" Carlos asked.

"No, Carlos, my Lord," Yahudit said in a serious tone, "It's far more than that. Yes, there is love. But yes, there is the New Religion, as well."

"Oh," Carlos said, looking a bit disappointed.

"Not to worry," Yahudit said. "It is not God's duty to worship, but to receive worship. All the hard work will be done by your worshippers. I am the first one, but many more will follow."

"Okay, dear," Carlos said. "If you say so."

"Do you love me?" Yahudit asked.

"You know that I do," Carlos said.

"Then, trust me," Yahudit said.

"Okay," Carlos responded with a weakened voice.

"Oh, here is our seafood linguini!" Yahudit exclaimed as soon as she saw her dish approach her.

"Wow, you seem more excited now than when we were about to get married," Carlos said with a visible disappointment.

"I was nervous, then," Yahudit said. "Now, I am not nervous."

"Oh," Carlos said, not looking convinced.

"Marriage is a splendid thing, but also a life-changing, momentous thing," Yahudit said. "Food just doesn't have that gravitas."

"Oh," Carlos said, being more convinced.

"Are you not happy that our food is approaching us?" Yahudit asked.

"Yeah, I guess so," Carlos said. "It's my first time trying seafood linguini as well, so I am a bit apprehensive."

"All will be okay," Yahudit assured. "It's going to be great; you will see."

Yahudit

"Here you are," the waitress said. "So, are you enjoying your meal so far?"

"Yes, it is fabulous," Yahudit said excitedly.

"So, your father is taking good care of you in Las Vegas?" the waitress asked. She was of Mexican descent and about the same age with Yahudit. Yahudit wondered if she had overheard any of their conversation and was being intentionally hurtful.

"He's actually not my father," Yahudit said, trying to force gentleness. "He's my husband."

"Oh," the waitress said with feigned remorse, "Please, excuse me."

"That's quite okay," Carlos said. Yahudit threw him a dirty look. The waitress smiled and quickly moved away.

"That was unpleasant," Yahudit said. "Don't you think?"

"She didn't mean anything by it," Carlos said.

"Of course, she did," Yahudit said. "She was being cruel."

"No, darling," Carlos said. "You are reading into things."

"No, I am not!" Yahudit said. "Why are you taking her side? Is it because she's Mexican?"

"Now, that's unfair!" Carlos said. As soon as Yahudit heard Carlos say that, she felt bad about pursuing the argument.

"I am sorry," Yahudit said. "I was just mad for you, that's all."

"No, you don't have to feel bad for me," Carlos said. "I consider myself mighty lucky, and I don't really care what people think or say. I love you. You are my wife. And that's that."

"I am glad we got married," Yahudit said to appease Carlos, who looked visibly agitated.

The seafood linguini was consumed in silence. Although Carlos protested that the waitress' comments did not affect him, Yahudit noticed a visible depression creep over

Carlos' face.   Yahudit was feeling a bit depressed herself because she realized that she had her first fight with Carlos. And over what? Her efforts to defend him! The only comfort during the quiet moments that followed the altercation was the sweet taste of seafood linguini. It just seemed to melt in her mouth. She swore that she would remember this seafood linguini, forever.

The magic show was waiting, and the excitement that Carlos had in his heart could not be contained. He was visibly excited. It seemed like he had never seen a magic show before. Come to think about it, Yahudit realized that she had never seen a magic show in her whole life, either. But Yahudit was not as excited as Carlos to see the magic show. However, she was excited that he was excited. She felt like a concerned older sister celebrating the joy of a younger brother who was experiencing something great.

Carlos and Yahudit had a seat close to the magic show. Carlos was beaming, but he was too focused on the magic show that was about to start to shine his sunny face in Yahudit's direction. Yahudit did not mind because Carlos was so happy. His happiness rubbed off on her.

The magician was dressed in a typical magician's outfit. He looked Eastern European, which lent credibility to his magic show.   It seems like magic done by magicians from former Czechoslovakia or Romania was authentic, or even real magic. Somehow, a blonde magician from Sweden did not seem to fit the genre of magic. Shouldn't a blonde man from Scandinavia be dressed in a Viking outfit or something?

The first magic show was pulling an animal out of a hat. But it was not a rabbit out of a hat; it was a dog. Yahudit reasoned that it is harder to pull off a magic show with a dog because it is hard to control his barking, whereas the rabbit does not really make an audible noise.   But what impressed the audience, it seemed, was not this tricky part of the show, but that the dog was really cute. All the "ah's" and "oh's" testified to the fact that the audience was focused on the furry star rather than the complexities of the magic. This was Las Vegas after all. Despite the Eastern European aura, the magician was, first and foremost, a showman. People seemed to enjoy the show. Carlos joined the audience in a loud applause. Carlos clapped so hard that Yahudit was afraid he would injure a vein in his hand.

The second magic show involved the Eastern European man throwing knives at his beautiful Scandinavian-looking assistant. She was tied to a rotating board, and he was throwing his knives at random. The female aide looked absolutely frightened. Yahudit wondered if she were in love with the magician, so that she was willing to risk her life. It is possible that they are in a relationship? Obviously, she did not enjoy being tied to the board, being forced to look straight at quickly advancing sharp projectiles in her direction.

Yahudit wondered if she could do something like that. Would she be able to do something she utterly detested because she loved someone? She felt that she could not. Although she was doing many things that she found difficult, Yahudit felt that essentially she wanted to do them. Finding something difficult to do is different than doing something against which each cell in your body militates against.

Yahudit looked at Carlos. It was obvious that he had taken a liking to the show. It did not look like it bothered him that this part of the program was not technically magic. But it was show business, and a darned good one at that. Carlos was happy to be there, experiencing new things, with the woman she loved. Yahudit smiled as she remembered that she was the object of Carlos' desire. Carlos did not seem like he noticed Yahudit looking at him. He was so absorbed in the show. Yahudit wondered if Carlos was always that focused. He seemed to be quite focused. Now, Yahudit was beginning to think that it was a part of Carlos' nature.

When all the knife throwing was done, the Scandinavian assistant gave the most beautiful smile of anyone that Yahudit had ever seen before. She looked like an angel, who has seen the glory of the Almighty God. And she was looking toward Carlos.

Yahudit

Why Carlos? Yahudit felt a pang of jealousy enter her heart. Why was she looking at him? Was it because she had deified him that no one could but appreciate him as a God? Has she undone herself? Yahudit felt jealousy mixed in with deep-seated worry. What was going on? She felt confused and felt a bit sick in her stomach. To make matters worse, Carlos did not seem to notice what was going on in her heart. In fact, he was looking directly at the Scandinavian aide! The nerve!

"The next show requires a volunteer from the audience," the magician said.

"A volunteer?" Yahudit said softly as to herself. Carlos looked at her.

"You should volunteer, Yahudit," Carlos said.

"No, no," Yahudit said. "Why don't you." As soon as she had uttered her words in a low-reflex response, Yahudit regretted it. She had been so nervous that she had uttered the words without thinking. Now, she was realizing the impact of her words. The Anointed One had compelled her God to act.

"If it is your wish, my dear," Carlos said, "I will."

"Oh, you don't have to," Yahudit tried to dissuade him.

"No, it's okay," Carlos said. "I am as good as my word." Carlos stood up and raised his hand.

"I see an eager volunteer over, here," the magician said. "Hilga, would you go and escort the gentleman to the stage?"

"Sure thing, Johannes the Great," Hilga chirped.

Yahudit felt like she could just scream. What? The Scandinavian goody-two-shoes was going to escort her husband to the stage? Escort? Is that like going out? Like going together? Yahudit did not like the term at all. Escort!

Carlos looked happy, and that irritated Yahudit even further. It was clear that Carlos was oblivious to the raging civil war in Yahudit's heart. At the moment, her jealous rage was beating her good sense and judgment.

"Don't have too much fun up there," Yahudit said as Hilga approached.

"Huh?" Carlos said, looking confused.

Yahudit

"Nothing," Yahudit said. "Do well, honey."

"Oh, you are going to have so much fun, Mr. Gentleman," Hilga said. Yahudit felt that Hilga said this just to spite her. She must have heard what she had said! How evil!

Yahudit glared at Carlos and Hilga walking side by side. It seems like Hilga was walking close to Carlos intentionally just to make her jealous. In fact, she was holding onto his elbow. It was altogether irritating. Yahudit just wanted to scream, but contained herself. Yahudit wondered why she was feeling so much jealousy. She had never fancied herself as a jealous person before. In fact, she did not remember a single moment when she felt so much jealousy. Now, she was as jealousy as the Stepmother in the Cinderella Story. What was happening to her?

"Thank you for volunteering," the magician said.

"I am glad to be here," Carlos said.

"Now, give our brave Gentleman volunteer a kiss," the magician said. Hilga hesitated. It was definitely not a part of the routine. And it did not seem like she was eager to, either. She was teasing Yahudit, but her heart clearly belonged to the magician. Now, he was selling her out. Yahudit squinted her eyes to see if she could detect an expression in Hilga's face. Hilga quickly kissed Carlos on his cheek, so Yahudit could not observe her expressions well. But Carlos' expression was clear to everyone. He was smiling. In fact, Carlos' smile ripped across his face like the sword slash of Zorro in his more graphic movies. Yahudit wanted to get a sword and make such a slash on Hilga's face. After the thought ran across her mind, Yahudit felt a bit ashamed for feeling such violence. She considered herself to be a person of peace.

"Now, we got the formalities out of the way, let's get to business," the magician said, full of smiles. "What's your good name?"

"My name is Carlos," Carlos said.

"What a good name!" the magician said with feigned enthusiasm.

"Thank you," Carlos said, looking a bit bashful.

"Are you afraid?" Johannes the Great asked.

"Me, afraid?" Carlos said, trying to sound tough, "Of course, not!"

"I am glad to hear that," Johannes the Great said, "Because this part will be scarier than the last part."

"Oh," Carlos let out a comment that sounded like he was afraid.

"You know how in high school, all the cool people bullied the nerds?" the magician said. "And all the nerds were afraid of all the cheerleaders, especially those with streaks of different color in their hair?"

"Yes?" Carlos said, more in the form of a question than in the form of an answer.

"Consider yourself the nerd, today," the magician said.

"Okay," Carlos responded.

"And you know who the scary cool cheerleader is?" the magician asked.

"No," Carlos said.

"It is Hilga," the magician said and pointed to his blonde assistant. Hilga tried to make a scary face. The audience laughed. Carlos did not look too intimidated.

"This is where you are supposed to make an expression of fear, Carlos," the magician cued Carlos.

"Oh," Carlos responded and tried to make an expression of fear. The audience laughed hysterically.

"But because we are for world peace," the magician said, "We are going to put you together."

"Huh?" Carlos responded. The audience laughed even louder.

"Not to be too afraid," Johannes the Great said, "I have you."

"Okay," Carlos said.

"You and Hilga the Cheerleader will go into that small cabinet together," the magician said.

"That cabinet?" Carlos asked. It was a small cabinet. The audience laughed.

"Why? Are you afraid?" the magician asked. The audience started to clap.

"Of course, not," Carlos said.

"Well, to play along with the game, you have to be at least a little bit afraid," the magician said.

"Okay, I am a little afraid," Carlos said.

"The truth, folks," the magician said to the audience. He received a loud applause.

"But remember, this is a family show," the magician said to Carlos. "No hanky-panky in there. It's not seven minutes in heaven, you know." The audience laughed.

"Of course, not!" Carlos said. The audience laughed even harder.

"Why? Don't you find Hilga attractive?" the magician asked.

"No, it's not that," Carlos said. Hilga looked slightly offended.

"You think Hilga is pretty, right?" the magician asked.

"Yes," Carlos said. "Who wouldn't?" Yahudit was raging mad at Carlos' comments.

"Well, go in there, and magic will happen," the magician said. "Come out when I tell you to."

Carlos and Hilga went inside the closet and they were body to body because the closet was too small. As Johannes the Great closed the cabinet door, he said, "Don't do anything I wouldn't do."

The audience clapped.

After closing the door, the auditorium speakers blared, "Hello, Is It Me Your Looking For?"

The audience laughed.

While the song was going on, the magician indicated to the audience to remain quiet.

At the end of the song, the magician said, "Carlos and Hilga, come out."

And there was no sound.

Yahudit

The magician walked over to the closet and opened the door. They were kissing!

"Now, that's magic," Johannes the Great declared. He got a loud applause from the audience. Yahudit felt like standing up and screaming, but she restrained herself.

Carlos was led out of the closet by Hilga. Hilga's lipstick mark was all over Carlos, who looked flustered. He had a dumb smile plastered on his face. Yahudit was mad. She was madder than hell.

"Thank you, Carlos," the magician said.

"Thank you," Carlos said in a feeble voice. The audience laughed and clapped as Carlos walked off the stage toward Yahudit.

"That is magic folks," the magician said again and drew another round of applause.

"The nerve!" Yahudit said to herself.

Carlos walked toward Yahudit with the dumb smile still on his face. It was visible that he was trying to wipe the smile off of his face. But it did not seem to work. Yahudit gave him a dirty look, but did not say anything. The magic show seemed to continue to something else, but Yahudit was not paying attention to that.

"It was just a part of the show," Carlos said defensively as he gazed upon his infuriated wife.

"Just a part of the show!" Yahudit repeated, irritated.

"Well, you asked me to volunteer," Carlos said, trying to build his case.

"Did I ask you to kiss her?" Yahudit asked.

"Shhhhh," Carlos said, looking around at other audience members. They were acting like they were looking at the magic show. Yahudit knew that they were looking at them furtively.

"It wasn't me," Carlos said. "It was all her."

"Uh-huh!" Yahudit said and turned around to another direction.

"Honey," Carlos said. "Please don't be mad."

"I am not speaking to you," Yahudit said.

Yahudit

"Don't be childish, Yahudit," Carlos said.

"Childish?" Yahudit said loudly. Then, she restrained herself. "Just see the show!"

"Okay," Carlos said and started to look in the direction of the magic show. However, Yahudit was visibly mad that he complied with her wish so quickly. Should he not have tried to appease her? Did he not care? Did he really like Hilga? Yahudit felt mad. She looked over at Carlos. He was actually looking at the magic show!

Yahudit felt a tear drop trickle down her cheek. This was unconscionable! How could he? Yahudit thought angry thoughts, nonstop. Carlos just kept looking at the magic show. She could swear that she saw a gleam of light in his eyes as he stared in the direction of the stage. He was surely looking at Hilga. Yahudit was sure of it. Yahudit was so upset that she was not noticing any of the magic show that was being performed up on the stage. All she could think about was the kiss. That kiss!

How could he do it? Did he not just profess his undying love for her? Was he just saying that without meaning it? Was he just going along with the relationship because she was a strong personality? Was she forcing him in any way to a relationship that he did not want? Was their marriage a sham? How could he? That kiss! That kiss!

Yahudit was bothered by the kiss. For her, it was a betrayal of his heart. A kiss is not just a kiss. Kiss symbolized so much more. It was a symbol of commitment. The magician knew this! That scoundrel, he did it on purpose! He noticed that they were a lovey-dovey couple, and he wanted to break them up. He could not stand seeing Carlos so happy with her. Yahudit became angry at the magician, who was out to destroy their axis mundi, the new world order that they were trying to create. He was like the serpent. He tempted Hilga to partake of his wicked scheme. And she in turn caused the fall of Carlos. Look at him! He looked all dreamy! This cannot be happening!

Yahudit

Yahudit allowed her thought to race faster than the top speed at which her red Porsche was capable of traveling. In fact, Yahudit allowed her thoughts to speed faster than the speed of sounds coming out of the magician the deceiver. In fact, Yahudit's thoughts were traveling faster than the speed of light that has not been surpassed by any human-made object, thus far.

Finally, the magic show seems to end. Carlos stood up and clapped. He actually stood up! Yahudit threw him a dirty look, but he did not seem to notice. Suddenly, a guy in a waiter tuxedo showed up and said, "Johannes the Great would like the pleasure of your company."

Before Yahudit could say a word, Carlos said, "Please tell him that we would be happy to."

"Please come this way," the waiter said.

"Okay," Carlos said. "Honey, come on. Let's go. We get to meet the magician."

"And his assistant," Yahudit said. As soon as the words passed out of her mouth, she was eager to go backstage and meet the woman who tried to steal her husband away. Yahudit had a word or two to say to the magician as well. Now, Yahudit could not wait to stand within striking distance from the magician and his assistant.

Carlos seemed happy by what he perceived as Yahudit's eagerness to go backstage. Yahudit thought it was so odd that Carlos was so oblivious to her sentiments. Was he a complete dolt? Or was he just insensitive? Did he not understand the significance of that kiss? That kiss! Did Carlos think that it was just like a handshake? Maybe, Carlos was faking nonchalance. Maybe, he really cared, but was trying to pretend like nothing was wrong because she was looking agitated. Yahudit tried to figure Carlos out, but could not.

Soon, they arrived backstage. The waiter led them to a room and said, "Please wait, here. The magician and his assistant will join you, soon." After these words, the waiter left. Carlos and Yahudit were alone in the private room of the magician and his assistant.

Yahudit

"Isn't this great?" Carlos asked. "We get to meet the magician!"

"And the assistant," Yahudit added to see his reaction.

"Yeah, and his assistant," Carlos said.

"But you already met her, didn't you?" Yahudit said in an accusatory tone.

"Who?" Carlos feigned ignorance.

"The blonde assistant," Yahudit said.

"Oh, her," Carlos said, trying to sound like he did not care.

"Or rather, your lips met her lips in a serious way," Yahudit said, sounding jealous.

"Come on, Yahudit," Carlos said. "You are not jealous, are you?"

"Jealous? Who? Me?" Yahudit said. "Just because your husband kisses a complete stranger in front of thousands of people, why should I care?"

"There are not thousands of people, here," Carlos said. "Besides, we did not kiss in public."

"So, you admit kissing her?" Yahudit argued. "You kissed her, didn't you?"

"No, it wasn't like that," Carlos said. "It was her, who kissed me."

"Why would she kiss you?" Yahudit asked.

"I don't know," Carlos said.

"But you did not put up a fight, did you?" Yahudit continued to be accusatory.

"Put up a fight?" Carlos said, raising his voice. "Did you see the size of the closet? Did it seem like anyone could put up anything over there?"

"I am sure something was up," Yahudit said.

"Now, you are being crass, Yahudit," Carlos said. "It's so unlike you."

"What do you know about me? You have known me how long?" Yahudit uttered in anger.

"Now, Yahudit, let's not say anything we will regret later," Carlos tried to reason with her.

"I will say what I want," Yahudit yelled.

"Shhhhhh," Carlos said. "People will hear you."

"I don't care!" Yahudit yelled even louder. "I don't care if people hear me."

"Please, Yahudit," Carlos said. Please be reasonable."

"Or what?" Yahudit said, going into the fighting mode.

"Please, Yahudit," Carlos begged.

"Okay," Yahudit said. "Consider this my honeymoon gift."

"Oh, thank God," Carlos said.

"But you are really insensitive, Carlos," Yahudit said.

"I am sorry," Carlos said, "Although I am not sure why I should apologize. I did nothing wrong."

"What?" Yahudit yelled again. "You did nothing wrong!"

"Okay, okay," Carlos said. "I am sorry. Please, let's settle down. The whole place is going to hear us."

"Alright," Yahudit said. "Let's see what the magician and his hussy have to say."

"You are not going to pick a fight with them, are you?" Carlos said apprehensively.

"No, of course, not!" Yahudit barked. "Why would I pick a fight? I never pick a fight."

"Uh, oh," Carlos said and sat down on a chair close to him.

"Why are you sitting down?" Yahudit asked.

"I just want to relax before meeting Johannes and Hilga," Carlos said.

"What? Are you on first name basis now," Yahudit argued.

"Well, I did kiss her," Carlos said.

"See, you admit kissing her," Yahudit barked.

"I am sorry," Carlos said. "It's not like I was trying to. It just happened. Besides, I could not move inside that closet. It really wasn't my fault."

"It wasn't your fault," Yahudit mimicked. "Listen to you shirk your responsibility."

"I am just telling it like it is," Carlos said.

"What if it was me in that closet, and it was the magician and me kissing?" Yahudit asked.

"Well, I would just say that it was a part of the show and move on," Carlos said.

"Yeah, right," Yahudit said.

"I am serious," Carlos said. "I wouldn't care."

"You are just saying that because it did not happen," Yahudit said.

"No, I am not," Carlos said. "I mean it."

"I don't believe it," Yahudit said.

"Well, believe you me, dear," Carlos said. "I am open-minded."

"And you are saying that I am not open-minded?" Yahudit argued. "You are saying that I am a narrow-minded tight ass."

"You do have that," Carlos said.

"This is not the time to be funny," Yahudit said, although she could not contain a smile from creeping out onto her visage.

"Okay, Yahudit," Carlos said, "Can we agree to be civil until our hosts arrive."

"Fine!" Yahudit said and turned around.

"Okay," Carlos said and remained quiet on his chair.

There was a moment of uncomfortable silence. The silence seemed to stretch out for hours. Yahudit looked at her watch and a mere ten minutes had passed. How long was the unbearable silence going to hover over their co-existence? Yahudit could not bear it any more. She longed for Carlos. She wanted Carlos to hug her. She wanted Carlos to squeeze her. She wanted Carlos to kiss her. Why was he just sitting there in silence, like he did not care? It was just too cruel. He was just too cruel. Oh, Carlos!

The door opened, and Johannes the Great and Hilga waked in.

"I am glad that you can join us," the magician said. "Is this your wonderful girlfriend?"

"She is my wife, Yahudit," Carlos said as he shook Johannes' hand.

"Well, it is really nice to meet you," the magician said as he lifted up Yahudit's outstretched hand. He kissed Yahudit's hand.

"Oh," Yahudit said, a little flustered.

"Please excuse my European ways," Johannes the Great said.

"That's okay," Yahudit said.

"This is my assistant, Hilga," Johannes the Great said to Yahudit without letting go of her hand.

"Nice to meet you," Yahudit said. The magician let go of Yahudit's hand, who in turn gave her newly released hand to Hilga. Hilga shook her hand like an American.

"Where are you from?" Yahudit asked.

"From Sweden," Hilga said.

"Welcome to our country," Yahudit said.

"Thank you," Hilga said. "Where are you from? Egypt?"

"No," Yahudit said. "I was actually born in the United States."

"But where are you originally from?" Hilga said.

"My family came from Iran," Yahudit said.

"Oh, the country with great tension with the USA," Hilga said.

"Well, we are Jews," Yahudit said and noticed Carlos throwing a quick glance at her.

"Are you, now?" Hilga said.

"Now, now," the magician said, "Why don't we get changed, Hilga, and then we can all go out for some late night snack. Of course, Carlos and Yahudit, you will be our guests."

"Oh, thank you," Carlos said enthusiastically.

"Thank you," Yahudit said politely, devoid of all enthusiasm.

"We'll just quickly get changed," Johannes the Great said. "You don't mind, do you?"

"Well, I want to take a quick shower," Hilga said. "You wouldn't mind, would you?" Without waiting for an answer, Hilga stepped into the small shower space in the room. The glass pane was transparent. The magician looked at his naked assistant showering.

"Small perks of the trade," Johannes the Great said to Carlos. Carlos smiled and stared at Hilga's naked body.

"Now, don't let me stop you, my husband," Yahudit said angrily.

"What?" Carlos said without turning around.

"So, Yahudit," the magician said, "How long have you been married?"

"We have been married about a day, now," Yahudit said. She looked over to Carlos, and he was still looking at naked Hilga. Yahudit wanted to say something.

"How did you meet?" the magician asked quickly, "You look like you have been a couple for a long time."

"Well, we haven't known each other too long," Yahudit said, not really paying attention to her answer. She kept looking at Carlos, but when she wanted to say something, the magician quickly jumped in.

"What kind of wedding did you have?" the magician asked.

"It was a Las Vegas wedding," Yahudit said.

The magician started to take off his magic outfit. "Really?"

"Yes," Yahudit said. She did not want to stare at the magician while he was taking his clothes off in his dressing room, but somehow he seemed to have held her enthralled.

"Did you have an Elvis preside?" the magician asked, as he took off his pants.

"Oh, yes," Yahudit said and realized that her voice was cracking.

"I think, I am going to quickly jump into the shower as well," the magician said. "You don't mind, do you?"

"No," Yahudit said instinctively as she saw him become completely naked. Did he have no shame?

Johannes the Great jumped into the same small shower as Hilga's.

"Hilga, are you not done, yet?" Johannese the Great asked. "You are giving them a quite a show."

"Oh, Johannes," Hilga said and rushed out of the shower. Carlos followed her naked form move out of the shower. He stared as she toweled off. Yahudit herself was somewhat taken aback. She could not help but to stare at Johannes the Great and his form through the shower glass door.

As soon as Hilga was dressed, Carlos turned around to see Yahudit staring at the naked magician.

"Yahudit," Carlos said, trying to start a conversation.

"Huh?" Yahudit responded, slowly turning toward Carlos.

"Wasn't the magic show great?" Carlos rushed some words.

"Yeah, it was great," Yahudit said, and she darted a look at the shower section of the room.

"Yahudit," Carlos said, trying to capture her attention. "Do you think they will tell us their magic secrets when we are eating together?"

"I think they already did," Yahudit said.

"Huh?" Carlos said.

"Oh, nothing," Yahudit quickly said. "I am not sure."

"Oh," Carlos said. "I hope so. I would like to learn some of their magic tricks."

"I bet you do," Yahudit said.

"Don't you?" Carlos said.

"Now that you mention it," Yahudit said. "Maybe, you are right. The magic trick might be worth learning."

"Yeah," Carlos said. "I knew you would come around," Carlos said.

"You don't know what it means," Yahudit said.

"Of course, not," Carlos said. "That's why it's magic."

"Yeah," Yahudit said. "You can say that again."

"Are you angry with me?" Carlos asked, satisfied that she seemed to be giving him full attention, now.

"No," Yahudit said. "Not any more."

"What changed your mind?" Carlos asked.

"It's magic," Yahudit said.

"Sounds good to me," Carlos said.

"Really?" Yahudit asked.

"Yes," Carlos said. "Magic is good."

"Of course, magic is good," Hilga said as she joined the conversation. She was wearing a slinky one piece dress that showed that she was not wearing any bra or panties. Carlos looked a bit embarrassed as he looked at her red dress. Hilga was brushing her long blonde hair.

"Yahudit, believe me," Hilga said, "Johannes the Great earned his title 'the Great' for a reason."

"He's that great?" Yahudit asked.

"Yes, he is," Hilga said. "I can personally vouch for his greatness."

"See, honey," Carlos said excitedly. "You are in good hands. You are going to learn a lot of magic tonight."

"Uh, huh," Yahudit said. "Do you know what you are saying?"

"Of course, I do," Carlos said. "Hilga, do you think he will show his magic?"

"Yes," Hilga said, "Johannes the Great will show his magic to Yahudit with pleasure."

"I am glad," Carlos said. Yahudit and Hilga looked at each other. Hilga had a wicked smile on her face. Yahudit felt nervous, thinking about the whole thing. Carlos seemed to be oblivious to the inaudible communication between the two women.

Johannes the Great was soon out and about. He looked unseasonably cheerful. It was like the shower had rejuvenated him with an extra dose of torbo-charge enthusiasm. He was more enthusiastic than he was during the show. Yahudit thought him almost bouncy in his mannerism and gestures.

"Shall we go for an exciting night on the town?" the magician asked. "It is going to be absolutely fantastic."

"Yes. Oh, yes!" Yahudit said enthusiastically. Carlos looked at her, a bit surprised at her newly acquired enthusiasm.

"Yes, we are going to have a good time," Hilga said.

"Yes, let's go," Carlos said.

All four of them walked out of the building.

"My assistant will be driving her car," Johannes said. "Should we all go in her car?"

"Well, I hate to leave my car, here," Yahudit said.

"It should be okay," Hilga said.

"I just feel better to bring my car along," Yahudit said.

"A woman who likes to be in control," Johannes the Great said. "That should be fine, but we don't want to get separated or lost, so why don't I ride with you."

"Okay," Yahudit said.

"Carlos, do you want to keep me company?" Hilga said. "I will be all alone."

"Okay!" Carlos said, and then he looked at Yahudit, who had an expressionless face on. "Is that okay with you, honey?"

"The magician may tell you secrets he would not want Carlos to know," Hilga quickly added.

"Well, I guess it would not be nice to have Hilga drive alone," Yahudit said. "How far is this place?"

Yahudit

"Not far," Hilga said. "Just about ten minutes away. Follow me, okay?"

"Okay," Yahudit said.

Carlos got into Hilga's car, which was a blue BMW, 7 series. Yahudit and the magician got in to the red Porsche. Yahudit followed Hilga off the parking lot.

"So, tell me, how did you get into magic?" Yahudit asked.

Johannes the Great looked at Yahudit and smiled. The short silence made Yahudit wonder if she looked cheesy asking such a schoolgirl question. She felt herself turning red.

"Didn't you know?" the magician finally broke what seemed like an interminable silence. "Everyone in Eastern Europe does magic. I was the lucky one who got out."

"You are trying to make me laugh, aren't you?" Yahudit said.

"Isn't that what men do with beautiful women? Try to make them laugh?" the magician said with a coy smile.

"You think I am beautiful?" Yahudit asked, looking at Johannes the Great.

"Why else do you think I came over to your table?" the magician said. "I was enthralled by your beauty."

"What?" Yahudit said, surprised.

"I came over to get a closer look at you," the magician said. "Carlos was an excuse."

"Really?" Yahudit asked.

"You don't know that power you have over men," the magician said. "Look at Carlos. He is completely under your control."

"You think so?" Yahudit asked, smiling.

"No doubt about it," Johannes the Great said. "And I envy his place."

"What do you mean?" Yahudit asked.

"You are his," the magician said. "You belong to him."

"I don't belong to anyone," Yahudit protested. "I belong to myself alone."

"But you are for him and him only," the magician said.

"No, I am not," Yahudit said.

"Really?" Johannes the Great asked with an innocent look. "But aren't you married to him?"

"Yeah, but," Yahudit said, "That does not mean that he owns me."

"Okay," the magician said. "If you say so."

"I do say so," Yahudit said.

"Wow, you are independent," the magician said.

"I am," Yahudit said. "And I belong to myself alone."

"Yes, I can see that," Johannes said with a mysterious smile.

"So, you are from Eastern Europe," Yahudit said, changing the subject.

"Yes, from Hungary," the magician said, "From the city of Budapest."

"Wow, it sounds enchanting," Yahudit said.

"Yes, it is," Johannes the Great said. "It is a magical place, where everything is possible."

"Oh," Yahudit said and felt a warmth come over her body.

"And I made magic my world," Johannes the Great said.

"That sounds awesome," Yahudit said.

"It is," the magician said. "It is awesome like the opening of the Red Sea by Moses. For me, it has been more magical than that."

"So, you know the story of Moses?" Yahudit asked.

"Yes," the magician said. "Moses stretched out his rod, and the calm water of Red Sea was split open, so that they could enter through it."

"The way you tell the story," Yahudit said, and then she was lost for words.

"Yes," the magician said. "I know the story very well."

"How do you know the story well?" Yahudit asked, curious.

Yahudit

"To tell you the truth," the magician said. "My father was a famous rabbi in Budapest."

"Really?" Yahudit said, surprised.

"Yes," the magician said. "Do you think less of me?"

"Why?" Yahudit asked, finding the question strange.

"I don't know," the magician said. "Because I am a Jew?"

Yahudit felt odd at the question being asked. He seemed sensitive about the issue. Yahudit wondered why. People in America were proud to be Jewish. It was like a badge of honor. Being Jewish was being privileged. Aren't many famous actors Jewish? Aren't many famous politicians Jewish? Aren't many famous writers Jewish? Aren't many famous businessmen Jewish? Aren't many famous professors Jewish? What was there to be ashamed of?

"Why does that matter?" Yahudit asked, curious.

"Well, you see," the magician said. "It matters to some women."

"Really?" Yahudit asked. It never occurred to her that it mattered to some women. "What do you mean?"

"Well, sometimes," Johannes the Great said. "When I tell women that I am Jewish, they start laughing or making some comments."

"So, why do you mention that you are a Jew, right off the bat?" Yahudit asked.

"Because that's what I am," the magician said. "And because I have to keep the memory alive."

"Memory?" Yahudit asked.

"Yes," the magician said. "My father and his family barely survived the holocaust. In fact, all of his relatives perished in the holocaust."

"How did your father's family survive?" Yahudit asked.

"Early on, they realized what was going to happen, so they went to Russia," the magician said. "They survived there. And that was where my father met my mother and married her.

Eventually, they went back to the land of my father's birth, where he worked as a rabbi."

"Wow, that's interesting," Yahudit said and looked at Johannes the Great, lovingly. "But how did you get the name, Johannes?"

"That's my stage name," the magician said. "But it is on my American passport as well. My official name is Johannes Mozart."

"Johannes Mozart?" Yahudit said and started to laugh.

"Yes, I know," the magician said. "I changed my name in America."

"What's your real name?" Yahudit asked.

"It's David Levi," the magician said.

"David Levi?" Yahudit repeated.

"Yes," the magician said. "That's what it is."

"It's nice," Yahudit said. "So Jewish!"

"Yeah," the magician said. "I know."

"So, why did you change your name?" Yahudit asked.

"Can you see David Levi doing magic?" the magician asked.

"I guess not," Yahudit said, and they both laughed.

"You know," Yahudit confessed, "I am Jewish."

"Really?" the magician asked.

"Actually," Yahudit said, "I was Jewish. I gave it up."

"Why?" the magician asked.

"It's a long story," Yahudit said. "Maybe I will tell you about it some day."

"I would like that," the magician said.

"Why did you give up your religion?" Yahudit asked.

"What makes you think that I gave up my religion?" the magician asked.

"Because you changed your name and everything," Yahudit said, surprised.

"No, I did that just for show business," the magician said.

"So, you are still religious?" Yahudit asked.

184

"You don't have to be religious to be Jewish," the magician said. "Theodor Herzl taught us that. We are Jewish and that's it."

"I don't agree. I think it is hypocritical to be Jewish without practicing the Jewish religion," Yahudit said.

"I think it is possible to be a secular Jew and a secular Zionist," the magician said.

"So, you are a Zionist?" Yahudit asked.

"Did I not come from the same land as Theodor Herzl?" the magician said. "Of course, I am!"

"Oh," Yahudit said.

"You know," the magician said. "I feel closer to you because we are both Jewish."

"But I gave up Judaism," Yahudit said.

"You cannot give up your Jewish identity," the magician said. "It is like leopard stripes. Can he give it up unless he is skinned alive?"

"You can always paint over it," Yahudit said. "Many people color their hair blonde, for instance."

"Yeah, that's what Hilga does," the magician said, changing the subject.

"Really?" Yahudit responded.

"Yeah," the magician said. "And her colored hair is the most real thing about her."

"What does that mean?" Yahudit asked.

"Precisely!" the magician said.

Hilga was pulling into the parking lot of a trendy restaurant. Yahudit quickly followed. The valet parked their car, and before they knew it, they were being seated at their special table.

The table was one of those semi-circular tables.

"Do you want me to go in first?" Carlos asked politely.

"No, that's okay, I will go in first," Yahudit said and started to move toward the inside of the table. While Carlos and Yahudit were talking, Hilga and Johannes the Great had moved around to the other opening of the table. As soon as Yahudit was clearly inside the table, Johannes the Great started to move toward the inside of the table from the other side.

"Hi," Yahudit said as she realized that she was going to be sitting next to Johannes the Great the whole time.

"Hey," the magician said, "It looks like we will be neighbors."

"You are so lucky," Hilga said, "Being sandwiched between two beautiful women."

"That I am," the magician said.

"How about me?" Carlos asked.

"Isn't it nice to be face to face with me?" Hilga said, like a manager doing some damage control.

"Of course," Carlos said and smiled to Hilga, who smiled back with a tease.

Hilga started a conversation with Carlos, "You know what I like most about you?"

"What?" Carlos said, looking giddy.

"You are so shy," Hilga said. "There is something attractive about a guy who is shy."

"I am not shy, am I?" Carlos protested.

"Oh, you are," Hilga said, "And I like you the more for it."

While Carlos and Hilga were engaged in a conversation, Johannes the Great started a conversation of his own with Yahudit.

"So, why did you decide to give up the Jewish religion?" the magician asked, "If I may ask."

"Sure, no problem," Yahudit said. "I just thought that Judaism was all a fake."

"Fake?" the magician asked.

"Yeah," Yahudit said, "Jews are always going around complaining, but it seems like Jews are the wealthiest in America."

"Well, Jews had to work very hard to get there," the magician said.

Yahudit

"That's fine," Yahudit said, "But Jews should stop complaining and making themselves out to be the victims. That's just not true. Jews have reached the top in America, and we rule it over the Gentiles."

"I see where you are coming from," Johannes the Great relented.

"Jews make it sound like it's only the Jews who suffer," Yahudit continued in her rant. "And when others make legitimate claims about their suffering, they just quash them."

"What do you mean?" Johannes asked.

"Look at the way the Palestinians are being treated in Israel," Yahudit said. "Need I say more?"

"But those Palestinians are terrorists," Johannes the Great said.

"I see you have bought into the lie," Yahudit said. "I was that way, too, until recently. Now, I know the truth."

"Don't tell me that the truth will set you free," the magician said.

"You read my mind," Yahudit said. "You are really a magician."

"Well, I try," Johannes the Great said. "But don't you think that Jews deserve a homeland?"

"I consider America my homeland," Yahudit said. "Don't you?"

"No," Johannes the Great said. "I consider Hungary my homeland, but it is easier to survive economically in the USA."

"See," Yahudit said. "You don't need a Jewish homeland. Neither do I."

"Yeah, but," Johannes the Great protested, "We are Jews, and we need our homeland."

"It's all nonsense," Yahudit said. "I hate to admit it, but it's Zionist propaganda."

"How can you say that?" Johannes the Great asked. "You are a Jew."

"What are you?" Yahudit asked. "Are you working for Chabad, now?"

Yahudit

"Don't make fun of me," Johannes said. "You know that I am not religious. I have given up my Jewish religion. I am a Jew, culturally."

"What does that mean?"

"You know," Johannes fished for words, "It means that I am Jewish in my identity."

"But you are a Hungarian-American who does magic under some Gentile name," Yahudit said.

"Ouch," Johannes the Great said, "That really hurts."

"I did not mean to hurt your feelings," Yahudit said. "But it is true."

"You are like the sabras of Israel," Johannes the Great said. "You shoot straight from the hip and spare no mercy."

"I am cruel to be kind," Yahudit said.

"That's what they all say," Johannes said, "But cruelty can never be kind."

"But cruelty can help someone," Yahudit said.

"Like whom?" Johannes asked.

"The person who needs help," Yahudit said.

"You don't know how people think, do you?" Johannes the Great said.

"Of course, I do," Yahudit protested.

"You are a mere child," Johannes the Great said, "Who has not known suffering."

"I am not a child," Yahudit said, "I am seventeen, and almost eighteen. I am a woman. And I have known suffering. What do you know about my life?"

"I know that you are a rich Jew who is playing the rebel," the magician said.

"How do you know that?" Yahudit said. "I mean, why do you think that?"

"I am a Jew, remember?" Johannes the Great said.

"Don't remind me," Yahudit said. "I am sorry that I found that out."

"Why?" the magician asked. "Does that break your notion of Johannes the Great, the fabulous magician?"

"Well, let's face it," Yahudit said, "You are a showman and a good one at that. You are not really a magician, are you?"

"Well, you will think differently in the morning," the magician said.

"What do you mean by that?" Yahudit said abruptly.

"It is just that you will think differently after all night of dancing," the magician said. "We are going dancing, tonight, aren't we?"

"Are we?" Yahudit asked.

"Of course, we are," the magician said. "Johannes the Great knows best."

"If Johannes the Great says so," Yahudit said, slightly sarcastically.

"And Johannes the Great does say so!" the magician said.

"Now, are you going to say, 'Open sesame?'" Yahudit asked.

"I will sure try," the magician said.

"It sounds like you are having a good conversation," Carlos said, abruptly disturbing the conversation.

"Oh, Carlos, don't talk to them," Hilga pleaded. "Please, talk to me!"

"Yeah," Yahudit said, "Don't be rude, Carlos."

"Okay, dear," Carlos said and went back to his conversation with Hilga.

"So, Mr. Son of a Rabbi," Yahudit asked, "Why did you leave Judaism, the religion?"

"I grew up in the Communist era and was indoctrinated in Communist ideology," Johannes the Great said. "One day, I woke up and said to myself that the Jewish religion was all too superstitious. I wanted something real, so I decided to trade in my Jewish religion for Herzl's secular Zionism."

"Just like Herzl himself," Yahudit said.

"Yes, just like Herzl himself," the magician said.

Yahudit

"So, here we are," Yahudit said, "Two former religious Jews who have traded their old time religion for something new."

"I guess you can say that," Johannes the Great said. "So, are you happy?"

"I thought so," Yahudit said. "I think so. Are you?"

"Yeah," Johannes said, "I think I am happy, too."

"Good," Yahudit said.

"Good," the magician repeated. "You know what?"

"What?" Yahudit asked.

"I feel closer to you, now," the magician said. "I feel like I have a bond with you."

"Definitely," Yahudit asked.

"What does that mean?" the magician asked.

"I don't know," Yahudit confessed.

"Would you like to dance?" the magician asked.

"How about our order?" Yahudit asked.

"My assistant will take care of that," Johannes the Great said.

"Okay," Yahudit said.

"Can you order us some food?" the magician said to his assistant. "We are going to go dancing."

"You don't mind do you?" Yahudit asked.

"Of course, not!" Carlos said with a slightly changed voice.

"Don't worry," Hilga said as Carlos watched the two of them walk away. "They won't do anything half as crazy as we did, today."

Carlos turned red.

"Would you like to order something?" a waiter asked.

"The usual, please," Hilga said.

"Okay," the waiter said and walked away.

"The usual?" Hilga said.

"Johannes the Great and I are regulars, here," Hilga said. "The usual includes all their best stuff. You will like it."

"Okay," Carlos said.

"You know, you are very agreeable," Hilga said. "You are like the perfect mate."

"What do you mean?" Carlos said, not knowing whether he should be offended or not.

"You go along with what the woman wants," Hilga said. "That is the secret to a successful relationship."

"Really?" Carlos asked, curious.

"Yes," Hilga said, "Women need to feel that they are in control, whether they actually are or not."

"Why do you suppose that's the case?" Carlos asked, amused.

"Vanity?" Hilga said. "I think it is vanity."

"Wow," Carlos said. "Is that why? But what about a humble woman?"

"There is no such thing," Hilga said. "Some pretend to suppress it, but it is for their vanity. Haven't you heard the saying? Vanity, Thou Art Woman."

"No," Carlos said.

"Oh, Carlos," Hilga said. "I have so much to teach you."

"And I am glad to learn," Carlos said.

"I could tell," Hilga said.

Carlos looked down at the table like a schoolboy who had just cheated on his homework and got caught.

"I am glad to teach you, everything," Hilga said.

"Really?" Carlos asked.

"Yes," Hilga said. "I like you."

"I am glad," Carlos said.

"Why don't you move over closer to me, so we can talk more quietly to each other," Hilga said.

"Okay," Carlos said and quickly moved over toward Hilga and sat on the seat that Johannes the Great had sat.

"See, nice and close," Hilga said.

"Can I touch you hair?" Carlos asked.

"Why? Do you like my hair?" Hilga asked.

"Yes," Carlos said. "I have never felt blonde hair before."

"Sure, go ahead," Hilga said and bent her head closer to Carlos.

Carlos stroked Hilga's hair like he was stroking his favorite dog. Hilga smiled underneath the weight of his hand.

"You know, you are like a little boy," Hilga said and smiled. "I feel like mothering you."

"I do have that boyish charm, don't I?" Carlos said and smiled.

"You have a very nice smile," Hilga said.

"Yahudit tells me that all the time," Carlos said. "Where is Yahudit?"

"They are dancing somewhere," Hilga said. "Don't worry. It's one of the restaurant's dance areas."

"Oh," Carlos said.

"Do you want to dance?" Hilga asked.

"I am kinda hungry," Carlos confessed.

"Okay, let's wait for food, and then we can go dancing," Hilga said.

"Sounds good," Carlos said.

"So, what did you think about the kiss?" Hilga asked.

"It was amazing," Carlos said. "But don't tell my wife that, okay?" Carlos looked around the room.

"Don't worry, Carlos," Hilga said. "My lips are sealed for you."

"I guess that's a good thing, right?" Carlos said, trying to make out what she meant.

"Well, not really exactly, but you know," Hilga said. "Gag me with a spoon!"

"Huh?" Carlos asked.

"Don't you know the Valley Girl routine?" Hilga asked.

"Valley Girl routine?" Carlos asked.

"Yeah, like, like, surf's up!" Hilga said and started to shake her long blonde hair about.

Yahudit

"I don't know what that is, but I like what I see," Carlos said.

"You know," Hilga said, "Blondes have more fun, you know, like, like, gag me with a spoon. Ditch your non-blonde wife and like, like, go with me."

"Okie, dokie," Carlos joked.

"Are you serious?" Hilga dropped out of her Valley Girl routine.

"Of course, not!" Carlos said. "I love my wife."

"I can work with that," Hilga said.

"Huh?" Carlos asked.

"No, nothing," Hilga said. "So, how would you rate that kiss on a scale from 1 to 10?"

"10. Definitely, 10," Carlos said.

"That awful?" Hilga said with a sad face.

"10! That's the best!" Carlos said.

"It's the worst in the Faterland," Hilga said. "Eins ist das beste. 1 is the best in our Aryan Nation."

"Aryan Nation?" Carlos said, alarmed.

"Yah-vohl! Herr, Commandant!" Hilga said.

"What are you saying?" Carlos asked. "What does that mean?"

"Don't know understand the Nazi joke?" Hilga asked. "Me, being blonde and all."

"I don't get it," Carlos said.

"Do you know about Nazis?" Hilga asked.

"Yeah," Carlos said. "Didn't they like conquer Europe?"

"Yes," Hilga said.

"And wasn't there some short Austrian guy who fooled all the Germans into believing that he was blonde and tall and Aryan?"

"Oh, we call him our own Nepoleon," Hilga said. "He was short and he fooled all of Europe as well."

"But you are not German!" Carlos said. "You are Swedish."

"Ya, ya, want some smorgasbord?" Hilga said.

"Yeah, please serve me up a dish of Schizophrenia, please," Carlos said, trying to play along.

"That's not funny, Carlos," Hilga said, pouting her lips.

"Are you trying to kiss me, girl?" Carlos said.

"What if I was?" Hilga asked. "Are you a rabbit and going to start running away?"

"I am not a rabbit," Carlos protested.

"I see a rabbit about to run away. There is no closet to hold the rabbit in," Hilga said. "Rabbit's gonna run."

"No, rabbit's not going to run," Carlos said. "And I am not a rabbit!"

"Prove it!" Hilga said.

"There!" Carlos said and kissed Hilga. As soon as Carlos moved in, Hilga held her hands around his neck and kept him in the kissing position. Carlos did not try to disengage himself.

At that moment, Yahudit and Johannes returned. Yahudit saw them kissing and was mad. She was going to rush and hit Carlos, but Johannes the Great restrained her.

"Come on, Yahudit," Johannes the Great said. "Let's not do anything that you will regret later. Let's go and cool off for a while."

"I don't want to," Yahudit said.

"It's always better to approach things with a cool head," the magician said. "Don't you agree?"

"Okay," Yahudit relented and allowed herself to be dragged away by the magician.

"I am sorry that something like that happened," the magician said.

"Sure you are," Yahudit said.

"What do you mean by that?" Johannes the Great asked.

"I am saying that you had a part in it," Yahudit said.

"What do you mean?" Johannes the Great said. "We were out there dancing."

Yahudit

"I don't mean about this," Yahudit said. "I mean about what happened tonight at the show."

"What do you mean?" the magician asked innocently.

"You planned to have them kiss in the closet, didn't you?" Yahudit asked.

"No, of course, not," the magician said. "It just happened."

"It's magic?" Yahudit said with a mean tone.

"What happened happened," the magician said.

"Just like what happened there just happened," Yahudit said angrily.

"Yes," the magician said, "Life happens. Things just happen."

"Things just don't happen," Yahudit said, "Unless you allow them to happen."

"Do you really believe that?" the magician asked.

"Yes," Yahudit said.

"So, did you allow yourself to fall for me?" Johannes the Great said out of the blue.

"What do you mean?" Yahudit said. "What are you talking about?"

"I can see it in your eyes," the magician said. "You have fallen for me. And I for you."

"What?" Yahudit said.

"I want you, Yahudit," the magician said and moved in to kiss Yahudit. Yahudit tried to move, but somehow she found herself unable to pull herself away from Johannes the Great. While kissing the magician, Yahudit felt guilt but also happiness. She felt confused.

After a full ten seconds of kissing, Yahudit slapped Johannes the Great. Johannes the Great looked like he was in a lot of pain.

"I am so sorry," Yahudit said and moved in to kiss him. They kissed longer this time.

"Shall we go?" the magician asked.

"Where?" Yahudit said.

Yahudit

"Away from here to a more private place," the magician said, "To anywhere we can be alone, together."

"Okay," Yahudit heard herself say.

Johannes the Great and Yahudit walked hand-in-hand toward the red Porsche. Yahudit did not feel any anger toward Carlos anymore. She felt a pang of guilt at what she was about to do. But she felt also an intense desire for Johannes the Great. For some reason, they connected at a different level. She did not feel the same around Carlos as she did around Johannes the Great. For some reason, Yahudit felt a sense of connection that was beyond the mere physical. She felt like she connected with him at a deeper level. At the level of soul to soul.

What was going on? Yahudit could not explain it herself. It was like nothing she had experienced before. Her whole being seemed to ache, but she did not know why. There, she was connected to a total stranger via his hand, and she was aching. What was going on?

Yahudit felt herself feel a bit dizzy. She was not sure if it was jealousy that was making her feel that way. After all, she had seen tonsil-wrestling of her husband. It was just like she imagined it had been inside the closet. So, he did participate. It wasn't like the girl put her lipstick all over him. He was into her! Yahudit felt jealousy. That was for sure. Hilga was beautiful. She was like a Barbie doll. And how often had she wanted to look like a Barbie doll! Ever since she was young, she wondered why the dark Iranian gene predominated in her body, rather than the light Ashkenazi gene of her mother's side. As she felt ostracism from pretty Jewish American Princesses with blonde hair at the Ashkenazi synagogue, Yahudit had wondered if she had been cursed by God for some fault committed by her forefathers. Sins of the fathers shall visit them to the thousands of generations. Was she a victim of someone else's sins? And in her high school, how often did she want to look like a Barbie doll. It was California after all. There were beach bunnies everywhere. They looked like Barbie dolls. Unlike Ohio, where it is cold during winter, Southern California was bikini-able all year around. You were fit, or you were out. It was a horrible place for a young woman. Yahudit managed to do the fit part. God knows how many hours of exercise per week kept her in that shape. But the blonde thing? That would not have worked. Even if she had colored her hair blonde, like Hilga, she would have looked freaky with dark, brown, Iranian skin.

Oh, how often had Yahudit wished she had blonde hair and blue eyes. She could identify with the protagonist in Toni Morrison's novel. Blue eyes meant everything. It meant what was possible in America for a young woman. Yahudit did not have it, so she could not be a bona fide Jewish American Princess. All her wealth meant nothing because it could not buy her blue eyes, blonde hair, and white skin. It was horrible to be Iranian. Her skin was too dark to look like it was baked golden brown on the beach. And it was permanent. So, when she saw her husband with a blonde beauty, Yahudit could not but feel the weight of all the years of blonde-anxiety rushing at her. What she wanted to be. What she hated herself for. Why she felt an inferiority complex. Why she thought all the boys did not go for her. Everything converged at that vortex in Las Vegas. Her paradise-to-be was turning out to be a hell-on-earth. Maybe the aching that Yahudit was feeling was feeling was not love for Johannes the Great, but rather pain of jealousy.

However, it was also possible that it was jealousy and the memory of her unfulfilled childhood desires that operated in pushing her toward someone with Jewish roots. Those damned Gentiles will do it to you every time. Excuse the French. Her father used to say. Her father was right. Those damned Gentiles will do it to you every time. Carlos was doing it to her at this moment. It seemed like Jews understood. Jews experience similar things. Yahudit considered the fact that she was feeling aching all over her body because somehow her body had become an amalgamation of the suffering of the Jewish people. She had become Jewish Suffering personified. She was carrying the weight of the sorrows of all Jews, like the Suffering Messiah in the Book of Isaiah.

Yahudit

But Yahudit did not want to think about her messianic role. Was she not supposed to be the Anointed One to usher in the New Religion with Carlos as God? What was happening now? Was she supposed to stand by and allow her God to do what he wanted? Would a good God do something like this? Yahudit did not want to ponder the gravitas of consequences of Carlos' actions for the New Religion. In fact, she did not want to think about the New Religion at all at the moment. Yahudit just wanted to get away. She wanted to get far away.

Johannes the Great was it. It was he who provided that escape. And it felt like love. Maybe it was a sense of relief. It could be a sense of gratitude for being salvaged out of a painful situation. Whatever the complexities of the feelings were, Yahudit was clear about one thing. She felt desire. She felt an intense desire for Johannes the Great. It was a desire that was transcendent. It was a desire that could only be described with the words, soul-to-soul. And it was an intense physical desire.

Yahudit desired the magician with all her DNA. She felt that every cell in her body wanted his body. She wanted to be close to him like no other living organism had been close to another living organism. She wanted to create an epochal shift in biological possibilities. She wanted to be glued to Johannes. She felt the intensity of aching in her body, and she felt dizzy by it.

Why did she want him so much? Why? It complicated things. It complicated things very much. A part of her wanted to scream in anger. Yahudit felt angry at herself for wanting him so much. She wanted to blame him for the desire that he created in her heart, in her soul, in her body, in her cells, and in every micrometer of her body. If she had not met him, she would not have felt such intense desire that was so wrong. It was so wrong. And it could not be. Could it? It should not be. Should it? Yahudit's mind was filled with anger at Johannes the Great because he sparked in her a fire that she feared would consume her. She felt that nothing would be left because the fire of her desire and, yes, love would burn her up.

Yahudit

But then, she felt the connection between herself and him. They were connected physically, although not intimately. She felt the energy and the power of that connection and desired for more. She felt the pressure point of the touch. She felt his flesh rub against her flesh. And she felt the electrifying heat of his being ignite her even further toward infinity. This happened all within the short walk to her red Porsche.

For some reason, Johannes the Great seemed to understand what was going on inside her; for, he spoke not a word. It was possible, of course, that he was strategizing how to get into her pants, but Yahudit quickly dismissed such a thought as it seemed to push the sacrality of her inferno experience to the realm of profane banality. She wanted to experience the other-worldliness of what she was going through without the intrusion of what would be completely ordinary and expected of mere mortals. Thus, Yahudit confined herself to the recesses of her mind the very possibility that it was just a physical transaction, however pleasurable the moments of corporeal intersection might turn out to be.

Yahudit reasoned with herself that it was not about physical pleasure. It was not about jealousy. It was not about anger. Rather, Yahudit convinced herself that it was about love. It was a sacral soul-to-soul love that was leading them on this journey to an other-worldly experience. She had already entered the inferno realm of infinite heat. She was determined to stay there with Johannes the Great and approach infinity with him. Is it possible to reach infinity?

At that moment of intense scrutiny, Johannes the Great chose to drop her hand and walk over to the other side of the car. Yahudit experienced the zero of infinity. Infinity will have to resume again. The pause in the approach to infinity must be zero, Yahudit repeated her thought in her mind again. She has to go from zero to infinity. In how many seconds? That was the question.

Yahudit stepped on her pedal and was ready to floor it. But she knew that she had to go out into the Vegas strip and into the desert before that would be possible. She had to remain in the realm of zero for a while. Infinity will have to wait.

"Where to?" Yahudit asked.

"Let's let the car take us," Johannes the Great said.

"You sure?" Yahudit asked. Did he know what approaching infinity meant?

"Yes, I am sure," Johannes the Great said.

"Okay," Yahudit said, and she drove towards the desert.

Yahudit felt free as she passed the lights of Las Vegas into the desert. It was as if Johannes the Great was not there. He seemed quiet. Awfully quiet. Yahudit turned to look at Johannes and saw that he had fallen asleep. He must have been quite tired. And the comfortable chair inside the red Porsche along with the soporific whiz of the Porsche engine must have lulled him to sleep. Yahudit did not want to wake him up. She looked at him closely for the first time and was able to scrutinize his face. He looked quite helpless in his sleeping state. This was such a contrast from the confident, always ready Johannes the Great, magician and entertainer par excellence. In a way, he looked like a child, who was tired out from the day's fun and games and now was sleeping off his exhaustion. Yahudit brushed his hair with her hand as a mother would her child who is sleeping.

"All men are like children." Yahudit's mother had told her once. "They just want to be the center of attention, and they always want to get what they want."

"Is dad like that?" Yahudit asked.

"Of course," Julia Kashiri said, "Your dad is a man."

"But it seems like you are always in control, mother," Yahudit Kashiri said.

"Appearances can be deceiving," Julia Kashiri said.

"Really?" Yahudit asked.

"The important thing is to make your man look good in public because in men's world there are lots of egos. A woman who can make her man look good in public will keep him for a long time. When I say that, I mean his heart. His heart will be in your hands if you make him look good in public."

Yahudit responded, "And in private?"

"In private, you remind him that you made him look good in public," Julia said. "And you should tell him that he is great. Men love to hear that. After that, whatever you want them to do, they will do. Men are simpletons. They just want their egos stroked. Once the stroking is done, they will follow you to hell."

"Mother!" Yahudit exclaimed.

"Well, I used the word in an allegorical sense," Julia said quickly.

"No," Yahudit said, "I was referring to your life's philosophy. It seems so calculating, so cold."

"Life is cold, child," Julia said. "Women are the weaker sex, and we have to be doubly clever to survive."

"But should we be dishonest?" Yahudit asked.

"Of course, truth is the best," Julia said. "But shouldn't you believe that your husband is the best? Should you not show that publicly? You should be wise and get the best out of it. Don't you want to be happy?"

Doesn't she want to be happy? Yahudit felt a tear drop trickling down her face. She looked again at the man-boy sleeping next to her, and she felt so lonely. She felt like she needed her mother. Never in her life did she feel like she needed her mother more than she did, then. She missed her mama. Where was she? What was going on with her? Was she too rash? Did she make a mistake?

Yahudit tried to wipe away her tears. Johannes the Great was no help. He was sleeping like a big lug. No emotion. No emotional support. Just satisfying his need to sleep. So selfish. So very selfish. Yahudit wondered if she had been selfish? Was she selfish to go dancing with Johannes the Great like that? Did that hurt Carlos' ego. Was it because his ego was hurt that he went and kissed Hilga? Was it his need for public affirmation? Did he feel like he was in a macho contest with Johannes the

Yahudit

Great? Was it her fault that Carlos felt the need to compete with Johannes the Great? To show him off? That he could take his woman like he had taken his? Was Yahudit the source of her own unhappiness? Had she ignored her mother's sole advice about how to handle men?

Yahudit wiped her tears and tried to look at her face in the mirror attached to the car. She looked fine. It is the secret of Babylon. Tears did not affect the Iranian skin. She looked at Johannes the Great, and he was still asleep.

No, it was not her fault. Yahudit tried to convince herself that it was not anything that she had done that caused a course of events which led to this point. It was, rather, destiny. It was meant to be. Had she planned to be at the magic show and meet Johannes the Great? No, they were the result of spontaneous decisions. Somehow, spontaneous decisions were linked by a chain into a logical process with real consequences.

Should Yahudit regret that she was sitting next to Johannes the Great and not next to Carlos? Yahudit was afraid to answer that question. She had made a commitment, and she was going to see it through. Isn't that what life is about? Following through with one's promises? But despite her resignation, Yahudit could not completely shake off the unnerving sensation that she was about to make the biggest mistake of her life, a mistake that would change the course of her core essence as she knew it and understood it. Still, Yahudit stuck by her decision to dispel all doubts that had impeded her thoughts and focused on going from zero to infinity.

Yahudit was afraid that Johannes the Great would be injured if he was in a sleeping state as she floored the red Porsche in the desert. Yahudit felt that she owed Johannes the Great, whoever he really was, at least that much, to be conscious in the event that this could be the last moment in his life.

"Wake up, Johannes!" Yahudit half-yelled and nudged the magician. "Wake up!"

"Uh?" Johannes the Great seemed half-conscious.

Yahudit

"Wake up," Yahudit said more softly, "We are in the desert and about to find out the top speed of this car. You want to be awake for this."

"Huh?" Johannes the Great asked.

"We are in the desert about to go as fast as this car can carry us," Yahudit repeated herself.

"Are you crazy?" the magician asked in a knee-jerk reaction. "Or maybe you are just kidding?"

"No, I am absolutely serious," Yahudit said.

"You can't be serious," the magician said.

"But I am," Yahudit said.

"It's dangerous," the magician said.

"You, of all people, are afraid of little danger?" Yahudit asked.

"I am of senseless danger," the magician said.

"But it's not that dangerous," Yahudit reasoned. "There are not any cars at this time of the night."

"There is a reason for that," the magician said. "It's pitched dark out here. It's very dangerous."

"Come on," Yahudit said. "A little danger never hurt anybody."

"That's not true," the magician said. "Many people have died because of what you call little dangers."

"You can't be afraid of death," Yahudit said.

"But I am," the magician said. "I am very afraid of death."

"Are you saying that you are a chicken?" Yahudit said.

"If that's what you want to call it," the magician said.

"You are not going to beg, are you?" Yahudit asked.

"Beg?" the magician said, alarmed.

"Beg me to stop the car?" Yahudit said.

"Of course, not," the magician said.

"I am glad that you have at least a little bit of pride," Yahudit said. "Here it goes. Hold on tight."

"Oh, please, Yahudit," the magician said. "Please stop. I beg you."

"You said you were not going to beg," Yahudit said as she sped her car.

"That was before I thought you would actually do it," the magician said.

"Here it goes," Yahudit said.

"No!" the magician said and closed his eyes.

"Wow, we are going at the top speed, I think," Yahudit said. "Open your eyes, Johannes. It's wonderful."

The magician opened his eyes and noticed darkness passing by him. The road seemed relatively straight. The speed was well over 100 miles per hour. The car started to shake.

"Are you satisfied?" the magician yelled.

"What?" Yahudit said. "Isn't this wonderful?"

"Yeah, yeah," the magician said.

"Okay, I think we can slow down," Yahudit said.

"Gosh, dang nabit," the magician said.

"What?" Yahudit said, after she stopped the car and drove it off the street.

"I am mad at you," the magician said.

"Why?" Yahudit asked.

"Would you not be upset if someone woke you up from sweet sleep and force him to go through a death defying feat?"

"Oh, come on, Johannes," Yahudit said. "You are being melodramatic."

"I can't believe you are patronizing me like that," Johannes the Great said.

"I am not doing anything of the sort," Yahudit said.

"Just because you are young and beautiful, you can't go around doing anything that you like," Johannes the Great said.

"Of course, I can," Yahudit said.

"No, you can't," Johannes the Great said.

"I can," Yahudit said. "See!" Yahudit went over to the side of Johannes the Great and got on top of him. She was facing him, and Johannes the Great looked simply shaken up.

"What do you say to this?" Yahudit said and kissed Johannes the Great on the lips.

Yahudit

Johannes the Great responded with kisses of his own, and they were interlocked in bilabial osculation for over a minute.

"Let's go outside," Yahudit said and pushed the door open. Yahudit stepped outside. The magician followed like a little puppy dog outside into the vastness of the desert, which was largely invisible due to darkness.

"So, are you afraid?" Yahudit asked, eyeballing the magician with a gaze of a temptress.

"Yeah, a bit," Johannes the Great said. "It's awfully dark out here."

"Are you afraid of me?" Yahudit asked.

"Now that you mention it," Johannes the Great said, trying to regain control with a joke. It did not work. Yahudit was not laughing or smiling.

"Do you know what I want?" Yahudit asked with the same serious gaze.

"Do I want to know?" Johannes the Great tried another attempt at levity. It did not work.

"What I want is," Yahudit said and paused for dramatic effect, "You."

"Urp," Johannes the Great audibly swallowed his nervousness.

"What I want to do," Yahudit said, as she was taking off his shirt, button by button, "Is to strip you down and hang you up like a Thanksgiving turkey."

"I don't know what to say," Johannes the Great said nervously. He was being serious.

Johannes the Great's shirt was off. Yahudit began to run her fingers through his chest and his stomach. Johannes the Great closed his eyes as if he felt something sensational. Yahudit moved in closer and held her face half an inch away from his face. She moved in further and put her lips by his ear. Her lips slightly touched his ear.

Yahudit whispered, "And I am going to pluck your feathers and butter your bare skin until you are juicy and wet."

Yahudit

Johannes did not say anything, but he began to breathe irregularly as Yahudit's hands gently caressed his torso. Yahudit felt strong in the mask of darkness, far away from civilization. She felt the need to empower herself as she felt the weight of helplessness pressing down on her. She needed to be free from the constraints of her expected role. She wanted to be the carver of the turkey and not the turkey to be carved.

Yahudit backed away slowly from him. She loosened the belt buckle of Johannes the Great. Then, she undid his button and unzipped his pants. Slowly, Yahudit pulled down Johannes the Great's pants. He was wearing boxer shorts made of red silk. His manliness was bulging out wanting to pierce the soft, silky matter. After the pants had fallen, Yahudit slowly ran her hands through his thighs without touching his essential matter. She could observe that it was growing harder and bigger. She felt amazed by it. It was like a miracle of nature that something could suddenly balloon up like that. She gazed at the growth, and she could feel a tug at her essential matter as well. A shot of desire shot up her spine to her brain and back down to her body to her groin. She wanted to be satiated. She wanted to be penetrated. She remembered the penetration of the night before by her husband, who made the experience beautiful. Although slightly painful, she felt the spurts of pleasure alleviate the tension of pain. She felt her desire increase and fluctuate in the moments of her first experience. She remembered how she experienced things she had not before, and how she tried to capture every second of that experience. She closed her eyes for a second to remember that moment. Then, she opened her eyes. Johannes the Great in his great extension still had his eyes closed.

Was he embarrassed? He had shown his cowardice and was afraid to see her face-to-face to see the disappointment in her face? Was he trying to enjoy the pleasure that seems to be shooting through his body at the moment, testified by his enlarged organ that seemed to be beating in visible regularity? Yahudit stroked his thighs further and noticed his body writhing a bit. He seemed like he was in pleasure, but it also seemed like he was in some pain. She could see his bulk moving inside the silkiness of the artificial clothing and wondered how it felt to have nature run his organ against the artificial stricture that was in her power to free. He seemed to be enjoying himself, so Yahudit decided to kiss his thighs and have him experience the wetness of her lips. She began to kiss up and down Johannes the Great's thigh and tried to match the pumping beat of his manhood. Slowly, Yahudit unleashed the force of her limber tongue onto his thigh. Like a snake exploring its territory, Yahudit encouraged her tongue to explore the vast territory of his thighs. They were like the desert, but did not smell like the desert. She smelled a musky odor as she approached the top regions of his tightness and felt intoxicated by it. It was a smell that she was not familiar with, but it seemed to awaken the primal desire in her heart. She could not contain herself any longer as she neared the regular beat of the drummer. The silky choir sang in unison as she felt the motion of the red silky body rubbing against her cheeks.

Slowly, Yahudit began to pull down the red boxer shorts. Yahudit was surprised by the whiff of strong odor trumpeting the glorious tower of his manhood, laid bare for a siege. Yahudit looked at it as she held his thighs with both of her hands. Without noticing, she had her nails biting into his skin. She felt a cold tremor run through her body as desire gripped her being. She could not take her eyes off of his natural sculpture, which she had elicited through her magic. It was the most beautiful thing that she has seen, she told herself. Gingerly, she laid her right hand on the pillar and held it. She heard Johannes the Great let out a shriek of pleasure and felt the beat of its heart. The more she squeezed, the more it seemed to beat, harder. With her left hand, Yahudit felt the softness of the two balls hanging down on the baskets of his body. Yahudit began to feel the shape of each ball and then squeezed the two balls together. Yahudit heard a yelp, so she gently released them. They hung on their respective baskets, looking like they were caught in the net and had to be released to play a next round of basketball.

Slowly, Yahudit moved her face toward the bastion of manhood without its infantry and soldiers to guard it. It was absolutely vulnerable. It was open to capture. It was there to be taken and conquered. Like an Amazonian warrior ready to make her conquest of the fiercest male warrior in the land, Yahudit moved in and kissed the visible opening of the tower. She heard an inaudible sound from Johannes the Great. She ignored it and kissed it again. Was it the kiss of death? Was it the kiss that betrayed? Was it a kiss of passion, a secret passion that an enemy has for the one whom he is supposed to hate? What to do? What to do?

Yahudit readied her archers and fired her tongue toward the helpless fort right before her. Her tongue dashed, and like a smart bomb, it did not miss a spot on the head of the greatest tower on the fort. She heard audible sounds coming out from above. Cries of help? Cries for mercy? Cries for more? Yahudit mercilessly continued to order the archers to fire. And her tongue circled the head of the fort, hitting bull's eye will every firing. She ordered the smart missiles to modify their patterns, and they rushed at the tower with the alacrity of a soldier who had trained for four years in military tactics and combat who was seeing his first battle. Like an eager soldier, Yahudit fired and fired with precision. And her tongue hit their targets. Her tongue pressed against various points of the head of the tower.

She realized that it was time for the army to move in. Archers had done their work. So, she moved her army with alacrity. Her mouth plunged wholesale into his tower, and Yahudit realized that the massive tower was completely besieged inside her mouth. Yahudit held Johannes the Great by his rear and squeezed his rear. As she felt the beating of the enemy troops and the life beat of their stand, Yahudit could not but help to order a strategic combination of advance and retreat. Soldiers pulled back and then advanced. The army pulled back and then advanced. Her mouth went forth and backwards. And the tower was helpless. Soldiers were falling by the thousands, surely. They were surrendering. But that was not enough. The Amazonian was going for a total conquest. She was going to make sure that the representative tower explodes and is no more.

So, Yahudit got her powerful forces ready for a last push to destroy the tower. She got her archers ready, the army prepared, and she made another plunge with all the forces in tact. They were moving in a strategic battle formation, working in synchronicity with each other. Yahudit moved her army faster and faster. The troops were exhausted, but the commander was relentless. Yahudit ordered more power, more force, more speed. The troops obeyed their captain, and moved in with forced movements. Yahudit saw that the enemy side was not going to surrender. In fact, it seemed like the tower was swelling up with reserve soldiers. Yahudit was not going to back down, so she ordered all her forces to work harder and work faster. She was going to destroy that tower and bring the enemy fort crumbling down.

She felt another surge of reinforcements tighten the tower. The beat was beating harder. And the tower seemed to be moving in a rhythmic motion as if the tower itself now has become a part of the enemy's last resistance. Yahudit was not going to give in or give up. That tower was going to explode. She heard the groans of enemy soldiers in the distance. They were in pain, although the noise sounded like pleasure. And she readied her troops. She paused for a second and felt the power of the thrust of the tower. Then, Yahudit plunged in with all her troops. Bam! There was an explosion. She felt it in her mouth. There was the oozing blood of the dead soldiers who died in the blast. Like a hardened Amazonian warrior, she drank their blood with eagerness. She swallowed and swallowed and relished the blood that was running down her mouth. Like a vampire, she exulted in the sweet smell of blood. Smell of victory. Smell of death. And for her, smell of life.

Yahudit

The enemy had been conquered. The fort was no more. The tower had fallen from its heights. What remained of it were ruins that hung weakly along the vast desert.

"Mercy," Johannes the Great said. "Mercy."

"So, you raise the white flag?" Yahudit asked, wiping away the evidence of her victory from her mouth and chin.

"Yes," Johannes the Great said. "I will do anything you wish."

"Good," Yahudit said. "Get into the car."

Johannes the Great got into the red Porsche. And as soon as Yahudit began to drive her car, he fell asleep. There was morning and there was evening, the fifth day. And Yahudit saw that it was good.

9

Carlos and Hilga finished their kissing. Carlos felt really guilty about the kiss. For some reason, this kiss was different from the first kiss. The first kiss had an excuse. They were confined in a closet, and their lips were inches away from each other. They could have just bumped into each other, and that would have been a kiss. But the second kiss was different. They were there, sitting in a public place. There was no accident there. There was no excuse there. They both wanted to kiss, and they did it. Everybody saw it. And Carlos knew that Yahudit could possibly see them, too.

"Where's Johannes the Great?" Carlos asked.

"He and your wife are dancing away on the dance floor," Hilga said. "Do not worry."

"What if she saw me?" Carlos asked, alarmed.

"No, she didn't see you," Hilga said. "If she saw you, would she not raise hell?"

"I guess, you are right," Carlos said.

"Of course, I am," Hilga said. "Let's just relax and enjoy ourselves, okay?"

"Okay," Carlos said.

"Look, here comes our food," Hilga said.

211

"Great!" Carlos said. "I am quite hungry."

"And the food will satisfy you," Hilga said.

"This thing is really good!" Carlos said. "What is it?"

"It is nouvelle cuisine," Hilga said, "And it is comprised of ostrich eggs, goose meat, and goat cheese."

"Wow, I don't think I have ever had any of those items before," Carlos said, "And now, I am having all of them in combination and in one sitting."

"Today is a day for new experiences, no?" Hilga said.

"Well, actually, a string of new experiences started a few days ago for me," Carlos said.

"Do you want to tell me about it?" Hilga said.

"Yes," Carlos said, "But I shouldn't."

"Why not?" Hilga asked.

"Because it wouldn't be right," Carlos said, "Or rather, it would not be fair to Yahudit."

"Why?" Hilga asked.

"Because it is about her," Carlos said.

"You can tell me, Carlos," Hilga said. "I won't tell her."

"Do you promise?" Carlos asked, looking at her beseechingly.

"Wow, you must love her," Hilga said.

"Yes, I do," Carlos said. "She is my wife."

"Okay, I promise," Hilga said.

"Few days ago, Yahudit and I ran away from our families to get married," Carlos said.

"You kidnapped Yahudit?" Hilga blurted out.

"Kidnap?" Carlos said, "What are you talking about?"

"Sorry," Hilga said.

"To continue with the story," Carlos said, "Yahudit and I ran away from our families to get married."

"It's like Romeo and Juliet," Hilga said. "Your families objected to your love?"

"To tell you the truth," Carlos said, "They don't know about us."

"It's like Romeo and Juliet," Hilga said. "They married in secret."

"Stop saying that it's like Romeo and Juliet," Carlos said. "That play is a tragedy, and both Romeo and Juliet die in the end. I don't plan on dying. I am sure Yahudit is not planning to die. We are going to live to be old and see many grandchildren."

"Okay, I am sorry," Hilga said. "It seems like all I am doing is apologizing since your anecdote started."

"Well, don't jump in with inappropriate comments," Carlos said.

"Okay, I am sorry," Hilga said.

"Stop saying that," Carlos said.

"Okay," Hilga said. "Please continue with the story."

"Should I be completely honest?" Carlos asked, seeking reassurances.

"Of course," Hilga said. "Would it not make you feel completely free to tell me the truth?"

"And you are going to keep the secret?" Carlos asked.

"On my grandmother's grave," Hilga said.

"Okay," Carlos said. "Here it goes. Yahudit, a few days ago, convinced me to take this car ride with her. At first, I thought it would be like a secret rendezvous. I thought it was going to be an afternoon out together. Nothing harmful. Nothing serious." Carlos paused for a second.

"And? And?" Hilga said, curious.

"And it turned into this," Carlos said.

"Where's the rest?" Hilga said. "Come out with it. Tell me the whole story."

"Okay," Carlos said hesitantly.

"Few days ago, Yahudit asked me out on a secret date, and I accepted. We went out to Venice Beach, and it was there that she revealed this plan for our lives. To get married and live happily ever after, together. But it involved leaving that very day, that very night. To hesitate would mean the failure of the plan. To go back to our homes would result in the death of our dream. Beyond all reason and desire to go back, we had to fight to leave right away without delay. Delay would mean tragedy. Lack of delay would mean success. We would leave our imprisoned states and ride the boat across the sea onto the land on the other side into happiness and victory. I understood what delay would mean. I understood that time was a capricious mistress. Time can love you one moment and then slaughter you the next. Time was against us. I was glad that Yahudit had the common sense to push me. Had I gone home, I would have not got out. And if I got out, it would have been too late. There would be troops of soldiers waiting to ambush us and destroy our escape. We would be caught, and then the firing squad would shoot us dead. The story would have ended in a Romeo and Juliet fashion, with both of us dead from a broken heart. But no, we did not hesitate. We did not go back to our homes, to our camps. We went forward. Thus, we were able to ride the boat to the other side, to the Promised Land."

"Wow, the way you speak with biblical imagery!" Hilga said, impressed.

"It's thanks to Yahudit," Carlos said. "I owe that language to Yahudit."

"And he is humble," Hilga said. "You are perfect, Carlos."

"That's what Yahudit said," Carlos said.

"Really?" Hilga said excitedly. "And she has captured me."

"Yes, she has," Carlos said. "I belong to her."

"And you like belonging to her?" Hilga said.

"Yes, I do," Carlos said. "That's why I married her."

"But you have known her for such a short time," Hilga said.

"Yes, I know," Carlos said. "But does love know time? Does love know place? Does love know reason?"

"You are so romantic, Carlos," Hilga said.

"That is because Yahudit inspires me," Carlos said.

"And me?" Hilga asked.

"You are beautiful," Carlos said.

"More beautiful than Yahudit?" Hilga asked.

"That's not a fair question," Carlos replied. Hilga looked at him for a moment and smiled.

"I guess it's not," Hilga said. "So, how beautiful do you think I am?"

"Very beautiful," Carlos said.

"Except for your wife," Hilga said, "Do you think that I am the most beautiful woman in this place?"

"By far," Carlos responded.

"Would you ever leave your wife for me?" Hilga asked.

"What kind of question is that?" Carlos protested.

"I am just curious," Hilga said.

"Don't you know that curiosity killed the cat?" Carlos said.

"So, how do you know that you love Yahudit?" Hilga asked.

"I guess, it just hit me from the sky," Carlos said.

"Yeah?" Hilga responded. "But that does not help me."

"Help you for what?" Carlos asked.

"I want to understand how men fall in love," Hilga said.

"Are you thinking about a man?" Carlos asked.

"Well," Hilga said and hesitated.

"I told you the truth, so it is your turn," Carlos said.

"That's fair," Hilga answered. "Yes."

"That's it?" Carlos said. "A single word answer? Come on, explain."

"Okay," Hilga said. "I have been in love with Johannes for a long time."

"Johannes the Great?" Carlos asked.

"Yes," Hilga said.

"And?" Carlos asked.

"But he does not seem to love me," Hilga said. "I want to understand how I can get him to love me."

"You sure that he doesn't love you?" Carlos said. "I could have sworn that he was crazy about you."

"Believe me," Hilga said, "He doesn't love me. I know he desires me, but he does not want to spend the rest of his life with me."

"That's interesting how you are defining love," Carlos said.

"Isn't love something special, something out of the ordinary?" Hilga said.

"I guess, you are right," Carlos said.

"What is more special than spending what is closest to eternity as a human being with the one that he loves?" Hilga said. "That is the sign of love, the desire to love forever."

"And you refer to marriage?" Carlos asked.

"Yes, of course," Hilga said. "Have you ever heard of anyone who did not get married, who stayed with a woman his whole life?"

"No, I guess not," Carlos said.

"Marriage is the sign of love, perhaps the strongest sign in the world," Hilga said, "Because it binds the marriage partners together by a vow and by law, two of the strongest signatures in our world."

"I see," Carlos said.

"It is the willingness to submit oneself to these two restrictive measures, the vow and the law, that makes love honest and real," Hilga said.

"You are quite deep," Carlos said.

"I know, I am blonde and supposed to be superficial," Hilga said, "But I don't fit the blonde stereotype, deep inside my heart."

"I am impressed," Carlos said and worried that he might say something wrong.

"It is the willingness to place oneself in such a restriction as marriage that testifies to the veracity of a man's love," Hilga said.

"So, are you saying that if a man doesn't want to marry, then his love is not genuine?" Carlos asked.

Yahudit

"Yes," Hilga said, "Because what a man values most is his freedom, or what some call the natural right of man."

"Hmmm," Carlos said in deep thought.

"A man who is willing to give up what is fundamentally important to him is the man who is genuinely in love," Hilga said. "A man who is not really in love would not want to get married; he will value his freedom above all else. For love to dominate his inner core and entire being, a man has to be willing to give up his natural right as a man and submit himself under the confines of marriage, which may be like a prison for some men."

"I am interested to hear that you don't think that a man truly loves unless he wants to marry," Carlos said.

"Think about all the restrictions once you are married," Hilga said. "Not including the legal aspects of it which bars freedom of movement and decision, there is a stated commitment and expectations that flow from it."

"Such as?" Carlos asked.

"Firs of all, within marriage a formation of family is expected," Hilga said. "Children are brought forth and generations are meant to be created consciously."

"You don't think that's the case with two people who love each other and just want to live together?" Carlos asked.

"No, because there is no absolute commitment involved," Hilga said. "Men know this. Marriage is a vow. It's a commitment, which is sealed. It is stronger than giving a person a man's word."

"Interesting to see the woman's perspective on this," Carlos said.

"Don't you think that men think about it in such a way?" Hilga asked.

"I am not sure," Carlos said. "We talk about football and baseball. We don't really talk about such things when men are sitting around. I think men try to ignore the subject. It is a stuffy topic."

"It's a stuffy topic for men," Hilga responded, "Because marriage is a form of confinement that a man places himself under, voluntarily. As much as he loves a woman, that does not change the fact that he is giving up the natural right of man to be married. He is willing to do so because his love has trumped his desire for freedom. In essence, he is choosing to be chained to the woman whom he loves."

"So, you don't think that a man loves truly if he does not want to marry?" Carlos asked.

"Yes," Hilga said. "A man is a liar when he says he loves, when he does not want to marry. The so-called love is not genuine. His I-love-you's are fake."

"Aren't you being too idealistic?" Carlos said. "You talk like some virginal youth."

"Far from the truth," Hilga said, "I have been around the block and back and then some. And what I have realized from knowing so many men is that men who truly love want to give up his freedom for his love and get married. That is the truth that my many experiences have taught me."

"That's interesting," Carlos said.

"Why?" Hilga asked.

"I thought women become wiser with experience," Carlos blurted out.

"What do you mean, wiser?" Hilga asked.

"I thought women who know men would understand a man's need for freedom and be willing to give it to him. You know that it is a natural right of man, then why would you not allow him to enjoy his natural right? Especially if you loved a man truly, would you not want to let him have that which is so valuable to him, such a part of him?"

Hilga answered, "But that's what love is. Love should be the most important thing for him, not the natural right of man."

Carlos responded, "But you did not answer my question. If a woman truly loved a man, would she not give up that which she desires the most, which is marriage?"

Yahudit

"But you are assuming that marriage is the most important thing for a woman," Hilga said. "That is simply not the case. Women value many things and like to be free, perhaps more than the men. Haven't you heard women being described as cats and men as dogs? Women are like cats because they don't want to be tied down. Cats are independent and do as they please. Dogs are loyal and essentially want to be close and to submit. A woman who gets married gives up far more. She will get pregnant, which will incapacitate her for eight months. She will suffer professionally. In contrast, men who get married advance professionally. He doesn't get pregnant. He doesn't have to carry a child in his stomach for eight months."

"Gee," Carlos said. "I guess you have a point there."

"Marriage is the purest earthly attestation of love," Hilga said.

"I guess you are right," Carlos said. "Yahudit wanted to get married right away."

"See, she loves you and wanted your love to complete her," Yahudit said. "I believe that no human being is complete alone. One is made complete through marriage."

"But there are so many people who get married who do not love each other," Carlos said.

"That may be true in some cases," Hilga said, "But a married person belongs, whereas a single person does not. It is the way of the world. How many cultures do you know, which does not have marriage of some sort? Do you think that humans got together in a huddle and decided to form marriage units? No, marriage ceremonies formed all over the world because it is a part of the natural order of things. It is the highest order for human beings. Because it is the highest form of natural and physical accomplishment, marriage as a phenomenon makes the members of that union special. Thus, even if the two did not, quote, love each other, they are a part of something that is special, which makes them special. That is why in societies where there are arranged marriages, you see the completion of

219

the natural order of things and love predominating as well. Marriage generates love even when there was none."

"You really believe that?" Carlos asked.

"Yes," Hilga responded. "Of course, I rather marry the person I love. But I believe that if I were to marry someone I did not, quote, love, I would still find love within the special order of the universe, the design of the natural order of things."

"So, why don't you dupe Johannes the Great into marrying you?" Carlos asked.

"I have tried, but failed," Hilga said. "I guess I am not smart enough."

"You are smart," Carlos said, "That's for sure."

"So, what am I doing wrong?" Hilga asked.

"I don't know," Carlos said.

"How did Yahudit get you to marry you?" Hilga asked.

"She just convinced me," Carlos said.

"Convinced you?" Hilga said.

"Yes," Carlos said, "She reasoned with me and we became married. She convinced me through practiced rhetoric. She was persuasive, I tell you."

"So, you didn't really love her?" Hilga asked.

"I did not say that," Carlos said. "I was definitely attracted to her. But I am not sure if it was lust or love. I guess men never really know the difference. For men, they just blend in."

"So, you are telling me that you were in a state of confusion and Yahudit straightened you out?" Hilga asked.

"I guess you can say that," Carlos responded. "Most men are confused and are not sure. I guess in your terms, men waver between their natural right to be free and their desire for love."

"Yeah?" Hilga asked.

"Men are not sure most of the time," Carlos said. "That's why a strong woman always gets her man."

"So, you don't think I am strong?" Hilga asked.

"I did not say that," Carlos protested.

"But that's basically the principle you are laying out," Hilga said.

"I guess if you put a gun to my head, I would have to admit that," Carlos said.

"You would probably lie and tell me what I want to hear if I put a gun to your head," Hilga said.

"True," Carlos said, "But that's the saying, you know."

"I know," Hilga said. "So, how do I get Johannes the Great to marry me?"

"You have to be consistent with him and wear him down with your charm," Carlos said. "You have to constantly let him know that you want him to marry you, and you have to convince him."

"But that's degrading for a woman," Hilga said.

"You can't have your cake and eat it, too," Carlos said. "You have to choose between your pride and marriage. It's been like that since the beginning of time."

"You think so?" Hilga asked.

"Sure," Carlos said. "Often, women choose their pride and, in effect, choose unhappiness."

"I did not think of it that way before," Hilga said.

"That's why the Good Book says that pride comes to fall," Carlos said.

"But it's so hard," Hilga said.

"Of course, it is because you are flesh and blood, a person with emotions, feelings, and fears," Carlos said. "And fear sometimes is the motivating factor that props up pride. Why do you think many people choose pride over happiness? It's the fatal flaw of women."

"How about men?" Hilga asked.

"Men have pride," Carlos said, "But you will be hard-pressed to find a man who won't speak to someone because of pride. Men duke it out and then have beer afterwards. That's the way men are. If men really had pride, such things would not happen."

"Interesting," Hilga said. "What do I do, now?"

"You will have to continue to persuade Johannes the Great," Carlos said.

"Why do you keep calling him, Johannes the Great?" Hilga asked.

"Because that's what he is," Carlos said.

"No, that is his stage title," Hilga said, "Johannes is his name."

"Well, I like calling him Johannes the Great," Carlos said.

"Suit yourself," Hilga said. "But you won't feel such warm fuzzy feeling for him if you knew what he was doing with your wife."

"What do you mean?" Carlos said, unnerved. "They are dancing, right?"

"They are dancing, alright," Hilga said. "But not the kind of dance you have in mind."

"You will have to explain yourself because I don't understand," Carlos said.

"Here it goes," Hilga said. "Johannes the Great is making a great play for your wife."

"No, I don't believe it," Carlos said.

"Believe you me," Hilga said. "That's what is going on."

"But he seems like such a nice guy," Carlos said.

"He's an entertainer, a magician, for God's sake," Hilga said, "Of course, he's going to look like a nice guy."

"And he seemed so nice to us," Carlos said.

"Of course, he was nice to you," Hilga said. "It is because he wants to get into your wife's pants."

"What are you saying?" Carlos asked, alarmed.

"It's a game to him," Hilga said, "With how many women he can score."

"That's so crass," Carlos said.

"I am telling it like it is," Hilga said.

"And what's your role in this?" Carlos said.

"I am Santa's little helper," Hilga said.

Yahudit

"Santa?" Carlos said, visibly upset.

"You would be surprised how many women consider Johannes the Great as Santa who gives her a great gift," Hilga said.

"Gift of infidelity?" Carlos asked.

"Yes," Hilga said, "Call it what you want. But you would be surprised how many wives Johannes the Great initiated into his great club."

"Why do you help him, if you love him?" Carlos said, aghast.

"It is because I love him and don't want to lose him," Hilga said.

"You must be kidding me!" Carlos said. "You cannot be serious!"

"But I am very serious," Hilga said. "I know that if I let him go or he lets me go, then that's the end of it. I love him, and I cannot have the end."

"But you are talking about helping him cheat with other women!" Carlos said. "There's a limit to everything. Should your love not limit help to those that would help you achieve the love, achieve the marriage?"

"In the idealistic world," Hilga said, "Yes. But this is not the idealistic world."

"I don't get you," Carlos said. "One moment, you say that love causes a man to give up his freedom. The next moment, you are saying that you are playing the role of the enabler for his affairs?"

"I told you that I love him," Hilga said, "But I have also told you that he does not love me."

"So, you have never made love?" Carlos asked.

"What a question!" Hilga said. "But I will answer that. Yes, I did make love to him."

"Why?" Carlos asked. "If you do not think that he loves you, why make love to him?"

"You can never understand," Hilga said, "Because you are not a woman."

"Try me," Carlos said. "I am really confused."

"I know he does not love me, but I want him to love me," Hilga said. "So, I want him to make love to me."

"That's so stupid," Carlos said. "Why would you make love to someone before you are sure they love you?"

"Love does not make sense," Hilga said.

"That's why you are not married to Johannes the Great," Carlos said. "If you were smart like Yahudit, you would be married."

"What?" Hilga said, visibly upset.

"She would not make love to me before we were married," Carlos said. "It was because I knew that I had to marry her before I could make love to her that encouraged me to marry her so quickly."

"You are joking, right?" Hilga asked.

"No," Carlos said. "Not at all."

"So, you are saying that my mom had been right all along?" Hilga asked. "Why buy the cow when you can get milk for free?"

"Yeah," Carlos said. "Something like that. Although that analogy does not work because cow can provide steak and ribs."

"Be serious!" Hilga demanded.

"Okay," Carlos said. "But I am serious about this. Your mistake is that you give him your body and then you deliver other women to him. You can never get a man to commit that way. You have to be possessive. You have to say he's yours and claim him as your territory. He has to know. Other women have to know."

"You talk like a cowboy out for a gun fight," Hilga said.

"Love is a battlefield," Carlos said. "You have to move your soldiers to win."

"How about you?" Hilga asked. "You are here debating with me while Johannes the Great is out there doing your wife."

"Please, Hilga," Carlos importuned, "Restrain your speech."

"Sorry," Hilga said with a suppressed smile.

"But they are going to be back after their dance, right?"

"Sure," Hilga said, "Or maybe they will sneak out to do the wild thing."

"Hilga!" Carlos said.

"Sorry," Hilga said, "But knowing Johannes, he's miles from here, now."

"Then, why did you say that they are still on the dance floor!" Carlos demanded.

"Remember," Hilga said, "I am Santa's little helper."

"You bitch!" Carlos said with a visible disdain.

"I am sorry, Carlos," Hilga said. "But this is a routine we put on many times. It's Johannes' idea. And what am I supposed to do?"

"You didn't have to help him," Carlos said.

"You don't understand," Hilga said.

"I do," Carlos said. "You are weak and you are as wicked as Johannes."

"No, don't say that," Hilga said as visible tears swelled up in her eyes. "I would just die. Just die! I care about what you think. I care about you."

"Oh, shut up," Carlos said. "You are saying that because you are Santa's little helper. What do you take me for? A fool?"

"No, Carlos," Hilga said. "I don't take you for a fool. In fact, I think I am falling in love with you."

"Come off it, Hilga," Carlos said. "You are lying to me like you lied about them dancing."

"That was no lie," Hilga said. "They were dancing. It's not my fault that you did not want to go and find out for yourself with your own eyes. In a way, you wanted to be near me. Admit it! You wanted to be by my side. You like me. Why else would you kiss me?"

"Don't change the subject," Carlos said.

"I am not changing the subject," Hilga said. "I think I am falling in love with you."

"But you just met me!" Carlos said.

"Didn't you just meet Yahudit?" Hilga reminded.

"But that's different," Carlos said.

"No, it's not," Hilga said. "When you kissed me inside the closet, I knew that it was a love at first sight. You wanted me, and you wanted me badly."

"It's jus lust," Carlos said. "It's not love."

"How can you know, Carlos?" Hilga reasoned. "It may be love, but you may not know it, yet. For my part, I feel like I am falling in love with you."

"That sounds fake," Carlos said.

"But it's not," Hilga said. "I like the fact that you kiss with passion. I like the fact that you desire me. I like the fact that you lust after me. I like the fact you sat there, ignoring your wife. I like the fact that you kissed me there for all to see. I like the fact that you made me the most important woman in your life at this moment. And I think I am falling in love with you for it."

"I didn't know that it meant all that," Carlos said.

"You are acting without conscious decisions because you are already attached to me," Hilga said. "I know you, and I can be a great couple."

"How about Johannes the Great?" Carlos asked, incredulous.

"You are absolutely right, Carlos," Hilga said. "You are the great one, not Johannes. You have made me see him for what he really is. You have shown me the truth. He is just using me. He doesn't love me. He doesn't want to be with me. But you do. You love me. You want to be with me."

"But, I can't wrong Yahudit," Carlos said.

"But she's wronging you," Hilga said. "She's cheating on you with a complete stranger. She's insulting you in public. She doesn't care about how you feel. She only cares about Johannes."

"No, that's not true," Carlos said. "She cares about me."

"Yeah?" Hilga said. "Then, where is she? She's in the arms of another man? You call that love? You call that caring?

And she married you! She convinced you to marry her. How could she do that to you!"

"Well," Carlos said hesitatingly.

"I want you, Carlos," Hilga said. "We will be great together. Just forget Yahudit. Forget Johannes. Let's just think about our love and what we can be together. You and me, we can go far. We can build something special together."

"Why me?" Carlos said, incredulous.

"Because, you showed me that you care about me, you want me, and you have shown me the truth. You have liberated me from Johannes' evil grip on me. You are my knight in shining armor."

"Really?" Carlos asked.

"Really," Hilga answered.

"No, I have to look for my wife," Carlos said.

"Don't be weak," Hilga said. "What would she think if you go after her like a puppy when she is amorously engaged with another man?"

"I am not a puppy," Carlos said.

"Then, prove it," Hilga said. "Prove that you are a man. Go with me."

"Okay," Carlos said. "I will."

"I knew you were a man, deep inside," Hilga said triumphantly.

"Of course, I am," Carlos said. "I am a man."

Hilga and Carlos stood up. Carlos paid the bill with the allowance that Yahudit had given him for emergencies. Hilga and Carlos left in Hilga's BMW. Carlos was silent as he sat in the comfortable chair. At first, he was deep in thought. Then, he fell asleep.

After a short period of sleep, Carlos was jerked awake by the weight of what he had done. He had taken the first step toward marital infidelity. It weighed heavily upon him. For some reason, it paralyzed him. Of course, it could have been that he had just awoken from a short but deep sleep after a long day of fatigue. But somehow, Carlos was sure that it was the pressure of his conscience, bearing down on him. He felt suffocated by it. He felt like the walls were closing in. Of course, it could have been that he awoke to a small space inside a moving car, that could easily give anyone claustrophobia. But Carlos was sure that it was the pricking of his conscience.

Carlos looked at Hilga. She was driving and seemed to be deep in thought. Maybe she was thinking about what he had said to her?

"Where are you driving to?" Carlos asked.

Hilga looked at Carlos and smiled. "So, the sleepy-head is finally awake?"

"Yeah," Carlos said and smiled back.

"We are headed to my place," Hilga said, smiling.

"Where is your place?" Carlos asked.

"It's not far," Hilga said. "It is just outside the main part of Sin City."

"Ah, the burbs," Carlos said.

"Nice and quiet, away from everything," Hilga said.

"So, you are a homebody after all?" Carlos responded.

"Of course, I am," Hilga said. "Marry me and make me a decent woman, Carlos."

"But I am already married," Carlos said.

"You can annul your marriage," Hilga said, "And we can get married."

"I can't do that," Carlos said.

"Why not?" Hilga asked, "Because you are a puppy?"

"No, I am not a puppy," Carlos said. "I am here with you, aren't I?"

"But you are still a puppy, who's afraid to take a leap," Hilga said.

"But you are asking me to break my marriage vows," Carlos said.

"I think you have already done that by getting into this car," Hilga said.

"Nothing happened," Carlos said.

"But something will happen," Hilga said. "And you want it. You want it badly. Admit it."

Carlos responded, "I am a man with weaknesses and desires. And you are incredibly attractive."

"So, you will break your wedding vows, but you don't want to make the commitment?" Hilga asked. "Am I like all those women in Johannes' eyes? Just a great lay?"

"How could you say that?" Carlos replied. "You know me better than that."

"I thought I did," Hilga said. "I thought you were decent, and you would do the right thing. I thought you would marry me and make an honest woman out of me. I thought you would be my knight in shining armor."

"I am," Carlos replied in a knee jerk reaction. "I can be."

"Then, why don't you?" Hilga said. "It is obvious that Yahudit does not need you. You are like her accessory. She is a confident, self-reliant woman who does not appreciate what she has. I am different. I know a gem when I see it. And I appreciate it."

"Of course, Yahudit appreciates me," Carlos protested. "Why else would she marry me?"

"She wanted a puppy, a pet," Hilga said, "Who does all the tricks she wants you to do without any of the benefits. You are thrown a bone. For what? For your honor or glory? No, for her amusement. She is out for herself and herself only. You are just an accessory."

"That's not very nice," Carlos said, feeling hurt.

"We are about telling the truth, tonight, right?" Hilga said. "Right?"

"Yes, I guess so," Carlos said.

"So, I am telling you the truth," Hilga said.

"I guess you are right," Carlos said. "It does feel like she does not need me."

Hilga exuded a flash of a radiant smile. "Of course, Carlos, Yahudit doesn't really love you. She only likes the idea of you. She only likes to have a puppy."

"Really?" Carlos asked, doubting himself.

"Yes," Hilga said. "I am different. I want a man. I want a man who will be there for my emotional needs, my doubts. I want my man to be strong, and you are that. You have shown me the way. You are my knight in shining armor."

"Really? Carlos asked, as if seeking reassurances.

"Yes, Mr. Knight," Hilga said. "You are the valiant knight in shining armor to save me. I want to be saved by you."

"How about Johannes the Great?" Carlos asked, compelled by doubts. "Aren't you in love with him?"

"You have shown him to be a mere mortal to me," Hilga said. "But you are like a God, who saves."

"That's what Yahudit said," Carlos said.

"She didn't mean it," Hilga said quickly. "Look at her, abandoning you after a day of marriage with a charlatan and a fake, who has pulled the same trick over thousands of women."

"Thousands?" Carlos asked.

"So to speak," Hilga said. "The important point is that I mean what I say. I need you, unlike Yahudit who considers you her mere accessory."

"Really?" Carlos said, seeking assurances.

"Yes, Carlos," Hilga said. "I will be true to you if you marry me and make an honest woman out of me."

"How about Johannes the Great?" Carlos asked.

"What about him?" Hilga said. "He doesn't love me, any way. And Yahudit doesn't really love you, either. We are doing the right thing. And they have to deal with the truth. The truth shall set them free. The truth shall set us free to our life happily ever after."

"I guess you are right," Carlos said.

"Of course, I am right," Hilga said. "Here we are. Let's go into the warmth of my sweet home."

"Wow, this is a nice place!" Carlos said.

Yahudit

"See, this home is waiting for you," Hilga said. "All you have to say is, 'I do.' And this home is yours."

"I can't," Carlos said. "Yahudit."

"You can," Hilga said, "Because you are a strong man and not a puppy."

"I don't know," Carlos said.

"Come inside and sit down," Hilga said gently. "I will fix us some drinks and let's chat a bit more."

"Okay," Carlos said.

The interior of the house was nouveau décor. Carlos liked her taste in bright colors; he felt cheered up by the brightness. The sofas, he thought, looked a bit like the ones out of Austin Powers movies, but found that it brought levity to the situation. There was so much discussion about difficult topics that Carlos felt overwhelmed by it.

Carlos wanted to see if he was falling in love with her. Hilga was attractive for sure. But was he falling in love with her or was he falling in lust for her? Did it really matter? Was there really a difference when it boiled down to it? Whether he married her for love or for lust, he was planning to be with her and be her knight in shining armor. What did it matter if it was lust or love? It was going to be legit.

But then, Carlos was faced with the daunting task of disengaging himself from his wife. They were already married. Their bond was sealed and legal. They were done for. How could he change that which had already been done? He could not undo it? What did it mean to annul a marriage? Could such action really undo that which was done? It was like a woman getting a surgery to make herself look like a virgin for her wedding night. Did it really undo anything? Was it cosmetic nature? To make the other person feel good? To make yourself feel legitimate? Did it have epic significance? Or, was it a one-way to lie to oneself?

Carlos felt a pang of pain in his side. He did not know why he felt it. But he felt that it had something to do with Yahudit. Maybe he was in love with her after all. Maybe he was crazy about her. Maybe he could only be happy with her. But did that all matter as he sat in this beautiful living room with an attractive lady, discussing canceling his marriage? Did his feelings account for anything or was he merely the victim of Fates that have engulfed his life? Was it his fault that Yahudit had run away with Johannes the Great? Was it his fault that she had, for some reason, decided to cheat on him? Was it his fault that Johannes the Great treated Hilga so badly and that she needed a savior? Was it his fault that he was the only one there to save Hilga? Was it his fault that without his help, Hilga would suffer all her life? Should he now turn his back on the destiny that had been thrust upon him? Should he walk away knowing that the most helpless woman he had known in his life was so close to salvation and that he was the only one to save her? Was it his duty to fulfill his destiny?

Yahudit brought him a drink. It looked like a home concoction of mixed elements. Carlos decided not to ask what was in it. He was too much in thought to divert his attention to that which was not directly relevant to the matter at hand. Surprisingly, Carlos felt nothing poignantly as the sense of duty that seemed to face him. He felt like a marine going to the frontlines to do his sworn duty. He was a knight in shining armor, ready to rescue a woman in need.

He felt like a man. He felt invigorated. He felt needed. He felt like his destiny was before him, and he felt alive again. This was life worth living for, to fight for the woman who needed him, the woman who loved him, the woman who needed his love, the woman to whom he owed his destiny and purpose in life. Hilga was his reason for existence. His divinity had meaning with her. It did not for Yahudit. Yahudit did not really need him. Yahudit wanted to do all things by herself. She strayed as she willed. She betrayed him as she willed. Hilga was different. Hilga was fundamentally dependent on him. What would happen to her if he dropped her? What would happen to her if he let her go? Could he live with the consequences of a woman lost because he let her go? He did not think that he could. He did not think that he could go on living a meaningful existence, if he did not rescue her. He was it. He was the only one who could. He felt the importance of his own existence weighing down on him like the pain of a hard day's workout which is also invigorating and rejuvenating.

Despite the gravitas of the whole situation, Carlos felt light, like he had just gone bungee jumping and realized that he was still alive. He felt like he could tackle anything. Surely, if the Fates have dealt him such a hand, they knew that he could handle it. And handle it, he will.

"Yahudit," Carlos said, "Let's do it."

"I am Hilga," Hilga said, upset.

"I am sorry," Carlos said, "I am just so used to calling Yahudit's name. Of course, I meant Hilga."

"That's okay," Hilga said, "After all, she's your wife. But thankfully, you will abandon that fake for this genuine item."

Carlos tried to smile.

Hilga sat down near Carlos and said, "How do you feel?"

"How do I feel?" Carlos repeated the question like a parrot.

"Yes, how do you feel?" Hilga repeated the question.

"I feel good," Carlos said, "Like a man with a mission."

"I am glad," Hilga said, "That's what I like to hear."

"So, what do we do now?" Carlos asked.

"What do you want to do?" Hilga asked. "We can do whatever you want to do."

"What I really want," Carlos said, "Is to make love to you."

"That's what I want as well," Hilga said.

"But we shouldn't, should we?" Carlos asked.

"No, we shouldn't," Hilga said, edging a big closer to Carlos.

"No, we shouldn't, " Carlos repeated, and he drew closer to Hilga.

"But I want to," Hilga said, inching closer to Carlos.

"I want to, too," Carlos said, and he moved himself visibly closer to Hilga.

Carlos began to brush Hilga's hair with his hand. Hilga felt like he was being slightly patronizing. Why did he stroke her hair, as if she were a dog? But his gentle stroke felt good, and she felt more relaxed with each stroke. She tried to ignore it because she did not know exactly what to say or do. It was somewhat unusual for a man who wanted to make love to stroke the hair of the woman to whom he wanted to make love. Hilga was a bit confused.

Carlos looked at Hilga, and she turned a way, because she felt a bit embarrassed. Being so near him and feeling his touch on her head was too much for her. She had made a commitment to him and that meant a lot. It was like giving herself up to him. It was like she had, out of her own volition, made herself into his possession. She felt vulnerable as she felt his hand on her head. She felt like she wanted his hand closer to her person than on her hair, which was hard to feel. He wanted to feel the texture of his hand on her flesh. She wanted to feel the warmth of his hand on her body. She wanted to feel the passion of his new love on her without any interference. His hand on her hair was just a tease. She felt that he was being mean, that he was being cruel, for not giving her all of him, but giving a part of him in a remote region of her being.

As Hilga turned her head away in confusion, Carlos brought his hand under her chin. He supported her chin like a stand to which a television was attached. And he swirled her head toward him. She looked at him. He was so close. But he was so far away. He was there right in front of her. She could feel his breath, but they were not touching. Except for his hand that was acting as a hinge to turn her head, there was no contact. Why could he not touch her face with his hand? Why couldn't he just touch her face with his face? Why wouldn't he just kiss her? They were so close; yet, they were so far. It was cruel. It was too cruel to be so close, yet withhold his affection. Hilga wanted to hate him for it, but she couldn't because she had already given herself to him in her heart. She hadn't told him so, and perhaps she never will, but she knew that she had given herself over to him, heart and soul. That was her secret. That was her assurance. That was her salvation. That was her testimony.

But she could not let him know. She could not say it. She could not even move her face out of the hinge formed by his hand to reach over and kiss him. She wanted him to make the move. She wanted him to bring the hinge closer to him and kiss her lips. Her lips were getting dry. She could feel it becoming parched. She felt a cold nervousness seize her. But her mouth was watering. She was thinking of all the possibilities that a kiss would bring about. All the anticipation. All that tension and desire, suspended by mere few inches. She could almost taste his kiss. She could almost feel his wetness intermingling with her wetness. She could feel his lips gently pressing against her and sending her temperatures soaring. She could almost feel it. She could almost guess how it would feel. But he was there with his hands hinging her face. And the hinge was motionless. All too disappointing.

Hilga looked at Carlos, face-to-face. She looked into his eyes and knew that he loved her. He loved her more than any other man had ever loved her. And she knew that she loved him more than she had any other man. She knew that what had started as a mere game was no longer that. She was genuine in her affection for him. What she had said before became a prophecy that was being fulfilled, now. Without knowing it herself at the time, she was inspired by the spirit of love which was only making itself fully manifest. HIlga wanted to move in closer to Carlos. Hilga wanted to grab Carlos' head and kiss him. But she couldn't. She did not know why, but she felt paralyzed. She feared. And she realized that she feared because she cared. She cared for him. She cared about what he would think. She cared about how she would feel if anything went wrong. Thus, she hesitated. She hesitated, and she hated herself for it. She should just move in and kiss him. She should just kiss him. All would be okay. All would be wonderful.

Being so close, looking into his heart though his eyes, the window to his soul, Hilga felt a bomb explode in her heart. She knew that he wanted her. She knew that he had given himself to her in the same way she had given herself to him. But there was the one missing element of physical consummation. She was so close to him. And she felt the aching pain of desire for them to share intimacy. She wanted it. He wanted it. They would explode with happiness sharing it. What was pushing it away? Why couldn't she just take charge? She realized that both of them had been struck by the same fear. Fear of vulnerability that comes at the true moment of love. Facing fear where there should be none, but feeling it because the power of love was so powerful, so consuming.

Then, Carlos began to move closer to Hilga. She felt his warmth nearing. She felt the destiny about to begin its fulfillment journey. She froze and awaited the touchdown. The moments seemed to pass by like a snail moving at a turtle pace. These were the longest moments in her life. Slowest moments of suspended silence.

"I can't," Carlos said, "It wouldn't be right with Yahudit."

"What are you saying?" Hilga demanded impatiently. "Yahudit is cheating on you with another man. She does not love you."

"But still," Carlos said, "I have to do what is right."

"Isn't it right for us to share us?" Hilga asked. "Does it not feel right?"

"I don't know," Carlos said.

"Carlos, look at me," Hilga said to Carlos, who had dropped his hand and was looking away. "Please, look at me."

"I can't," Carlos said, "I feel so embarrassed."

"You do not have to feel embarrassed," Hilga said. "You are my hero, my redeemer."

"But I am a weak man," Carlos said, "I am here about to cheat on my wife."

"No, you are not weak," Hilga said. "You are strong. You are, here, because you want to make things right. The world has gone haywire. Your wife is out, doing the wild thing with the man I thought I loved but was using me for his own carnal pleasures, and with other women. He had no regard for my feelings. For him, I was not a person. And Yahudit has proven that she does not regard you as a person. She could have had the decency to go out secretly and cheat on you. But no, she chose to humiliate you in public by going away with that man. She did not care how you felt or for your love. Yahudit cared only about herself and her pleasure with that man. But you are different, Carlos. You are a strong man. You showed me how things really are. You have given me the courage to break out on my own and be with the man I truly love, a man who will be good to me. That is you, Carlos. You are a truth-giver and a savior. And you are a hero to me."

"I guess you are right," Carlos said, looking up at Hilga.

"Of course, I am," HIlga said, "You are my hero. You are a great man. And this is the right thing to do. You and I, we are right. We are what makes the world right."

"You think so?" Carlos asked.

"I know so," Hilga said. "Don't you feel good when you are with me?"

"Yes," Carlos said.

"See?" Hilga said. "It feels good, so it is right. We are right. We are meant to be together. Don't you feel that?"

"Yeah," Carlos said, "I guess so."

"You know so, don't you?" Hilga asked, seeking stronger reassurances.

"I know so," Carlos said. "You are absolutely right. We are meant to be together."

"Kiss me, you fool," Hilga said.

"Okay," Carlos said, and he kissed Hilga. Hilga kissed Carlos back.

"How was that?" Carlos asked.

"It was good," Hilga said. "Was it as good for you as it was for me?"

"You can't even begin to imagine," Carlos said, giving Hilga his signature Mexican smile.

"I want you to go further," Hilga said.

"But we shouldn't," Carlos responded.

"Why not?" Hilga asked.

"Because we are not married, yet," Carlos said.

"Yeah, but we are going to be married, right?" Hilga reasoned.

"Yes, but," Carlos said.

Hilga cut him off, "So, it is not like you would be committing adultery."

"But it is," Carlos said, "I am still married to Yahudit."

"But Yahudit is unfaithful to you," Hilga said. "She is not fit to be called your wife."

"That may be, but that does not still change the fact that we are married," Carlos said.

"But you promised that you would marry me," Hilga said and started to cry.

"Hilga, please," Carlos said, "Please, do not cry. I don't know what I will do if you keep crying."

"I will stop only if you give me another kiss," Hilga said.

"Okay, Hilga," Carlo said and kissed Hilga again. This time, Hilga held onto Carlos and would not let him go. She held his face with both of her hands. She looked at him, trying to pull away.

"Please, Carlos," Hilga said, "Don't pull away. I need you."

"HIlga," Carlos said helplessly. "What am I going to do with you?"

"I know you are trying to give your heart to Yahudit," Hilga said.

"I am not," Carlos said, "I am giving my heart to you."

Yahudit

"I can still feel your heart longing for Yahudit," Hilga said.

Carlos looked at Hilga. He could not look away because she was holding onto his face. He desperately wanted to look away. Anxiety gripped him, and he felt suffocated.

"You don't love me any more," Hilga said and started to cry again.

"Oh, Hilga," Carlos pleaded, "Please, don't cry. You are killing me."

"How can I kill you?" Hilga objected. "I don't have a gun."

"You are like a cancer patient, dying away," Carlos said, "And I feel helpless, standing by and watching you die."

"But that's not true!" Hilga exclaimed. "I may have cancer, but you are the doctor who has found the cure for it. All I need is your love. All I need is for you to love me and not Yahudit."

"How can I?" Carlos blurted out.

"So, you do love Yahudit!" Hilga said. "You really don't love me." Hilga started to wail.

"Oh, Hilga," Carlos importuned, "Please stop. It is not you who have cancer. I was wrong. It is me who has cancer. And you are my cure."

"Really?" Hilga said, looking at Carlos intently.

"Yes, Hilga," Carlos said, "You are my cure. I know that, now. I know that your love for me is intense. You love me in ways Yahudit never can. And I know that my salvation is only possible with you, Hilga. You are my cure, a panacea."

"Do you mean it?" Hilga asked, slowly letting go of the intense grip on Carlos' face.

"Yes, Hilga," Carlos said. "I never meant anything so seriously as I do now. You are my cure. You are exactly what I need."

"Then, you will stop loving Yahudit?" Hilga said with dead seriousness.

"Of course, Hilga," Carlos said, "For you, anything. For you, I would jump off the Bay Bridge."

"I don't want you to do that," Hilga said. "I want you to live. I want you to live forever with me."

"Yes, Hilga," Carlos said, "Why should we talk about death when we have found life? Why should I dwell in darkness when I have found the light? Why should you gaze upon a man headed for death when he has just been cured of cancer?"

"Huh?" Hilga said, confused.

"You are my life, Hilga," Carlos said, "I know that Yahudit was the one who had to go before to show the one who was to come. You are the one. You are the one."

"I am?" Hilga said, still confused.

"Yes, Yahudit was just preparing the way," Carlos said. "I realize now that she is not worthy to tie my shoe lace."

"Shoe lace?" Hilga asked, dumbfounded.

"Yes, you are the one," Carlos said. "Yahudit has led me to you, the one who will make me into who I am destined to become, not in title only but in the metaphysical and existential sense. You are the one."

"Wow," Hilga said, "This is a bit overwhelming."

"You say this?" Carlos asked. "But it was you who broke the levies of the dam. You are the one who allowed the violent torrents to flood the city. You are the one."

"Wow, Carlos," Hilga said. "I don't know what you are exactly saying, but I feel really turned on. Come, kiss me."

"You shall have that kiss," Carlos said, "And many more to come." Carlos kissed Hilga in a series of kisses, as if he were kissing his niece. Hilga looked up, a bit surprised.

"You are such a darling," Hilga said, triumphantly.

"Not as much as you are," Carlos said. "I can just kiss you like this, forever."

"I think, this is the right time to move into the inner chamber," Hilga said. "Come, my love, onto paradise."

Carlos followed Hilga, who tugged at him as she sped through the corridor.

Yahudit

"Wow, you are eager," Carlos said.

"I am eager for your love, Carlos," Hilga said. "Come, satiate my desire."

"I will try," Carlos said, overwhelmed.

"Not to worry, darling," Hilga said, "All you do is magic."

At that moment, something snapped. Maybe it was the built-up tension that had pervaded the whole room and the living space around them. Maybe it was the desire of his libido that had been held back far too long right in front of a woman whom he considered the most attractive woman whom he had seen in his life. Maybe it was the promise of deeper pleasures that her voluptuous kisses portended. It may be the complete and utter reliance of a woman that made him feel like a complete man for the first time in his life. Whatever it was, Carlos snapped. He became a wild beast, only to be controlled by one woman, who had taken his self-control.

Carlos ripped Hilga's clothing in two. He split the clothing the way Moses split the Red Sea. And he was ready to stretch forth his rod and touch the life-giving, or life-taking, waters of Hilga. Carlos beheld Hilga, who seemed stunned at what he had done. The look of shock was still in her face. But strangely, even miraculously, the shock faded, and something altogether different entered in its place. Carlos could not quite put his finger on it, but he could have sworn that it was a look of admiration. It was a look that Hilga had never shown before, during the short, but intense, time that Carlos has known her. She looked at him as a child looking at his superhero. She looked at him with wide eyes, as if she had seen the real Santa Claus. She looked like she just had a conversion experience, and he was the messiah, in whom she had placed her complete trust. Carlos was taken aback by her admiration. For a second, he hesitated. But only for a second.

Carlos recaptured his passion, like a lion who smelled the flesh of a deer, live and young, ready to be pursued, killed, and consumed. Carlos looked at the exposed breasts of a woman who looked even more beautiful without clothing than with it. He could see her pink nipple, erect and pointing, like a cherry on a freshly made ice cream sundae. Her breasts stood erect like a sculpture piece at the Louvre. He knew that this was the moment that he had waited for. It was the moment when he would break all barriers in his experience of passion. He knew that he was on a verge of nervous breakdown as he began to feel himself suffocate at the beautiful white breasts that were bare before him, more august than any sculpture he had seen on TV, internet, or in real life. There she was, flesh and blood, but something far more than that. It was magic. He was in magic. He was about to be joined to magic.

Carlos stood amazed as his blood pumped all over his body, and he could not feel anything. He tried to wriggle his toes and could not feel it. He had become mummified before the Helen of Troy. Or was he playing that role?

Carlos quickly pulled Hilga's dressed down. Soon, he was facing a woman with only a thong. With impatience, he pulled the last remaining clothing down. And he gazed at her form like a man who had just seen a UFO. It was not like it was the first time he had seen her naked. He had been in her dressing room. But it was the first time he realized what he had. He had eyes, but he did not really see before. He had a brain, but it did not really compute before. But a switch had been turned on.

And he knew that he wanted the moment to last, forever. Even before he laid his hands on her. Even as he gazed at her naked body and knew what would come next, Carlos did not want the moment to end. He felt the sadness of evanescence impeding his judgment. He grabbed her and hugged her and broke away from the routine of a savage tiger who wanted to consume his prey. He wanted to lie next to the deer and cuddle it. He did not want the moment to end.

Hilga grabbed his arms and pushed them away, like a mama bear who was out to protect her young. Ferociously, she pushed him away. This shocked him. He did not know what to do. The fear of the loss, the desire to hold on to the moment had incapacitated him. The woman realized it. Like an Amazonian, Hilga pushed him again. He took a couple of steps back. It was as if she wanted to bait him. It was as if she was intentionally trying to get him pissed off. He felt the pain of the push, but did nothing. He stared at the undulating movement of Hilga's voluptuous breasts that were more beautiful than any sunset he had seen in Southern California. He could not take his eyes off of the pink nipples that stood erect and pointing at him. It seemed to instruct him to do something. But he found that he had not yet mastered the language needed to understand the communication. Every part of the Amazonian spoke, and Carlos understood not a word, not a sign, not even a bit.

Hilga seized control. She ripped his clothing off like a vulture which drops down, kamikaze-style, to pick at the carcass that had to be consumed in such a manner, over and over again. Carlos moved about like a helpless animal, who had been killed in a single gun shot wound to the head. He noticed his clothing flying about, but he could not follow the pattern of the undress or the direction of his ubiquitously flying UFO. Hilga was in complete control, and he was completely helpless.

Hilga threw the naked body on the bed, like a teddy bear that had been discarded. But soon, like a child who seemed to have grown wary of her teddy bear who really was not, Hilga jumped on the bed. Carlos and Hilga both moved on the bed due to the quake generated by the Amazonian wrestler going for a pin. All Carlos could do was to marvel and allow to be done to his body what the Amazonian desired. He stood there, staring at Hilga's female form, flying about. Her hair was spread across the skies, and all the Carlos could see was her hair. All that he could smell was the smell of her perfume, mixed in with her female scent. And he could feel the pressure of her soft body on him, but it was moving around so fast that he could not quite fathom what was going on. All he knew was that ecstasy was exploding in his body and imagined that he was coming as closest as possible to what women call, orgasm. He had never felt that way before.

Yahudit

He tried to gain consciousness. He was conscious, but not really. She was moving so violently around him. Her hands were everywhere. Her hair was everywhere. Her smell was everywhere. She was omnipresent. There was not a place where she was not. Carlos stood in awe. And he felt her body moving back and forth on his body and her sweat and his sweat intermingling, like the commingling of the waters at the bottom of the waterfall. Carlos felt the pain of the friction mixed with the pleasure of the soft, wet body, rubbing against him. He felt excited, and it seemed like the pleasure was only mounting further and further. And then, it came. The volcanic eruption, so forceful and so all-encompassing that his whole body shook in trembling wonder. And it kept coming and coming. The volcano erupted, but the explosion happened internally in another's body. And then, he felt the hot lava of his inner being flow down all over him. He felt the powerful scent of the eruption and copulation of natural forces. And he felt the vestiges of pleasure pull at him at his epicenter. Then, it was gone. All the pleasure and all the desire. He was a mountain that had lost all its power in the eruption. But the earth seemed to move, still.

Carlos looked up and saw Hilga. She was still moving as if the mountain had not exploded in the eruption. No evacuations. Just the ever presence. The tectonic motion of earth's plates. There was no more. Did not this Mother Earth know? There was no more to give.

"Oh, just a little bit longer." Carlos thought he heard her say. He felt embarrassed and assured himself that he was just imagining those words. It was merely his male inadequacy, the fear that all men had at the worst possible moment.

"I guess we have to take a break," Hilga said and shook her head. She looked disappointed.

Carlos was afraid to ask. He was afraid to speak. He was afraid to hear her say anything at that moment. He felt fragile, like a thin glass place that would just break when touched. But no plate breaks merely from touch. But even the strongest plate can be broken in two with a strong movement of the earth that shatters the known world. The world known to Carlos was fragile. It was very fragile at that particular moment.

Carlos reached up. He pulled himself up, like a cripple who was about to participate in Special Olympics. He pulled himself up and held onto Hilga. He dragged her down with him. No longer was there two right angles formed by their bodies. There were two parallel lines, juxtaposed to each other. For some reason, Hilga did not move. It was as if Hilga understood. It was as if Hilga wanted to be gracious.

Carlos wondered why Hilga had not faked it. Maybe, this truth-telling was not so good after all. She faked nothing and let the truth out. He felt so vulnerable in the moment of unspoken truth. He began to doubt all that he was, all that he could be. He doubted all about himself.

Why could she not have faked it? Why? Did she want to humiliate him? Did she want to make him feel like nothing? Was this some sick joke that she was playing on him? It was so cruel. It was so heartless. Carlos could feel the tears dropping down his cheeks as he lay there holding onto Hilga. Carlos was afraid that she would push him away, again. He was afraid that she would bully him around, like she did just a few minutes ago.

"Please, don't leave me," Carlos said. "Please do not leave me, Hilga."

"Shhhhh," Hilga said, not moving from her spot. "I am not going to leave you, my darling Carlos. I am not going to leave you."

"Please, Hilga, don't leave me," Carlos said, as if he had not heard what Hilga had said.

"Shhhhh," Hilga said once again. "I am not going to leave you, my darling Carlos. I am not going to leave you."

"Good," Carlos said. "If you leave me, I am going to kill myself."

"Shhhhh," Hilga said reassuringly. "I am not going to leave you, my darling Carlos. I am not going to leave you."

Yahudit

Under the weight of her body, feeling the cold sweat of theirs mixed with his own bodily fluids, Carlos fell asleep. It was cold. It was very cold. And Carlos felt the weight of the whole world upon him. He did not know what he dreamt, but he had a chain of nightmares in a chaotic fashion. The next morning, he awoke and found himself, alone and naked, in someone else's bed. He could still smell all the scent of the night before, and he wanted desperately to wipe the smell off. He felt sticky and icky. Carlos jumped into the foreign shower and cleaned himself in a systematic fashion, as if he were in a prison.

When he wiped himself dry and walked back to the room naked, he noticed a note written for him. It asked him to meet her for lunch at an Italian restaurant. He saw the address and the phone numbers written on the piece of paper. He quickly got dressed and stuck the piece of paper in his pocket. He called a taxi and went to the place where he was to meet her. Carlos had become Hilga's slave. He would do anything that she wanted, as long as she would not leave him. Carlos realized that he had signed up for a life-time of indentured servanthood.

When he got in the taxi, Carlos checked his messages on his cell phone. There were messages from Southern California. He ignored them. Then, the final message was from Yahudit. It was a simple message that stated that she had annulled the marriage and that she had left. He could keep the apartment. She had left money for him. She had left a lot of money for him. One hundred thousand dollars. The bank account only belonged to him, now, and he could do what he wanted with the money. But she had left. She realized that she had to go back. She realized that he was not for him. She realized that she was not the messiah. She realized that he was not her God. She realized that she missed her parents. She missed her friends. She missed her world.

Carlos could not believe that this had happened. Now, he was condemned to slavery, for sure. It was not he who was God. It was Yahudit who was God. And it was she who made them, male and female. It was she, who made him a suitable helper for Hilga. How capricious God was. How could Yahudit the God Almighty do this to him? She brought him out of Egypt, out of the land of slavery, to show him where he was to worship, to receive worship. But the Exodus was not for salvation. The Exodus was to bring him to death in the desert. For forty years was he damned to wander the desert? Would he be punished for idolatry? Was she saying that he had broken the covenant and now must suffer the consequences as a covenant breaker? Was he condemned to toil to satiate his slave-owner with the fallen body that left eternity behind?

Yes, God made them male and female, and condemned them to death for eating of the tree of the knowledge of good and evil. But was this God also the Serpent who had tempted? Where was this God? She was far away from Las Vegas, the Sin City. He could see all this before him. The horrible things to come after the days of creation.

Carlos tried to focus on happy thoughts. He had Hilga. It was not like he had nothing. He had a helper to cope with everything in the new world. God made them, male and female. There was evening and there was morning, the sixth day.

10

Before long, Carlos was at the Italian restaurant. He was dumbfounded. The moment he walked outside of the taxi cab, Carlos realized that he was lost, completely lost. He was lost to Yahudit. He was lost to himself. And he was lost to the world.

"Hi, Carlos!" Hilga chirped.

Carlos walked up to her and hugged her. He needed a hug.

"Oh, Carlos," Hilga said, "You are so sweet. There, there."

Carlos stood there, hugging Hilga and being hugged by Hilga. It felt good for him to feel love, to be loved. He hugged her tighter and tighter. And she reciprocated.

"What's wrong, Carlos?" Hilga said gently. It was as if she understood him. It was as if she read his mind. It was as if she realized what it was that was troubling him. It was as if she knew.

"I," Carlos began. "I am happy that I have you."

"That is so sweet," Hilga said.

Carlos meant to continue and tell the whole story, but after the interruption, he lost his train of thought and the nerve to continue.

"Do you want me to order everything?" Hilga asked. "You don't seem like you are in a condition to choose."

"I am actually not in the condition to eat," Carlos said.

"Of course, you are, darling," Hilga said. "You just don't know it, yet. When you see the food, you will realize how hungry you really are."

"If you say so," Carlos said with resignation, "I am sure you are right."

When the waiter came over, Hilga uttered some words quietly. Carlos did not catch all the things that Hilga had said to the waiter, but he assumed they were related to the food that she was ordering for him.

"We are all set," Hilga said.

"Good," Carlos said and looked at her. "Thank you."

"No problem," Hilga said.

"Yahudit is gone," Carlos said.

"I told you so," Hilga said.

"You mean that she left with Johannes the Great?" Carlos asked.

"I got a message on my cell phone that he told the management that he had quit," Hilga said.

"What?" Carlos asked. "That's crazy!"

"Yeah," Hilga said, "And he did not even have decency to say goodbye to me in person."

"Just like Yahudit," Carlos said.

"See, I told you so," Hilga said. "They ran away together."

"That's just crazy!" Carlos said, feeling the pain of being jilted.

"Is it?" Hilga asked. "Isn't that what you and Yahudit do?"

"Run away together?" Carlos responded, surprised.

"Yeah," Hilga said, "You ran away together, didn't you?"

"I guess you are right," Carlos said. "However, Johannes the Great can't run away. Doesn't he have those magic shows to perform?"

"Actually," Yahudit said, "Last night was the last day on the contract. He could go on performing, but he is not obligated to."

"So, what's going to happen to the magic show?" Carlos asked, curious.

"The big wigs will find some schmuck magician to fill in the place," Hilga said. "There are many of them around in Las Vegas."

"You don't seem too angry about Johannes the Great leaving," Carlos observed.

"Well, Carlos," Hilga said, "Why should I? I have you, right?"

"Right," Carlos said and smiled. "You are absolutely right."

"You are not upset about Yahudit leaving, are you?" Hilga asked.

"Who? Me?" Carlos asked as he fished for words in his mind. "Oh, no. Of course, not. I have you."

"We are the happy couple, aren't we?" Hilga said.

"Yes, we are," Carlos said.

"All's well that ends well, no?" Hilga asked.

"Of course," Carlos said.

"So, when are we going to get married?" Hilga asked.

"Right after the meal, honey," Carlos said. "Yahudit left the message that she annulled the wedding."

"That's great!" Hilga said enthusiastically.

As Carlos ate his meal, Hilga jabbered on and on like a little school girl in love for the first time. Carlos realized that Hilga was right, that the food was heavenly. During the moments that he looked up from his food, he noticed that Hilga did not really touch any of her food. She glowed absolutely radiantly as she talked on and on. She was excited and visibly happy.

Yahudit

Carlos told himself in his mind that he was a lucky man, that he had made the right choice. He had gone out of a humiliating situation with his head and dignity intact. Here she was, his own wife, gallivanting around town with the known playboy of Sin City, and here he was, the schmuck who did not know better. He could have ended up being the ignorant fool, the class clown, the town jester, but Hilga saved him from all that. He was the hero of the story. He was the one who was ending up with the Barbie doll prize, a trophy wife. He was the lucky one.

How did he become so lucky? When did he become so lucky? He did not remember when he was ever lucky growing up. It seemed like it was all the other boys who had the luck. They got the pretty women. They won the prizes. They were the teachers' pets. They were loved by their friends and family. He felt utterly alone growing up with his mother. His father had died, trying to cross over the border. He was shot by a border guard, whose wife left him the night before. The jilted lover wanted something to kill, and he founded in his illegal running across the border.

Life was hard growing up in the United States as an illegal immigrant, whose whole family spoke Spanish . His mother only had an elementary school education, and she did not finish that either. She had depended on her husband for survival, and he got himself killed at the border. She had to learn to cope; she had to learn to survive. She began by cleaning houses for Gringos. The whites were nice, Carlos' mother always had said. She was a simple woman, and she did not care that they did not pay even the minimum wage. She did not care that they did not give her food to eat or give her break time. They drove her like a slave, but Maria, Carlos' mother, was always happy. She said that they had to thank God for what they had. They had to thank God for what he had given.

They went to mass, every Sunday, and his mother forced them to wear their Sunday best. Carlos resented his mother at first, but began to appreciate the merits of the Christian religion.

As he observed how vigorously the local priest worked for illegal Mexicans, he became moved and personally decided to be a Christian. He wanted to become a priest. But that desire was thrust aside as he met Marina, a Mexican woman at the church, who seemed like a wholesome young woman.

Carlos and Marina dated and got married right away, because Maria, Carlos' mother, insisted that it was wrong to fornicate before marriage. Carlos wanted to so badly. And so they were married at the age of eighteen. Then, Marina found that she liked sex way too much to stay a demure Christian. She started to cheat on Carlos behind his back at her work as a maid in a Gringo home. She acquired a taste for other men, and Marina was constantly unfaithful. She moved from one house to another house whenever she was about to be found out by the wife of the boss. Marina acquired a lot of trinkets along the way along with a slew of phone numbers of desperate and lonely men, whose wives did not give them respect as men, who were all too eager to shower gifts on Marina, who made the men feel like men.

Eventually, one of the Gringo bosses divorced his wife and married Marina. She was an illegal before so the marriage was not officially on record. She did not even have to get divorced. She just married her Gringo boss. Since he was Jewish, although a secular one, he did not care about her Catholic marriage to Carlos. After they got married, they moved far, far away, as the Gringo got a new and better job in Northern California. The house was left to the jilted and divorced wife.

Carlos was alone with no marriage on paper. He was an illegal until George Bush granted immunity and citizenship to three million illegals in the United States. That's when he became a citizen. Technically, he was single. Technically, he was a widower. He had couple children, who thought their mother was dead. But Carlos was married in the eyes of the church. And the priest knew what Marina had done. But he was an honorable man and kept the secret for Carlos, even among the local priests.

Yahudit

Carlos had felt a guilty conscience for a long time and refused to work in areas with large number of Mexicans. It suited him fine that he had a job working with Jews who did not ask him many questions. Then, he met Yahudit. Until he met Yahudit, Carlos was a lonely man, jilted by his first love, living a lie of a life, officially, with his wife supposedly dead.

Yahudit had changed everything. Whereas no one gave a damn, Yahudit cared. Not only did she care, she took him away from everything. The Jewish kosher kitchen had become a self-imposed exile, a self-imposed prison. Yahudit took him out of his incarceration and gave him freedom. He was free in Las Vegas. No one knew him. No one knew his past. No one really cared about his past. Hilga only cared about his present and his future. He liked that. He thought he was very happy.

Carlos decided that Yahudit was the beginning of his luck. With such thoughts came gratitude rather than resentment toward Yahudit. Carlos looked at Hilga talking lively in front of him as if he were her everything, and he knew that he had reached his paradise. It was all thanks to Yahudit and her crazy ways. Wherever she was, Yahudit can know that she will always be the angel of his life.

With happiness pervading through his being, Carlos ate his food. He thought about the marriage that was to come and the new life that he will start with Hilga in Las Vegas. They will be happy. He just knew it.

Contrary to what Hilga had presumed, Yahudit did not leave with Johannes the Great. The night was so humiliating to "control freak" Johannes the Great that he had decided to go back home to Eastern Europe for a visit. He felt that he would burst if he did not go back home. So, he bought a plane ticket right after Yahudit dropped him off and flew off without a suitcase. He had his credit cards and ATM cards with him. And having being an itinerant magician for a long time, he knew that everything else could be bought or acquired. So, he flew off with nothing but the clothes in his back. And Johannes decided to make a new life back home in Eastern Europe.

Yahudit

Yahudit did not know what was going on in Johannes the Great's mind, nor did she care. She just wanted to get away. She felt ashamed that she had cheated on Carlos with Johannes. She was curious, and it was this curiosity that killed all that she had worked so hard to build. Her New Religion was gone. She could not believe in it any more. She missed home and longed for all that she had despised few days before. So, she took her car, made some phone calls, including a call to have the marriage annulled, and she took off in her red Porsche. She drove as fast as she could toward Southern California. Her mind was numb, and she could not think. All she could think about was getting back in time.

She arrived home, safe and sound. Her mother was still with her parents, recovering from her nervous breakdown. Her father was still somewhere in an exotic place, filming some blockbuster movie. She found her home empty, but full of food. She ate and ate, especially ice cream and chocolate, and cried herself to sleep. Although she could not put her finger on it, she felt sad. She felt the weight of sadness press down on her like a big avalanche crushing happy skiers on the mountain slopes of California.

She missed Shabbat services. But she decided to go to her Hebrew Sunday School. No one seemed to notice that the whole world had been changed that week. They held classes as usual. She did not miss any class since the Hebrew Sunday School meets once a week. The classroom was comforting for some reason. She arrived early so there were hardly any students there.

She sat there and wondered what was to be. It wasn't like she just woke up, yesterday, and realized that something was wrong. She knew for a long time that something was not right. But she did not want to believe that there was anything wrong. She did not want to doubt. It cost too much to doubt. It cost her her peace of mind.

She thought back to that day. It was a day of jubilation. It was a day of elation. It was a day of enlightenment. But on the other hand, it was a day when she lost something. A day when she lost everything. It was a bittersweet day which she cherished.

She started to read her Psalms in Hebrew. She was the best student at her Hebrew school. She went faithfully every week and did the homework faithfully each time. She valued her acquired knowledge of Hebrew. She liked the fact that her parents complimented her on her Hebrew skills. It made her feel important. It made her want to learn more.